William Buell Sprague, William Coombs Dana

The Life of Daniel Dana

William Buell Sprague, William Coombs Dana

The Life of Daniel Dana

ISBN/EAN: 9783337333577

Printed in Europe, USA, Canada, Australia, Japan

Cover: Foto ©Raphael Reischuk / pixelio.de

More available books at **www.hansebooks.com**

THE LIFE

DA   D.

S   R,

BOSTON

J. E. TILTON AND COMPANY.

1866

PREFACE.

THIS memoir was nearly ready for publication in the autumn of 1860. It is hence, in every respect, a relic of the past.

The writer of most of these pages has attempted little more than a narrative of his father's life. What he was, appears from the testimony of others, and from his own writings. They who revered and loved him living will look with indulgent eye on this tribute to his memory — a simple column, to which another hand has added the Corinthian capital.

W. C. D.

TABLE OF CONTENTS.

CHAPTER XIII.

1837 — 1844.

CHAPTER XIV.

1845 — 1853.

CHAPTER XV.

1854 — 1859.

CHAPTER XVI.

1859.

APPENDIX.

THE LIFE

OF

DANIEL DANA, D.D.

CHAPTER I.

1771–1785.

ANCESTRY. — EARLY YEARS.

ABOUT twenty years after the landing at Plymouth, Richard Dana, whose father had left France in consequence of the persecution against the Huguenots, came from England to this country. He married and settled at Cambridge, Mass. His eldest son (who died in infancy) was born in 1649. On record is a deed of land sold by him April 20, 1656. His membership, and that of his wife, in the Cambridge Church, was as early as 1660. At an advanced age, he died suddenly at Cambridge, April 2, 1690. It appears, from the Probate Records of Middlesex, that he left no will, and that his estate was settled by agreement, signed April 16, 1691, by his widow, four sons, and three sons-in-law.

From Richard Dana are descended, as is supposed, all of the name in this country (with slight exception). Through him it would seem that a Huguenot origin might be definitely assigned to the family. But some imagine — as the name is found on both sides of the channel — that Richard was descended from William Dane (or Dana), Sheriff of Middlesex, in the reign of Elizabeth, whose coat of arms (the motto, "*Cavendo Tutus*") may edify those of easy faith in such matters.

What Richard Dana's motto was, or whether he had any, may be doubtful : we can more easily tell what it might have been. "*Ubi libertas ibi patria*" suits well his history.

Of the four sons of Richard who survived him, Benjamin, born 1660, who died at Brighton (then Cambridge), was the father of Joseph, born A.D. 1700, who lived for some time in Pomfret, Conn., and is called "Joseph Dana of Pomfret," in several deeds of land about the middle of the last century. He died at Lebanon, N.H. He was grandson of Richard, and grandfather of Daniel Dana. His son, Joseph Dana, D.D., of Ipswich, Mass. — born Nov. 13, 1742, graduated at Yale College, 1760 — was sixty-two years pastor of the South Church in that town.

Daniel, second son of Joseph and Mary (Staniford) Dana, was born at Ipswich, July 24, 1771. His mother died when he was not a year old. How tenderly her place was after a time supplied, appears from incidental allusions in later years. The thought of her whom he had never known was kept alive by the remark, sometimes made to him in his childhood, "I should know you, Daniel, from your resemblance to your dear mother." *

* She was step-daughter of the Rev. Nathaniel Rogers of Ipswich. She died May 14, 1772, in her twenty-eighth year. That she was lovely and beloved, appears in a letter still extant, occasioned by her death, from "Joseph Dana of Pomfret," then living at Ashford, to his son at Ipswich. The letter breathes a deeply religious spirit.

Years ago, aged persons in Ipswich spoke of him as one who " was never a boy." One incident, however, may slightly modify this judgment. Usually a model of filial duty, he, nevertheless, one day when there was no school, left his home, *sponte suâ*,—no leave asked,—and strolled away to the Farms, an attractive part of his father's parish. To the subsequent paternal interrogatory, "But why did you not ask leave?" the naïve answer was, "Because I didn't think you would give me leave." It was in keeping with the history of one, who, from the beginning to the end of his long pilgrimage, was *truthfulness itself*.

His love of music was early developed. Whilst yet so young as to drop the *r* in " trouble," and put *d* for *j* in "joy," he would sing (in unconscious prophecy),—

> " Through all the changing scenes of life,
>   In trouble and in joy,
> The praises of my God shall still
>   My heart and tongue employ."

When eight years old, he commenced studying Latin; the next year, he began with Greek. At twelve, he was reading " Seneca's Morals " as a pastime. At that time (1781–1783), the sessions of the Supreme Court at Ipswich were attended by Rufus King, who became a great object of admiration to the young student of Cicero. To hear him plead was more attractive than any recreation. He thought, that, if any modern orator resembled the great Roman, it must be Rufus King.

Shakspeare was an early favorite. He felt the charm of that sublime, all-comprehending genius; whilst whatever was morally objectionable found in his pure mind nothing to adhere to. Many were the noble sentiments and choice expressions made familiar at this early period, to be reproduced in after years. One of these that recurs to memory might have been taken as the motto of his life: —

"Let all the ends thou aim'st at be thy country's, thy God's, and truth's."

How genial were the influences of home, how nutritive to mind and heart the atmosphere of his father's house, those can best understand who remember the venerable pastor at Ipswich. When Dr. Joseph Dana was eighty years of age, his appreciation of the Latin classics was still perfect. More than one of his grandchildren, domiciled with him in childhood, can vividly recall the enthusiasm with which he inspired them in the study of Virgil and Cicero, and the singularly happy art with which he sought to waken into life the germs, not only of literary taste, but of noble and generous moral sentiment. The story of Sinon was made to render more impassioned the detestation of cunning and treachery; the episode of Nisus and Euryalus, and similar passages, were brought home in their pathetic power to the feelings; but admiration of the great poet was always to stop short of any tolerance for the barbarous pugilism of Dares and Entellus, which drew forth only indignant protest.* So, too, whatever in the great orator was below the standard of

---

* That his own moral training had been not dissimilar, appears from an incident once related by him of his childhood. An unseasonable fall of snow had driven some quails to take refuge, through the open door, in his father's house at Pomfret. The children at first counted on a welcome addition to the larder; but their thoughts took a different turn when their mother said, "My sons, never hurt any creature that *confides* in you!"

His mother was Mary, daughter of Francis Fulham, of Watertown Farms, Weston. See Appendix.

Christian ethics was distinctly repudiated. Even now, after the lapse of forty years, the ludicrously disparaging tones still linger in the ear, with which he would repeat Cicero's " *Trahimur omnes* LAUDIS *studio,*" &c., in contrast with the superior dignity and nobleness of Christian motive. It may safely be inferred, that, in the freshness of his earlier days, his sons found their home a place of genial nurture.

When not yet fourteen, Daniel, in connection with his brother Joseph (two years older), was encouraged by their father to commence a singing-school. The need was doubtless urgent; for the tradition is, that, in those days, the pastor's wife, seated in her chair in the centre of the square pew, had often much difficulty in preserving the gravity of the juveniles around her, under the moving effect of the uncouth sounds from the singers' seats. At the opening of the school, not the expected thirty or forty, but one hundred pupils made their appearance. The school was divided, and four evenings in the week occupied, instead of two. Its success was great, and its "linked sweetness long drawn out" beyond any possible imagining of the youthful teachers; for some of those introduced by them into the choir kept their places there *forty years!* In the old South Church in Ipswich, there might be seen, years ago, in the long gallery fronting the white-haired pastor, a row of grave, elderly men, the graduates of his sons' singing-school forty years before. Very grateful to his feelings was their long fidelity; albeit time added to the music some quavers not set down in the books.

Soon after, the brothers commenced also a high-school for young ladies. This they successfully con-

1*

ducted till they left home for college. The report has
come down to us that the school of these juvenile
teachers was remarkable for the perfect order and decorum which their presence maintained.

Their father, absent on a visit to Boston, writes, June
17, 1785, to his son Daniel, then not yet fourteen,
"This is five o'clock, and it naturally puts me in mind
of your schools. Pray be enterprising in both, so as to
engage, if possible, a lively attention in the misses to
their respective parts, and render those parts pleasing
to them. And, before all things, study to approve
yourself to God, my dear, in every thing you undertake, and depend on him for his aid, who can help you
through every difficulty, and make your work easy."

CHAPTER II.

1786—1788.

COLLEGE LIFE.*

"Whilst the brothers were thus occupied at Ipswich, their father paid a visit to the home of his parents, at Lebanon, N.H., a few miles from Dartmouth College. This was in the autumn of 1785. He took with him an axe, in order to hew for himself a carriage-road over those rough and wooded hills. He attended the commencement exercises at Hanover, and, dining with the college faculty, mentioned to some of them that he had two sons prepared for college. Profs. Ripley and Woodward soon after took him aside, and proposed receiving the students into their families, while he in return should receive under his roof and parental training two or three of their children. This proposal was accepted, and the good news conveyed to the brothers before the return of their parents to Ipswich. Prof. Smith came to Ipswich the ensuing winter, examined them, and pronounced Daniel, as well as his elder brother, prepared for advanced standing in college. They reached Hanover in season for the second term of the Sophomore year. The following letter presents the writer as he was at the age of fourteen:—

* Near the close of his life, some reminiscences of his college days were obtained from him by one of his daughters. The narrative in the first part of this chapter is from her pen, which has also given efficient aid to the entire biography.

7

"Dartmouth College, 7th February, 1786.

"Honored and dear Parents,—

"We have now passed more than a week at this place, and find it exceedingly agreeable — indeed, it could not well be otherwise, when we have such a good father and mother here; but I cannot express how I long to see you and my dear sisters and brother. It seems as if I had been from home a month, and was never to see you again. Pray let me have a letter as soon as possible.

"When we came here, we found that our class had got through algebra, and were studying geometry; therefore we began upon geometry, and have now advanced so far as to recite with them. We find them very agreeable and kind, and have been so happy as to form some little acquaintance with some of them.

"I have not time to write a long letter, therefore, after much love to all the family, must conclude by subscribing, my dear parents,

"Your dutiful and affectionate son,

"Daniel Dana."

A letter, two years later, refers to the sudden death of Prof. Ripley, and shows the deep impression it left upon his heart. As I sit to-day by his bedside (Jan. 28, 1859), he refers to it in earnest and pathetic tones, as if it were a grief of yesterday. He repeats, for the first time, perhaps, in seventy years, the opening and latter half of the closing stanza of Professor Smith's Elegy : —

"From earth's dark regions to the skies,
Saints, joyful, take their flight, and rise;
The tears are wiped from all their eyes.

Released from care, released from pain,
Ne'er to be vexed with sin again,
They live, they love, rejoice, and reign.

The resurrection of the just,
While we dear Ripley's corse to dust
Convey, affords us joy and trust."

Among his fellow-students there was one who received him, at first, with warm courtesy, and paid him those marked and kind attentions best adapted to win the heart of an unsophisticated youth. But before long he received evidence of this young man's moral worthlessness, and quietly withdrew from his society. Between him and several others of his class there arose friendships strong, tender, and enduring. First among these chosen ones was Arnold, of Providence, whom he described as by far the most brilliant and attractive member of the class. Next was Hyde, afterwards the Rev. Dr. Hyde of Lee, Mass., who, after an interval of long years, wrote him, "I loved you at college; and I have loved you ever since." There was Montague, too sensitive and reserved for the attainment of a high degree of what the world counts success. In the class next succeeding was Daniel Hardy, regarded at the time as the brightest intellect within the walls of Dartmouth,—handsome in person, and ardent in character.*

On the 17th of September, 1788, he took his first

* About thirty-five years afterwards he was much gratified by a visit from Daniel Hardy, still of fine personal appearance, and vivacious (though he had been a little unsettled) in mind. Their conversation was very interesting, and their singing together delightful. He said of Mr. Hardy, after he had taken his departure, "I remember, as if it were yesterday, how he appeared on the stage at Dartmouth, in the bloom of youth, of fine person, reciting Collins' 'Ode on the Passions;' his very voice was music."

degree. Of the four appointments given out for the
day, instead of the usual number, three, his was a
Greek Oration.

It was with surprise, not sympathy, that he had listened to the expressions of pleasure with which some
of his classmates anticipated their emancipation from
the restraints of Alma Mater. To him, it was quitting
a loved shelter to embark upon an uncertain sea.
Within her halls, and engaged in pursuits most congenial to his tastes, he had secured the love of his
revered teachers, and, by his zealous study of the Greek
and Roman immortals, particularly Homer, had obtained the specially warm approbation of that good
man, and lover of the classics, Prof. Smith.

Here, too, had he felt the first more conscious actings
of a Heaven-directed love and joy, which were destined
to burn higher and purer as the years and ages should
roll away.

He could not remember the time when he had lived
without prayer and serious reflection; but it was
during his junior year, that he was conscious of more
decisive resolutions of self-consecration. He attended
the meetings of some of the students for conference and
prayer, and for verbal and written discussion of questions in divinity; but his not being a member of the
Church probably deterred him from taking a prominent
part. On a subsequent visit to Ipswich, he connected
himself with the church of which his father was
pastor."

During his college course, and for several subsequent
years, his history is chiefly supplied by his father's letters. To those who find biography in nothing more
useful and attractive than as it reveals the influences by

which character has been formed, the extracts that follow will not seem irrelevant or too numerous. Not without interest, in addition to their wise and pious counsels, is the glimpse afforded of New England three-fourths of a century ago, and the picture so unconsciously given, so undesignedly left to a future generation, of a Christian family, all whose members have passed away, save two, — then in earliest childhood, now in honored old age. *

The letters that follow cover a period already passed over in the narrative. At the date of the earliest of them, the younger of the brothers was in his fifteenth year. At the close of his long life they were found carefully preserved. The indorsement on the first is, " Hon'd Father, Feb. 6th, 1786."

" To Messrs. JOSEPH and DANIEL DANA, Dartmouth College.

"MY DEAR BOYS, — Since you left us, we have received two letters with the signatures of DANIEL, one from Newburyport, the other from Pembroke. We suppose it highly probable that others, bearing the signature of JOSEPH, may be on the way, and at any rate consider you as *one* in all your letters, and shall treat you as one in ours. It has contributed not a little to our comfort to hear of your progress so far; and when I contemplate you, as I now do, as having arrived at the desired place of your destination, I am still more comforted than before. When I think of you as engaged, with a number of fine associates, in prosecuting your delightful studies under your worthy instructors, I must felicitate you and myself, painful as the separation is to us here, and I suppose to you also. I thank Heaven, there is no need that I should stim-

* Appendix.

ulate you to diligence in your studies, unless you are altered from what you were with me.   As to method in study, and the best means of preserving your ideas &c., it is probable you may receive advantage by hints from others; and I wish you to pay great attention to such hints upon these heads as you shall receive from time to time from your instructors; for much depends on having a good plan of study, and much time has been laboriously thrown away, in many instances, for want of it.   For which reason, *Quanquam a Cratippo nostro haec te assidue audire atque accipere confido,* * yet it is a wonder if I shall not be officious enough sometimes to throw in such thoughts as occur to me. For the present let me only desire you in general to write as much as you conveniently can, and let me have the pleasure (I am pretty sure it will be a great one) of seeing, when you return, your collections, remarks, &c.   I have said, heretofore, what I wish you to do upon Cicero de Oratore, if you shall find time for it.   Suppose you should do something similar upon all your most valuable authors, — more or less as you shall find time, — reviving withal that method you once begun with, of noting down, at first going over, the pages, and parts in pages, which contain the most striking passages, especially sentiments, and what appears most worthy to be reviewed and remembered.

"Let me also recommend to you to have each of you a memorandum-book in which to lay up your own thoughts: I mean any valuable ideas upon any subject which may occur to you or which you may meet with in conversation. Let this be a perfect miscellany, without form, order, or connection, except that you

* Vide Cic., de Officii, p. 102.

will put down, first, ideas and observations on the subject which first occurs, and as many as naturally and easily occur at the time, and then strike them off, and distinguish them by No. 1, No. 2, &c. You will find this of great use to habituate you to thinking; and it will be a magazine from whence you will be able to fetch out great part, perhaps, of what you will want, when you come to composition upon any interesting theme. But I must have a care not to burden you beyond your bearing. Be not so studious as not to take care of your health, or neglect necessary action.

" Toil strung their nerves, and purified their blood."

This is good philosophy, and it will hold of walking, or any well-chosen exercise.

" But with all your attentions to health of body and improvement of mind, my dear children, remember the one thing needful. Let the sacred Scriptures be honorable with you, as the most important and estimable of all writings; and let prayer be your constant and delightful exercise. Those that honor him, God will honor; and those who despise him shall be lightly esteemed. "

"Ipswich, Feb. 12, 1780.

" We miss you much this evening, as, indeed, upon every Lord's-day evening. We want our fine bass and fine counter to make up the harmony.* Yet, if you

---

* A reminiscence may be appropriate here in respect to the writer of the above. " He was enthusiastically fond of music, particularly of a sacred character, for which he had a fine voice and an exquisite ear. His family will never forget his rapt appearance, when his eight children united with him, as they sometimes did, in singing in four parts the morning or evening hymn around the domestic altar; and when, in

may, where you are, give true praise and worship to
your God and Saviour, and if you may be fitted for
some eminent service in Christ's kingdom, what a
favored parent shall I be! This, my dear young friends,
I am pretty sure, is my principal wish for you; and all
things else are small compared with this. In this idea
and hope I grudge no care, no labor in your behalf, nor
any expense within my power, which may promote the
important design.

"I have been trying to drop some hints to-day on
seeking the things which are Jesus Christ's. And I
will add for your sake, dear youth, as I cannot now
discourse to you every day, that if, in all your studies,
you seek the things of Jesus Christ, and set it before
you as your *primum* and *ultimum* to serve his great
purposes, he will bless your studies, and you shall find
a certain solidity attending all your acquirements.
Otherwise there will be a vacuum which nothing can
fill. Seek, then, with your whole souls, the true knowledge of Christ, and look to it that your hearts are
attached to his interest. Let nothing divert your attention from this object. Let nothing prevail with you to
treat it as being but of secondary consequence."

Writing to them, June 1, 1786, just after his return
from the funeral of the Rev. Mr. Hale of Boxford, he
says, —

"It appears a high blessedness to be a good man,
and especially a faithful minister of Jesus Christ, even
though one is called off early. I have been not so

the height of his excitement, he would unconsciously leave his seat, and
station himself in different parts of the room, and even in the entry, with
the hand over one ear, the better to enjoy the concord of sweet sounds."
—*Letter of the Rev. Samuel Dana, in Sprague's Annals, vol. i., page 600.*

solicitous for you to have long life, as that you might be the friends and servants of the best of Masters, and go home to him when he shall please to call you, — be it earlier or later."

In a letter of Feb. 14, 1787, alluding with great grief to the then recent death of Prof. Ripley, he adds at the close, "How consoling do you imagine it was to me to find, in the last letter from your dear paternal friend that I am ever to receive, this honorable mention of you both: 'Their steady application and agreeable deportment must make them scholars and secure them friends."

In another letter, he speaks of procuring for them some cloth — "Parson's Gray " — of American manufacture, and adds, "I wish, that, in such a time as this, an example of this kind might be given by the classes as they are graduated."

The financial disorder of these times is indicated in another letter, in which the writer speaks (with no dissatisfaction) of having got together " *two dollars* " towards the payment of his sons' bills. How much of the Continental currency these answered to at that time is not stated.

To these letters may be appropriately added one from the Rev. David Tappan, afterward professor in Harvard College.

"NEWBURY, April 26, 1788.

"DEAR SIR, — The esteem and affection which I bear to your excellent parents give me a lively and sensible interest in every thing which contributes to their honor and happiness. And as wise, virtuous, and dutiful children are eminently their parents' joy and crown, so I cannot but take a sincere part in the satisfaction which your good father and his amiable consort derive from this source. I particularly rejoice in the agreeable characters, both in a moral and literary view, of his two sons at college. With mingled admiration and pleasure have I contemplated the remarkable smiles of heaven which have attended his laudable but arduous undertaking to give them a liberal education, particularly, in blessing them with *two successive fathers* at the university, whose generous patronage and provision have so greatly lessened the trouble and expense of carrying them through a collegiate course, — a consideration which, I doubt not, has had its weight with you and your brother, to engage you to the best improvement of advantages granted to you in a manner so distinguishing. You have undoubtedly felt that such a wise and grateful use of your privileges was the just expectation both of heaven and earth, — was a sacred tribute which you owed to your God, to your friends, to your fellow-creatures, and to yourselves. I rejoice to hear that you have appeared to act under the governing influence of these ideas. I especially thank you, my dear sir, for the pleasing proofs which your letters and other productions, sent to your Ipswich friends, have given of your attention and proficiency, as well as of a good and feeling heart. I hope the pleasure which you hereby give, not only to your immediate connections, but to all who love them and you, will be an additional stimulus to a mind so generous as yours to go forward in the unbounded field of knowledge and virtue. Amidst all your other studies, you will not forget that religious 'wisdom is the principal thing,' and will therefore make this the great centre and scope of all your literary pursuits and acquisitions, devoutly referring and consecrating them to the superior interests of God and his Son, of Christian truth and holiness. With the best wishes for your welfare in all respects, and that of your brother, I sub-scribe, your sincere friend,

"David Tappan.

"P.S. You will much oblige me by favoring me with a share in your epistolary correspondence."

2*

CHAPTER III.

1788-1791.

A Year at Hanover. — Two Years at Exeter.

Having been appointed Preceptor of Moor's School, in connection with Dartmouth College, soon after graduation he entered on his new duties. To a youth of seventeen, the position must have been one of weighty responsibility. That the separation from his brother and fellow-students, and the transition from the republican freedom and abounding joyousness of college life, could not but cast some shade over his spirit, those can well understand who have been placed in similar circumstances.

His father writes, Feb. 1, 1789, "Very unexpectedly, Mr. President called on us to-day for a short time. I am happy to hear the agreeable account he brings of your health, your conduct, and the good acceptance you meet with. . . . Adieu, my dear son. You are much upon my heart. Continue to make me happy as you have done; and get as near to God as possible, and prepare to do something for him which shall eminently glorify his great name."

"March 8, 1789. — We feel for you most tenderly in your present solitude, and must have a visit in your vacation, short as it is, if you can make it convenient. But pray, if you do come, do not encumber yourself in this bad season with a poor horse. I have but little news to tell you. We have this day been following to

18

the grave Mr. ——, in his ninety-second year. Poor old man! May God grant you and me to lay up in a better manner against the time of need. 'Are you prepared, master,' said honest old Cato. 'Oh, no!' said the poor man, 'I have left that alone.' May Divine mercy, my dear child, prevent us. There is not in the universe a more foolish creature than man left to his own imaginations."

In another letter, his father says, "I rejoice that the affairs of your school are in a good train, and that I hear you mentioned, from time to time, with so much honor."

While thus occupied at Hanover, measures were in progress to transfer him to a still more honorable and eligible position. The founder of Phillips Academy, at Exeter, an institution of higher rank and on a more ample scale than is usually indicated by the term Academy, was desirous to secure his services. His father writes, May 31, 1789, —

"As long ago as April Court term, Judge Phillips, of Andover, who is one of the trustees of Exeter Academy, inquired after you with a degree of earnestness; and since that time I have had opportunity of conversing at large with him at his own house. I now enclose to you an extract of a letter which I have received from him lately.

[*Extract, May* 14, 1789.]

"'After your friendly visit, I wrote very soon to my uncle at Exeter, and have received his answer, the purport of which is that it would be agreeable to him to see your son Daniel placed in the Academy at Exeter as soon as he can be obtained with propriety. He wishes you to write to your son by the first opportu-

nity to prevent his making any engagements that will
interfere with this proposal. If he should not come
till the commencement at Dartmouth, it is wished that
he should succeed Mr. Abbot in the station he now
holds. Interim, if your elder son will undertake as a
brother instructor with Mr. Abbot it will be agreeable
to him (my uncle); and he proposes the same compen-
sation which was given to Mr. Abbot when he first
engaged.

"'As transient conveyances of letters are very uncertain, would it not be well to write more than one letter
to your son,' &c.

"You will see that the younger Mr. Phillips is in
earnest to obtain you. So, I find, is his uncle, at Exeter, the founder of the Academy, whom I have seen
lately. I understand by Col. Phillips that he has written lately to Mr. Woodward on the subject; that he
also relies on a general promise Mr. President made
him in the winter, that he will not oppose your coming.
On my part, I have complied, as you see; and it is my
desire that you enter into no engagement which will
interfere with the proposition now before you. I have
gone upon the supposition that you are engaged where
you are until commencement. After that we expect
you to return to us, and be at liberty to go where
Providence points the way.

"Write me as soon as possible your whole heart.
Write me fully upon all your affairs. I hope it will be
agreeable to you to be nearer to us if heaven sees best.
. . . "Shall I congratulate you that our beloved
Washington appears again, and greater than ever?
Shall I pray you to set him before you as a model, and
drink deep into his spirit? I think I may; for I be-

lieve it to be a spirit from above, and wish it were everywhere diffused."

The following was written four days later.

" To Daniel Dana, Preceptor of Moor's School,
Dartmouth College.

"Dear Sir, — I was at your father's this week. In his usual kindness, he showed me a letter from Judge Phillips. You are to be invited, I know not but you are already, to Exeter Academy. You know that I wish Moor's School well; but Exeter Academy is an important affair. I rejoice on two accounts, — theirs and yours. I think it may be to your advantage to go to Exeter. That Academy is pretty well endowed; it has a large fund; it needs a good preceptor, and it will flourish. Go, dear brother: you have always one friend while remains

"Timothy Dickinson.

"Newbury, June 4, 1789."

His father writes (July 19, 1789), " You will come as soon as may be after commencement. Yet I must not oppose your taking Exeter in your way, as your brother will be there, at Col. Phillips's; and this may preclude the necessity of going thither again till you have had something of a vacation."

Near the end of autumn, Mr. Dana went to Exeter, where he was received with the utmost kindness by Col. John Phillips, the founder of the academy, under whose roof he passed two happy years. In later times he said of Col. (Judge) Phillips, that he had never since known a layman so well read in theology. His father writes (Dec. 16, 1789), " I expected, indeed, that you would enjoy yourself in that worthy family in which Providence has placed you; but to observe the reasons of satisfaction upon which you lay the strongest emphasis raises my pleasure still higher."

A little remnant of the "patriarchal institution" still lingered in New England at this time. Col. Phillips had an old and indulged black servant, to whom one day, with affected gravity, he said, " Well, ——, as you have been a faithful servant a good while, and are now getting old, I think I shall *give you your time.*" The veteran left the presence without reply; but in the passage to the kitchen was overheard soliloquizing, " Massa say he *gib me my time.* What I do wid *my time?* He gib 'em to me, I *no take 'em, no hab 'em* " (with indignant emphasis).

At Exeter, Mr. Dana found cultivated and genial society; and there commenced the warm and enduring friendship between himself and Mr. Abbot, who for fifty subsequent years gave celebrity to Exeter Academy, being honored with such pupils as Daniel Webster, and others of distinguished name.

Near the close of his first year at Exeter, his father writes (Nov. 14, 1790), —

" I am still desirous that you should read the Scriptures in the way I have sometimes hinted, noting for review such parts as strike you more particularly, and making your own remarks in writing, as briefly, or as much at large, as the present impression leads you; noting some for subjects of conversation with proper persons, or of more particular inquiry. And I could wish you to transcribe for more perfect remembrance, many of the more sublime or otherwise remarkable passages, in the prayers, thanksgivings, benedictions, of inspired writers; or in the descriptions, prophecies, or discourses upon great subjects. This is a favorable season for treasuring up what it will be useful through life to be well stored with.

"Your aunt Fisher really entertained herself and us in telling how you are beloved at Exeter.

"When you have read Sheridan as much as you desire, we should be glad of him here ; yet do not hurry yourself. I think that Sam is now in a good way as to Latin and Greek ; and I shall try to make him an English scholar."

A youth from Ipswich — then at Exeter Academy — used, in after years, to speak of Mr. Dana's great popularity as a teacher. His classical attainments were in high repute ; and " the older scholars were always glad when his turn came to officiate at prayers."

His pleasant memories of Exeter appear in a letter to his friend, Mr. Abbot, March, 1793 : —

"Your observations on satirical wit are too true, and too frequently exemplified. Indeed, what passes under that name is generally neither more nor less than the malice of the heart a little disguised by the paint which the imagination lends it. What a hateful composition ! And yet how often do we see the possessors of it admired, flattered, envied, and imitated.

"It is impossible to speak on the subject of wit, and not call to mind the circle in which, with you, I have spent so many hours, equally delightful and improving.

And I am sure that if it ever was found pure, and unalloyed by any odious mixture, it was there."

CHAPTER IV.

1791–1793.

THEOLOGICAL STUDIES AT IPSWICH. — TEACHING. — ENTRANCE ON THE MINISTRY.

AT the close of his second year at Exeter, he was urged to continue there as a permanent instructor; and many proofs were given then, as in subsequent years, of the high estimation in which he was held by the Phillips family: but his heart was set on the work of the ministry; and, near the end of autumn, 1791, he returned to Ipswich, "hoping (as he says) to be uninterrupted in the study of divinity" with his father. But he was soon pressed, with an urgency which he could not refuse, to take charge of the classical school at Ipswich. This was a serious impediment to his theological studies; but he had already made considerable advance in them. Several common-place books still extant, in which he had followed out the suggestions of his father's letters, were probably begun at Exeter.

His theological studies must have been, to borrow Dr. Chalmers' expression, rather *intensive* than *extensive*. It appears from the memoir of the Buckminsters (a biography of unique interest) that "Dr. Dana of Ipswich" was one of those with whom Dr. Buckminster desired that his gifted son should study divinity. But the facilities of theological education then were no more in proportion to those possessed now, than was the slender library of the Ipswich pastor to the well-

24

filled shelves of modern seminaries. Still, what is gained in surface is sometimes lost in depth; and, however Mr. Dana might have prized the magnificent exegetical aids which German scholarship has elaborated, the (so-called) philosophic theology of Germany could never have been otherwise than repulsive to a mind so earnest and reverent in its search for the pure and simple truths of divine revelation. He had seen, before he left college, the effect of a little taste of German criticism in unsettling, for a time, the religious convictions of a highly esteemed fellow-student. This had left a deep impression on his mind.

Nor is it likely that German mysticism, any more than German skepticism, would have fascinated one who, within the limits of human knowledge, desired clear ideas clearly expressed, and, beyond those limits, regarded bold speculation on sacred themes as an intrusive impertinence.

> "And fools rush in where angels fear to tread"

was a favorite quotation with him in later life; and not less so the conclusion of Cowper's beautiful apostrophe to the author of the "Pilgrim's Progress:" —

> "And not with curses on his art that stole
> The gem of truth from his unguarded soul."

His school at Ipswich closed with an exhibition. One of the dialogues was from Addison's Cato. Consulting his elder brother as to some mode of softening the expression, "Ten thousand curses fasten on them both," the latter gravely suggested one that he thought "not more than half as bad;" namely, "*Five* thousand curses," &c.

3

Oct. 7, 1792, he writes Mr. Abbot, expressing his great regret at being unable to be with him at the exhibition at Exeter: "And so the little dream of happiness in which my fancy has now and then been rioting is vanished; but all the powers on earth shall not hinder my being with you in imagination, and, what is more, in affection. I will go with you to the venerable mansion; at examination, I will be at your elbow. I will attend you to the Doctor's and to the meeting-house. I will have my share in your pleasures and your vexations, in your anxieties while something is yet to come, and your lightness of heart when all is over."

What Mr. Dana was as a *friend* appears very vividly in his letters to Mr. Abbot.*

In May, 1793, he received licensure, of which the following is the record :

"*To whom it may concern, greeting,* — These certify that Mr. Daniel Dana, A.M., appeared before the Essex Middle Association, at the Rev. Mr. Levi Frisbie's, Ipswich, May 14, 1793, for trial and approbation as a candidate preacher of the gospel of Jesus Christ, and that, after hearing him deliver an excellent discourse, on Heb. ii. 3, 'How shall we escape if we neglect so great salvation ;' and receiving satisfactory answers to a large number of questions upon the fundamental doctrines of religion, both natural and revealed ; and the modest declaration of his faith and hope in the Lord Jesus, and of the motive of his offering himself to be a candidate for the work of the gospel-ministry, — cheerfully and unani-

---

* A package of these letters, returned after Dr. Abbot's decease, has supplied some valuable passages to this biography.

mously voted, that they can, and do, approbate and recommend the said Mr. Danial Dana, as a qualified candidate preacher of the gospel of Jesus Christ.

Attest, JOHN CLEAVELAND, *Moderator.*"

The above certificate was accompanied with a kind letter from " Father Cleaveland," as he was then called. He had been a chaplain in the old French war, and in the war of the Revolution. He writes, —

" I hope God will endow you with a strong faith, and make you to be a burning and a shining light."

Preaching his first sermon soon after at Ipswich, Mr. Dana was haunted with the idea that the people must be disgusted by his vociferation, but was relieved, upon coming out of church, by his father's good deacon expressing warm approbation, but begging that in future he would " try to raise his voice a little."

He still for a time continued his studies at Ipswich, from which place he wrote thus to his friend at Exeter, July 11, 1793 : —

" Yours, give me leave to say, is the most friendly, agreeable, instructive, and encouraging letter that I have received this long time. Your ideas on the subject of *preaching* and *preachers* have my complete acquiescence, though some of them were in a great measure new to me. 'Tis true there are many trials and difficulties attending the employment ; and probably these are still increasing ; but, after all, there are so many things in it which must be so exactly congenial to every good mind, so many which to such an one must bring a present reward, that, if any one who has engaged in it and has any tolerable prospect of success, does not find it the principal source of his pleasures, it must be a melancholy symptom *of something wrong within.* And to me there appears in the expression of the great and good apostle a *heroism* that casts into shade all the displays of the kind that ever I read in any poet in my life: 'But none of these things move me; neither count I my life dear to myself, so that I might finish my course with joy, and the ministry which I have received of the Lord Jesus, to testify the gospel of the grace of God.'"

How he spent the latter part of this year we learn from a letter written by his father, addressed to "Mr. Daniel Dana, preacher of the gospel at Hampton." The writer says (Dec. 6, 1793),—

"Though we always part with you with regret, yet we enjoy the thought that you are acting an important part on the stage of life, and the animating hope that you will be made a blessing to mankind.

"Though I know but little of Hampton, I have presumed that you will pass your four weeks not disagreeably. Mr. Merrill called yesterday (being still one of the committee), and wished to know whether you had other engagements beyond your four weeks at Hampton; as they would wish to engage you again for New Rowley if you are at liberty."

The writer's good horse had met with some injury (a serious matter when there were no stage-coaches). He says in a subsequent letter, "We are trying what good provender can do to raise up the spirits of our faithful Rosinante. Already the good creature looks much better. . . . Sam is doing finely. You would smile to hear how popular he becomes. Scholars are still coming in to him; his number more than fifty. . . . I have another letter from Mr. Cabot, dated Jan. 3.

He speaks of Congress as 'surrounded with difficulties which require the exertion of every virtue to encounter.' I believe they are ; and we must pray for them accordingly." Jan. 21, 1794, after alluding to "the kind reception everywhere met with thus far" by his son, he thus proceeds : " Mr. S—— preached for us in the afternoon of last Sabbath ; sound, solemn, but in his manner less agreeable than at the first. If a preacher, by bringing his heart up to his work, and losing himself in it and in love to his auditory, comes more and more into nature and simplicity as he advances, 'tis a good advance truly. It sometimes happens that the longer one goes a candidating, the more recourse he has to art and labor and unnatural tones to recommend him. I have always been happy to hear of you as a child of nature, and very free from every kind of affectation ; and the best way I know to preserve it is to let one's heart go more and more into the truth he delivers, and expand more and more in the way of kind affection to his hearers as he addresses them."

On the third day of February, 1794, the church at Hampton gave him a call to become their pastor. There had been some local dissensions among them, and the call was not unanimous. His answer in the negative was accompanied by the following letter : —

" HAMPTON, March 15, 1794.

" DEAR SIR, — I cannot persuade myself to take leave of a place in which I have been honored with tokens of the most cordial friendship, by numbers whom I highly esteem, without repeatedly expressing my grateful, affectionate sense of their kindness. It is with many painful sensations that I now part with them. It is, however, if I know my own heart, a sense of duty

3*

which has prompted my conduct: a regard not only to my own happiness (which I think myself allowable in consulting in a certain degree), but to that of the people in this place.

"I know that it has been frequently suggested, that there is no probability of there being, at any future time, a greater degree of union, if so great, as there is at present. Such observations have always given me pain; but they would have given me much greater, if I had supposed them sufficiently grounded. Give me leave to ask whether the probability is not on the contrary side? Is it not *highly* probable, that, when each part of the town has had a share of disappointment, many obstacles to their union which *have* existed will exist no more? Since both may now set out on terms perfectly equal, is not the prospect somewhat promising, that there may be hereafter a harmony and union nearly complete? To have been the instrument of preparing the way for this will ever afford me the highest satisfaction; and that it may soon take place is my most ardent wish. Above all, let me entreat of those who have been desirous of my tarrying to keep up no party or contention on my account; for they may be assured that nothing will give me equal pain. Let me entreat them never to relax their endeavors to effect a union in some preacher who will be likely to do good; since, if they humbly and diligently wait on Heaven in this way, there is great reason to hope that their desires may ere long be accomplished.

"You will please to communicate what I have suggested to as many as you shall think best; and permit me to subscribe,

"Your cordial friend and servant,

"Col. Jonathan Garland."　　　　　　　　　　　"D. Dana.

That he gained the confidence of those who were at that time divided, appears from an official note, written years afterward, when the pulpit at Hampton was again vacant, Dr. Appleton having been called to the presidency of Bowdoin College. It commences thus : —

" HAMPTON, Jan. 6, 1808.

" Rev. DANIEL DANA.

" SIR, — The town and Congregational society have instructed their committee for supplying the desk, not to introduce any gentleman as a candidate until he shall have received a recommendation from you, &c."

CHAPTER V.

1794.

COMMENCEMENT OF HIS MINISTRY AT NEWBURYPORT.

By invitation of the session of the Presbyterian Church in Newburyport, he commenced preaching there on the 23d of March, 1794. An immediate interest was awakened, and a movement made for the continuance of his services. In this church, Whitefield had preached; beneath its pulpit, his mortal remains still rest.

In a letter dated April 9, his father says, "We certainly ought to bless God for so favorable a reception still given to you. And when so much cordiality is shown by so respectable a society, and an invitation given which is thought to express the general, if not the universal wish, the opinion of your friends here is, *that you should comply with a grace.* You have no need to be cautioned against carrying an air of presumption as to the final issue. Nor, on the other side, against so committing yourself as to be precluded from deliberating hereafter upon any questions of form and order which may come in the way."

The wisdom of this last counsel was made very conspicuous by subsequent events.

On the 13th of June, a call to the pastoral office was given him by the church, and on the 19th of the same month, "at a legal meeting of the Presbyterian society,

32

Hon. Jonathan Greenleaf, Moderator, it was voted to concur with the church in giving Mr. Daniel Dana a call to settle with us as a minister of the gospel. Yeas, 112; nays, 10."

This is termed in the church records, " As full a meeting as is almost ever known." The result was perhaps as near an approach to unanimity as could have been expected in their peculiar circumstances. In addition to older causes of dissension, the previous year they had been nearly equally divided as to a candidate; and the discordance thus excited was not likely to be soon removed. But the ten negative votes were of importance, as seven of them were from church-members, including some from the session.

Another difficulty in the way of accepting the call was the exceedingly isolated position of the church. From its origin, it had stood very much alone. Whitefield, and after him Gilbert Tennent, had preached in Newbury. Great religious excitement followed, of which one result was, that large numbers, connected with the First and Third Congregational Churches, dissatisfied with their pastors, withdrew, and were ultimately united in a new church, which adopted the Presbyterian form. But this they were not permitted to do peacefully. Their secession was regarded as disorderly; and as, in those days, the law exempted none but " Churchmen, Anabaptists, and Quakers " from parish taxation for the support of the parish minister, this bitter element was superadded to the usual asperities of a church feud, that they were compelled to contribute to the support of the minister they had left. Their unhappy experience of Congregationalism as sustained by law, and the hope of securing exemption from its burdens, led them to adopt the Presbyterian form of government; but still it was not till 1770 that they entirely escaped the clutches of the parish tax-gatherer.

Great prejudice existed against them during the life of their first pastor, Rev. Jonathan Parsons, a good and able man, the friend of Whitefield. His successor, the Rev. John Murray, a native of Ireland, educated at Edinburgh, was a popular pulpit orator, and not wanting in talent, energy, and religious zeal; but, unhappily, he was chargeable with some moral obliquity in having early made use of credentials not quite genuine. This sin of his youth, however repented of, had not been ecclesiastically forgiven. Leaving the presbytery of Philadelphia, and, as he thought, their jurisdiction, he found — or made — (being himself a large part of it) a presbytery in Maine, that recognized him. In those days, there being no general assembly, each presbytery, and sometimes each church, did what was right in its own eyes. After Mr. Murray's settlement at Newburyport, " a very considerable proportion of the neighboring clergy declined intercourse with him. This threw back an odium on his character, in which it was impossible his people, however blameless they might have been, should fail to participate. Their harmonious intercourse with many of the surrounding churches, during the whole ministry of Mr. Murray, was interrupted."*

Dissensions also sprung up among themselves. During the long sickness which preceded Mr. Murray's death, a young missionary of Lady Huntingdon's school, who, at his suggestion, had been employed as his assistant, caused a large secession from his church.

* Rev. S. P. Williams's "Historical Discourse," page 35.

The splendid voice and eccentric originality of Mr. Charles W. Milton could not but produce a sensation; and Mr. Murray, declining in health and years, saw crowds of his late admirers rushing after the stranger who could charm them with oratorical thunders louder than his own. They formed a separate church, and, by a mode of instalment quite their own, made Mr. Milton their pastor. Thus was one more added to the circle of neighboring churches between which and the Presbyterian no friendly feeling existed. Indeed, at this time, it held but little intercourse with the numerous Congregational churches which were near, and almost none with Presbyterian churches, these being few and remote.

Must this state of things continue? If so, could he identify himself with it? These were questions which the pastor elect could not avoid, and which he met with the simplicity, frankness, and decision which belonged to his character. The following paper is in his handwriting: its date is July 10, 1794: —

"HONORED AND BELOVED, — In the call lately presented, you have given me such proof of your candor and esteem as commands my warmest gratitude. Nor will I attempt to conceal the agreeable impression which has been made upon my mind by the general appearance of this Society, the solemnity and decorum of the public assemblies, and the acquaintance which I have had opportunity to form with a considerable number of individuals.

"But, before I give that definitive answer which will involve in it consequences of the greatest moment, permit me, in full confidence of that candor which you have ever shown me, to open my heart upon certain points which to me are interesting, and to you, as I humbly conceive, an object deserving attention.

"It cannot, my respected fathers and brethren, have escaped your notice, that, united as we are in the great essentials of religion, our habits, with respect to discipline and form of government in the church, have been different. It is therefore justly expected of me, on the supposition of accepting the call, that I come prepared to accommodate myself to the existing methods of practice in this society, so far as yourselves, upon a deliberate view, shall judge necessary and conducive to your best edification.

"And if, when this is done, there shall remain other points in which I may be indulged without injury to your religious interests, may not such indulgence strengthen instead of weakening our union? as, in that case, it will have mutual accommodation for the bond of it, which is perhaps one of the most pleasing and lasting bonds.

"I have, then, no questions to move respecting the internal order and government of this society. If the church shall judge that an administration by a chosen eldership will best answer, in this place, the ends of that government which our Lord has ordained, I can cheerfully acquiesce in it.

"But, in regard to communion of churches, I cannot refrain from wishing that this society, if I am to be received into it, may be equally open to Presbyterian and Congregational connections. And I submit it to consideration, whether, in the present state of things, it would not be gain rather than loss, to recur, in this respect, to the original form in which this church was settled.

" All are sensible that many circumstances are materially different since the church first joined itself to the presbytery; and it is obvious, that, when a presbytery is so diminished that a sufficient number for council upon important occasions cannot be included without extending to a very great distance, the privilege to each church so connected is much diminished: being confined to it for council becomes inconvenient; attending its meetings, laborious. Indeed, there is not vicinity enough for sufficient knowledge of the state of each particular church to give the best advice upon all occasions, or for affording every assistance which need may require.

" It is therefore submitted, *whether, returning to the liberty of choosing (as well as affording) council among Presbyterian or Congregational churches, as shall be found convenient, will not be a resuming of a real advantage, both for doing and receiving good.*

" One thing is certain: that it would much enlarge the influence of a respectable church, so conveniently situated as this is for active fellowship with a large number of Christian societies; and it will happily cherish that generous Christian love which finds a high pleasure in embracing and tenderly uniting itself to all good men, of whatever denomination. I frankly acknowledge, my honored fathers, that with me this is a favorite object; and I can scarcely entertain a doubt that it would be agreeable to you.

" As to this town in particular, where of necessity we most often mix and converse together, permit me to say what a happiness I should esteem it, to see Christians of different congregations as united and harmonious as possible, and to be at liberty to improve that

4

candid reception with which I have hitherto been indulged in the other societies, to my own advantage,
and to the promotion, as far as in my power, of the
common cause of Christianity.

"I have brought up those considerations which perhaps ought to have the principal weight. It may be
of less consequence to others, though to me it is a circumstance which comes near home, that my most endeared
connections are among ministers of the Congregational
way, whom I must find it both unnatural and painful
not to honor, upon all occasions, with particular affection, or not to have as near connection with as with
any others in all religious or ecclesiastical transactions.
If such a sacrifice were necessary for the common interest of Christianity, I hope I should not decline it;
but, if it is not, your candor, my honored fathers and
brethren, I doubt not, will wish to relieve me.

"Let me entreat your fervent prayers, that the great
Head of the Church may prepare me for his sacred
work, and make every part of duty plain to me; that,
if I come to you, it may be in the fulness of the blessing of the gospel of Christ.

"May it please him to direct the concerns of this
society to his own glory and their highest edification,
is the constant prayer of your affectionate brother and
servant in the gospel,   "D. DANA.

" To the Presbyterian Church and Society in Newburyport."

It is interesting to observe how expressive this docu-
ment is of the spirit and principles which marked his
whole subsequent life. He was at this time not quite
twenty-three years of age.

This paper deserves to be read with the same discrimination with which it was written. It is by no means, what it has been more than once in print represented to be, an invitation to the church to *renounce Presbyterianism*, and become Congregational. " Communion of churches," is its subject; and what it suggests is " to recur, *in this respect*, to the *original form* in which this church was settled," which was *Presbyterian*,* but not of the exclusive, isolated " form " which Mr. Murray's difficulties had tended to create. Its founders, in the preface to their platform of government, say, " We shall readily join with those churches that explicitly declare they have not departed from the ancient faith." Again, two years later (1748), in a petition to the General Court, they say, " Your petitioners beg leave to suggest that they never intended, because they were Presbyterians, which respects the form of church government only (according to the general understanding of the words), that therefore they could not attend the worship of God in a Congregational church; but their difficulties are of a higher nature, and concern doctrinal points, which bind their consciences," &c.

" The form of government was, at first, one which might properly be called independent Presbyterian." Soon after its organization was completed, " negotiations were commenced, which, at length, resulted in a connection with the Presbytery of Boston." " They often protested, that, by becoming Presbyterians, they had no intention to withdraw from free intercourse with their Congregational brethren." †

---

* " The founders organized this a Presbyterian church." Rev. Mr. Vermilye's " Historical Discourse," page 40.

† Rev. J. F. Stearns' " Historical Discourse," pages 34, 35.

It was to *this* "original form in which this church was settled" — not Congregational, but liberal Presbyterian — that the paper refers. The question which pressed on the writer of it was, whether, by accepting the call tendered to him, he would be held to ecclesiastical non-intercourse with his own father (whose counsel he was constantly seeking), and with the good and eminent ministers, frequent visitors at his father's house, who had looked kindly on him from his childhood, and had taken a deep interest in his prospective usefulness in the gospel ministry. This appears very plainly in his father's letters at that time, still extant. In a letter, written by himself to his friend Mr. Abbot, he speaks of the presbytery as numbering but four or five active ministers, two of them "at the distance of one hundred and thirty miles" (nearly a week's journey in those times), and all personally strangers to him, and adds, that to be ordained *exclusively* by these would seem to him "too much like a renunciation of former connections, even the nearest."

"Active fellowship with a large number of Christian societies" is the subject of the paper, in contrast with severance of the writer's "most endeared connections," — separation from those ministers whom he must "find it both unnatural and painful not to honor upon all occasions with particular affection, or not to have as near connection with, as with any others, in all religious or ecclesiastical transactions."

In response to this appeal, the session (perhaps the church) "voted unanimously, that we still adhere to the constitution of this church, and our connection with the presbytery, and desire further to hold ministerial and church communion with such other ministers and churches as are united with us in the great fundamental doctrines of the gospel, in the same manner as heretofore practised in this church."*

An affirmative answer was now given to the call. More than two months had elapsed since it was tendered.

Hitherto Mr. Dana had not been brought into contact with Presbyterianism, which was, indeed, very much an exotic in New England. Still it is observable that the paper he presented to the church intimates no scruple as to personal connection with Presbytery. But, in after years, the esteem and veneration which he felt for the great and good men with whom he became acquainted at the meetings of the general assembly and other church judicatories, and the conservatism of that system, so much in harmony with his cherished tastes and principles, gave it an increasingly strong hold on his convictions and preferences. Still, wherever the great essential doctrines of the gospel were adhered to with equal fidelity by Congregationalists and Presbyterians, he counted the things in which they differed of far less importance than those as to which they were agreed.

At that time (1794), the church in Newburyport had not adopted the constitution of the Presbyterian Church in the United States. This it did at a later period, under his own ministry. But, even under that constitution, Presbyterianism was not precisely the same then as now. In 1791, all Presbyterian ministers who chose to be present were invited to sit as corresponding members of the general assembly.† Ten years

* Stearns' "Historical Discourse," page 58.
† "Life of Dr. Alexander," page 96.

4 *

later, the famous " Plan of Union " with Congregationalists was adopted by stanch Presbyterians. There
was nothing *then* anti-presbyterian in such communion
with neighboring Congregational churches as was
plainly essential to the welfare of the solitary Presbyterian church in Newburyport.

After the acceptance of the call, there still remained
some difficulties as to who should be invited to officiate
at the ordination. His father writes (Sept. 28, 1794), —

" It is of very great consequence to waive, and in a
friendly way to check, all discussion respecting the late
pastor, and the comparative merits of those who did
and those who did not exchange with him. The real
question is, whether any thing shall now be done to
cloud the prospect of general harmony with good men ?
The question, is whether every thing should not be done
to cherish that harmony ?

" The session have voted to hold communion, &c.,
and very properly ; but a pointed discrimination, now
set up, would go far to defeat that intention, as it would
be lifting up the standard of hostility against many
whose gifts might have afforded much comfort and edification to the society.

" If you shall become a member of the presbytery,
as you expect, in case of settling here, you will be
among the first to treat them with due honor, and to
have as much intercourse with them as their situation
will admit ; but every one sees that your exchanges
must be chiefly with others who are nearer, &c."

He writes again, on the 6th of November, —

" Be cheered, my son, by the evident tokens of divine
favor upon you. Your prospects as to having a united
and affectionate people are as promising as almost any

one's in these times. Have, then, but one care now,
that of being a blessing in your important sphere."

In the end, all things were arranged satisfactorily;
and, on the 19th of November, 1794, he was ordained
and installed pastor of the Presbyterian church in
Newburyport. The following is extracted from the
"Newburyport Herald" of Nov. 21, 1794: —

" On Tuesday evening last, the Presbytery of Londonderry, agreeably to previous appointment, together
with a number of corresponding Congregational ministers, convened in this town for the purpose of attending
to the final trials of Mr. Daniel Dana, in order for
ordination to the pastoral care of the Presbyterian
church and congregation here. On Wednesday, the
public solemnities were performed, in the meeting-
house, in the following order: the Rev. Mr. Noyes
of Southampton made the introductory prayer. The
Rev. Mr. Dana of Ipswich preached the sermon, from
Acts xx. 24. The Rev. Dr. M'Clintock of Greenland
made the consecrating prayer. The Rev. Mr. Morrison
of Londonderry gave the charge. The Rev. Mr. Miltimore of Stratham gave the right hand of fellowship;
and the Rev. Mr. Frisbie of Ipswich the concluding
prayer. The candor and catholicism displayed in the
combination, so entirely harmonious, between the ministers of different denominations, and that upon so
important and conspicuous an occasion, must give sincere pleasure to every friend of that religion whose
prominent feature is charity. A numerous and respectable company of singers afforded, by their performances, high pleasure to a large audience, who displayed
through the whole solemnities a degree of attention
and decorum worthy of remark and commemoration."

The sermon, and the other parts of the ordination service, were published by request; as also the sermon of the pastor on the sabbath following, from 2 Cor. ii. 16, "Who is sufficient for these things?"

At this time commenced his long connection with the Presbytery of Londonderry. He found in that body, then, and in succeeding years, fathers and brethren of congenial sentiments with himself, and in character worthy of his high respect and esteem; and by them he was always beloved and honored. With the Rev. Dr. Morrison of Londonderry, his friendship was specially warm and intimate. His relations to the presbytery appear to have been uniformly pleasant, from the period of his reception to it, in the freshness of his youth, to the day when another generation of its members gathered around his couch to bid farewell to the patriarch whose pilgrimage was then nearly at its close.

The Rev. James Miltimore, who took part in his ordination, continued his friend and neighbor for more than forty years. The kind manners and the venerable, benignant aspect of that good man are still fresh in memory.

From this year (1784) to the end of his life, with the exception of an interval of five and a half years in New Hampshire, Mr. Dana's residence was in that beautiful town (now city) of Newburyport, which the passing stranger easily recognizes as one of the "pleasant places" of the earth, and of which her native sons, however long and far removed from the localities dear to childhood, speak always with enthusiasm. One who has been a traveller in many lands, may yet look with undiminished delight on the long line of beauti-

ful residences in High Street, with their terraced
gardens and grounds; and on the magnificent prospect
thence of land and sea in the clear light of a summer's day, or when autumn sheds a mellow lustre over
the round hills on the banks of the Merrimack. Nor
has there been wanting to Newburyport a goodly heri-
tage of intellectual culture and religious influence.
Many honored names are associated with her history,
either as natives or residents; and scarcely any place in
the land, of similar size, has supplied an equal number
of members to the clerical profession.

In a letter written Nov. 23, 1794, a few days after
the ordination, his father says, "You have an important sphere of usefulness. The kind reception you meet
with the multitude of that numerous society is certainly encouraging in regard to the progress of the
gospel. And it is not a duty to indulge anxiety as to the
opposition; though you would not despise any one
who has a soul. That happy combination of qualities
mentioned by the apostle deserves your remembrance
and mine: 'God hath not given us the spirit of fear,
but of power, and of love, and of a sound mind.' May
you be filled with such a spirit, and by it rise superior
to every opponent and every difficulty!

"The solemnity and decorum observed by that great
assembly, and the tender affection appearing in so
many, comfort me much upon every remembrance.
Be animated, my son; be strong in the grace of Christ,
our blessed Master. Let your performances carry more
and more of freedom. And, especially, let them express a *heart* which loves your people, and ardently
wishes their eternal good.

"Adieu,　　　"J. DANA."

CHAPTER VI.

1795-1800.

WITHDRAWAL OF THE MINORITY.— PASTORAL DUTIES.
—YELLOW FEVER. — INJURY TO HIS EYES. — SUC-
CESS AS A PEACE-MAKER.— MARRIAGE.

DURING the earlier months of his pastoral connection,
Mr. Dana's principles were tested by the course pursued by those who had been adverse to his settlement.
They declined to acquiesce in the decision of the
church and the presbytery. Nothing was objected to
him personally, except his *youth ;* but his preaching
seemed to some not sufficiently *doctrinal.* They missed
doubtless, some phrases long familiar to their ears;
as, from the isolated position of this Church, one style had
long prevailed in the pulpit. Divine truth in the simplicity and symmetry of its scriptural forms is not so
attractive to some as are the idols of scholastic manipu-
lation. His style had been formed on classic models;
and, instead of restricting himself to a few favorite
topics, he aimed to introduce his hearers (to borrow
his own expression) to the "whole generous circle of
scripture truths." It is remarkable, that, of the long
list of his printed discourses, none are more replete with
doctrinal instruction than some of the earliest of the
series. *   The presbytery were perplexed with no

---

* The Second and Third, from John vi. 29, and Eph. iv. 30, may be
specified.

46

doubts; their final action had been unanimous, and accompanied by a special testimony to "the orthodoxy, piety, and prudence" of the young candidate for ordination.

Nevertheless, agitation was kept up for several months; and at length the minority secured the services of an older minister, the Rev. John Boddily (of Lady Huntingdon's school), who in July commenced preaching in the house of one of the elders. They next proposed, that, as a peace-measure, he should be settled as colleague with the pastor. This proposal was not acceded to. In October, the presbytery finally decided to give them a separate church organization. They, however, dropped connection with the presbytery, which was only resumed, after many years, by their successors.

It must be admitted that the course pursued by these dissentients, if it had not the sanction of presbytery, had at least that of immemorial usage. They were a very respectable minority; their wishes had been thwarted; quiescence in such a case would have been contrary to all local precedent. Whether from the extreme asperity of the east winds on that exposed coast, impregnating the atmosphere with the seeds of rankling irritation, and making the "*dolce far niente*" of Italy a thing impossible, or from the deeper interest felt there than elsewhere in ecclesiastical affairs, — whatever the cause, physical or moral, certain it is, that, from the earliest times, there had been among the churches in that region an unusual amount of what the poet calls "harmony not understood." Coffin's "History of Newbury," one of the most honest histories ever written, reveals an odd state of things between the first

settlers and that ripe scholar and exemplary man,
Thomas Parker, pastor of the first church in Newbury.
For some twenty-five years, one-half of his congregation faithfully attended on his edifying preaching on
Sunday, and then quarrelled with him all the week
about church government; his Congregationalism being
not as Congregational as theirs. At one time, claiming
to be a majority, they even assumed to " suspend " him
from his pastoral office, kindly adding, however, " In
the mean time, as a gifted brother, you may preach for
the edification of the church if you please " (!).

In the case to which our narrative refers, a separate
church organization was plainly the true solution of the
difficulty. It gave the dissentients liberty to follow
their preferences, whilst it left to the pastor a congregation amply large and thoroughly united and homo-
geneous.

It may well be supposed, however, that the agitation,
of many months' continuance, which preceded this
result, put to a severe test the equanimity (not to say
magnanimity) of one whom nature had endowed with
sensibilities both generous and acute.

Rev. Mr. Carey of Newburyport wrote to a friend,
that he " looked on with admiration at the blended forbearance and spirit of his course toward the malcon-
tents." The following extracts are from his father's
letters during this time of trial.

" Ipswich, July 30, 1795.

" I am very well satisfied with what has been done;
and doubt not that He who hitherto has conducted
your friends and you in a way so unexceptionable will
be with you and them in what remains. For the rest,
wait on the Lord, and keep his way, and be under no

discouragement from any appearances. I have thought, and still think, that a minister of right character, conducting with prudence and resolution, would be very likely, in the course of things, to have a congregation to his wishes, in such a place as you are in; and, to me, all things seem tending to that point. You have the consciousness of not driving off anybody by bad doctrine or offensive conduct. If still they are irreconcilable, be thankful if they will be good enough to withdraw, and try to comfort themselves with some other preacher.

"And God Almighty grant you more and more of every virtue; and bring you nearer to himself than ever, advance you to higher usefulness than ever, by all these trials of faith and patience."

In another letter, he says, "It is pleasing to see how the zeal of your friends is kindled upon the present occasion." — "Oct. 24. We hear nothing lately but that all is quiet and happy with you." — "Nov. 4. The general current of accounts respecting the state of your society, and your prospect of greater comfort and increasing usefulness, is favorable and animating."

"Jan. 20, 1796. Refer all to that superior wisdom which best knows how to govern the church and the world. It is but a little way, at best, that we can see before us. There is nothing but what the over-ruling Power can turn to good; and these considerations should teach us, perhaps, to be less strenuous against any thing except plain moral evil." — "March 28, 1796. I am comforted to find what a united and cordial society you now find yourself connected with. You have nothing to do but to go on preaching and living

5

that divine gospel which you have embraced. God will take care of the rest."

But the most remarkable passage occurs in a letter of May 29, 1795: "Those restless spirits are doing you more good than perhaps they design, and much more, perhaps, to Zion."

These words came true in a sense which the writer could not have divined. Thirty years afterward, when Mr. Dana's "doctrine" and "life" had become "fully known" to a whole generation of his townsmen, this same church that had seceded from him, re-called him to Newburyport by a most cordial invitation to become their pastor; and that relation he sustained to them till his final resignation of the pastoral office in 1845. They who separated from him in his youth were unconsciously building a church for him in his later years.

From a statement of the whole matter placed on the records of the First Presbyterian Church, the following extract will suffice: —

"From all these things, we realize an additional bond upon us to strengthen the hands and the heart of our beloved pastor, whose eminent abilities and excellent spirit, approved through so many and great trials, at so early a period of his life, carry a new and additional commendation of him to our esteem and affection." *

The pledge here given was fully redeemed. From the beginning to the end of his pastoral connection with this church, their warmth of attachment was unfailing.

He was early called to unusual conversance with

---

* The statements, thus far, of this chapter are based wholly on documents. The writer remembers no allusion of his father to the subject.

those scenes that touch the deepest sensibilities of a pastor. There was much sickness in town in the year 1795. He officiated at fifty funerals,—nearly one every week. From this it may be judged how much of his time was given to the sick and dying.

The next year, Newburyport was visited by a scourge almost unknown in that latitude—the yellow fever. It was generally fatal. Dr. John Barnard Swett, his physician and friend, being asked by some one, "What is it?" replied, "It is death; I can give it no other name." Visiting freely among its victims, Mr. Dana was much exposed, and his life was near becoming a sacrifice to his sense of duty. One morning, Dr. Swett and himself met at the bedside of one in the last stage of the disease. Having an appointment to fulfil at Gloucester, he set out, perhaps the next day, feeling slightly unwell at the time. On the road, he became so ill as barely to be able to reach his father's house at Ipswich. The fever was upon him, and he was brought very low. On his recovery, he heard with much grief the news which had been kept from him,—the death of his beloved physician.

In a few weeks the pestilence disappeared. Dr. Buckminster of Portsmouth wrote him, Oct. 14, 1796, "I rejoice that God has preserved you through the sickness with which you have been visited, and that he has so far removed the scourge with which he has been visiting Newbury, as that the inhabitants are returning to their deserted dwellings."

He afterward referred to this illness as having suggested to him a valuable lesson as to the manner of approaching the sick and dying. An aunt with whom he was a favorite (the wife of Dr. Joshua Fisher of

Beverly), coming into the room when he was much prostrated, could not suppress her emotion. He remembered the excitement and exhaustion which this caused to himself, and learned hence the need of consideration of the physical state of those in similar circumstances to whom he came as a spiritual guide and comforter.

His visits to the sick were always singularly prized. Once, when called up at night for this purpose, he asked the messenger, "Is not Mr. M. her minister?" The answer was, "Mr. M. is her minister when she is well, but you are her minister when she is sick." How often was his presence like the entrance of a ray of heavenly sunshine to the darkened room of the afflicted and sorrowing! The tenderness of his sympathy, the aptness of his quotations from the Bible and from his favorite, Watts, and those prayers which seemed to bring heaven so near, made him pre-eminently a minister of consolation to the sick and dying. "When the ear heard him, then it blessed him; and when the eye saw him, it gave witness to him. The blessing of him that was ready to perish came upon him." Many, it may be presumed, in the course of his long pastoral experience, saw in him the realization of that beautiful ideal, —

> "Beside the bed where parting life was laid,
> And sorrow, guilt, and pain, by turns dismayed,
> The reverend champion stood: at his control
> Despair and anguish fled the struggling soul:
> Comfort came down the trembling wretch to raise,
> And his last faltering accents whispered praise."

He often spoke with pleasure of the answer once given by an aged man, dying, to his question, how

death appeared: " Death — it seems like a dark valley;
but I think I can see light beyond!"

His pastoral duties occupied so much time in the day,
that he was obliged to extend his hours of study far
into the night. Before he was aware of danger, he had
inflicted a lasting injury on his eyes. In addition to
the suffering and annoyance to which he was subjected
at the time, he was compelled to use green spectacles
as a protection almost to the close of his life. This
greatly impaired the effect of his performances in the
pulpit, as far as the expression of the eye was concerned. It was only near at hand that one could fully
enjoy its pleasant light, enkindled by genial converse or
inspiring recollection. The evil was partly compensated by the greater freedom and animation of sermons,
which, thoroughly prepared as to their topics, were otherwise extemporaneous. The solemn stillness and profound attention of his numerous auditory, re-acting upon himself, gave him stimulus and support. Where
his eye most naturally rested, not far from the centre
of the church, there sat one (to whom he afterwards
sustained a near relation) whose eyes, never wandering
from the speaker, and often suffused with tears, told how
deeply the heart was moved. He felt that he could
scarcely preach if Mr. Coombs were absent.

How serious was the obstruction, during these first
years of his ministry, to written preparation for the
the pulpit, appears from an advertisement to two discourses, delivered April 25, 1799, the day of national
fast recommended by President Washington : —

" To those who heard these discourses, and who
have requested their publication, the author would
suggest, that, as he was necessitated by the feeble state

5*

of his eyes to deliver them from very imperfect notes, it has been impossible to recollect, in every instance, the precise expressions originally used."

This he also speaks of as " having much retarded his progress " in respect to publication. Notwithstanding this, two other sermons of his had been printed by request the previous month.

In 1798, his father writes, " I am glad that you begin to harmonize the neighboring societies. Continue in your good wishes and endeavors for still more of the same kind ; though time perhaps may be required."

Time *was* required where discord was so inveterate. Dr. Alexander, visiting Newburyport three years after this, found six churches in which he could preach, between whose pastors there was little or no exchange of pulpits.* But Mr. Dana's efforts to counteract what he publicly rebuked as a " narrow, contentious, censorious spirit " were in the end successful. Already (1798) he had obtained an act of amnesty from his church to the Congregational church formed by secession from it before his ministry commenced. He was on friendly terms with the Rev. Mr. Boddily, the pastor chosen by those who had withdrawn from himself. When Mr. Boddily's death occured, in 1802, he was called on by them to preach the funeral sermon. He labored also to smooth the way to an exchange of pulpits with Dr. Spring, who, having been often at his father's house, had known him from his childhood. But some could not easily forget that Dr. Spring had responded to Mr. Murray's proffered hand by putting his behind his back. Mr. Murray, among his friends, made reprisals on Dr.

* "Life of A. Alexander, D.D.," page 256.

Spring by a sly hit at his Hopkinsian heresy, quoting with great gusto from Watts, —

" What mortal power from things unclean
  Can pure productions bring?
  Who can command a vital stream
  From an infected Spring? "

Thus, with one blow, did he both vindicate orthodoxy and avenge himself; a playful revenge, however, if we may trust the tradition that he was of a forgiving temper.

Between Mr. Dana's church and that from which it had separated in 1746, no complete amity subsisted till (in the same spirit which had dictated his own appeal for Christian union before settlement) Rev. Leonard Withington, in 1816, made it a condition of his acceptance of the call to the First Church in Newbury that past differences should be forgotten.

Before the termination of Mr. Dana's first pastoral connection, pacific relations had been established between all the churches. Their dissensions had become merely historical.

The record of an event, most important to the happiness of his life, belongs to this period. On the 30th of December, A.D. 1800, he was united in marriage with Elizabeth, daughter of William Coombs, Esq., of Newburyport.

CHAPTER VII.

1801–1806.

RELIGIOUS EXCITEMENT IN NEWBURYPORT. — REV. MR. MILTON. — ADELPHI SOCIETY. — PUBLICATIONS. — LETTERS FROM DR. MORSE.

EARLY in 1801, great religious excitement prevailed for a time in Newburyport. Mr. Dana seems at first to have been hopeful that much good would result; but such extravagances and disorders, more novel then than since, were soon mingled with it, as caused him solicitude. After preaching, young men would rise in the galleries and exhort; great confusion followed. He was present, on one occasion, at a united meeting at Mr. Milton's church, the headquarters of the excitement, when the agitation was extreme; and groans and shouts began to be heard throughout the spacious and crowded edifice. He rose, and with deep and calm solemnity said, "The Lord is a God of order, not of confusion." The effect was instantaneous; the vast auditory was hushed into solemn stillness. There must have been something strangely impressive in the scene, to have been described, as it was forty years afterward, by one who said, that, as he rose in that excited, tumultuous assemblage, "he looked more like an angel than a man."

The following from a letter of his father, dated Feb. 14, 1801, expresses, doubtless, his own sentiments at

the time. It is also instructive, as showing how often
the same scenes are reproduced, and how much the
same counsels are needed, in religious excitements,
from one age to another.

"Reviewing your letter, and the scenes I witnessed
lately, with some other things I have heard since, makes
me yet more decided that a stand must soon be made,
in a Christian way, against the eccentricities which prevail. I will not say in the most positive manner what
ought to be the first step: whether some ministers
should first be earnestly entreated in a private way,
and convinced, if possible, that the lead they have
given, if persisted in, will ultimately bring the utmost
disgrace on the work of God, and mislead (perhaps to
their ruin) many more than it benefits; or whether the
first step should be a solemn consultation of the several
ministers, with a delegation from their respective
churches of some of the most discreet and unexception-
ably Christian men, and friends to heart-religion and
the work of God.

"I am struck with the ruinous tendency of bringing
forward persons to perform public parts who (besides
many improprieties which ought to have a candid al-
lowance made for them) mislead in essential points
those who look up to them, and diffuse a bad spirit.
I was struck with the indiscriminate manner in which
all who cry out seemed to be *approbated* with very little of inquiry into their views or convictions, and with
very few cautionary hints of the danger of resting
without a foundation, — without thorough conviction,
or genuine conversion, faith, and repentance. I was
struck with the ungracious manner of praying over
sermons, and about ministers. It is too plain that *some*

who give the tone cherish such prejudices against ministers at large as are very unjust, and more plainly in persons so little informed as they are ; and they betray a censoriousness which goes to pull down all who do not think well of all these eccentric movements. They pray accordingly, and others by their example are led into it.

"If Mr. Milton did pray in the manner I hear he did on Thursday evening, I think it clear that he should know soon that others cannot go with him, unless he will retract and desist."

Of the " Mr. Milton " here mentioned, it may be said, in extenuation of any early mistakes, that without some deviation from ordinary rules and modes of action, he could not have been consistent with himself. He was a man of unrivalled eccentricity. By this, as much as by his mental vivacity, and the still more potent charm of a wonderfully strong, and at the same time musical voice, he had gathered a large congregation in Newburyport. He interpreted, in a very literal sense, the injunction, " Cry aloud, spare not, lift up thy voice like a trumpet." Clear, sonorous, trumpet-like, were the tones that rung through the whole neighborhood during his hours of public service.

Exchanging pulpits once with a clergyman at some distance, whose strength lay rather in mind and heart than lungs, and for whom a church had been built with special reference to the easy transmission of sound, Mr. Milton's first utterance nearly brought the whole congregation to their feet. In the afternoon, all Marblehead came together to hear this son of thunder. Not content with giving notice, before sermon, of a third service, he wound up the benediction in stentorian tones, with " Amen ; remember the *lectur'*."

He often abruptly closed his long prayer just as he appeared to be in the middle of it. As an instance of summary despatch, many will recollect the frequent petition, "Bless Bible societies, missionary institutions, tract establishments, and sabbath schools." This was varied sometimes with "Blessings on the head of Robert Raikes, the founder of Sunday schools!" begun on a high key, and descending with heavy cadence to the close.

He carried on a life-long wordy war against Antinomians,— a safe one, however, as there was no respondent; at least, none answered to the *name.* These invisible antagonists he sometimes floored with the petition, "Save us from the sweet *pison* of Antinomianism."

As Mr. Milton was as eccentric in person as in character,— very short and very broad, with a profusion of black hair flowing down his shoulders — the contrast between him and his nearest clerical neighbor, when seen together, was sufficiently striking. But, though opposites, they were never antagonists. Their orbits never intersected. And doubtless there were mingled with Mr. Milton's peculiarities, sterling traits of character, which, equally with them, accounted for the long fidelity to him of his large congregation.

In these years, there existed in Newburyport what might be termed a "Young Men's Christian Association,"; except that mutual improvement, rather than the spiritual direction of others, was the main object. Mr. Dana obtained from his father some counsels for their guidance : such as that there should be "*great simplicity,* — as little of parade or profession as may be ; that each shall religiously beware of every appearance of ostentation or spiritual pride in any form, in a particular manner not to make a righteousness of their meetings;" &c. That the " Adelphi Society" mingled good works with their faith, a proof is extant to this day, in the shape of a piece of plate presented to the pastor's wife, on occasion, probably, of the transfer of their meetings from the parsonage, where they had been warmly welcomed in the winter evenings, to the residence of Mr. Richard Pike, one of their most valued members.

In contrast with the pietism which sometimes springs up in distorted forms in the fervid atmosphere of animal excitement, more than one of Mr. Dana's earlier publications delineate, in the light of example, the fair proportions of that religion, deep-rooted, symmetrical, and mature, on which the gentle dew of heaven sheds down its silent nurture. He gives this beautiful picture of a good man, in a sermon occasioned by the decease of Mr. Benjamin Moody, an elder in his church :—

" There is a peculiar *pleasure*, as well as propriety, in paying honor at death to those excellent men who through life shrank and retired from their own praise. And if religion is the highest glory of our nature, and if to have much of the spirit of Christ is to be eminent in religion, I must confess I have known no man, personally, who has appeared to me more worthy of honor and everlasting remembrance, than he whom we now lament.

" He prized the *peculiar doctrines of Christianity*. They not only supported him in death, but sweetened and adorned his life ; while his life recommended *them*, and powerfully demonstrated how superior is a religion animated by the pure principles of the gospel, to every

thing besides that bears the name. The very spirit of
his Master breathed in his temper, and shone out in his
life. Where shall we find a man of such an affectionate, uniting, healing spirit; so ready to leap over those
barriers which bigotry erects between Christians; so
free from that narrow, contentious, censorious spirit,
which (I grieve to say it) has done such infinite mischief in this place; so ready to take to his arms and
heart the friends of God wherever found, and with
whatever society connected; so ready to throw the veil
of candor and compassion over their infirmities; so
zealous for the *love* and *peace*, as well as the truth and
purity, of the gospel; so distant from the affectation of
pressing unhallowed passion into the service of religion;
so ready to bear and to forbear, to become any thing,
every thing, or nothing, so that Christ may be honored
and his cause promoted?

"Never have I heard from the lips of man *prayers*
which to me appeared more of a nature to solemnize
and elevate the mind, to enkindle and cherish the spirit
of devotion. He conversed with his God as a friend;
yet who ever perceived in the prayers of this good
man, any thing even remotely bordering on unbecoming
familiarity or irreverence?"

One of his earlier efforts as a pastor had been for the
promotion of sacred music, which he found in a lan-
guishing state. He determined to devote two morning
and two afternoon hours, each week, to the gratuitous
instruction in music of such young ladies and gentlemen as were disposed to attend. In his circular of
invitation he says, "It being his duty, and, as he trusts,
his first desire, to consecrate his time and services to
the best and highest interests of the people of his

6

charge, he will endeavor, from time to time, to call the attention of his young friends to the all-interesting subject of *religion ;* and he most ardently wishes them to consider this as a principal object of the plan proposed."

A young lady, whose residence was just opposite the parsonage, obtained the consent of her parents, though their religious views differed widely from his, to attend his singing-class. There she received her first religious impressions, and from that time developed a character of singular loveliness. She died young, not long after her marriage. A brief memoir, introducing a selection from her writings, was prepared by him.

In 1805, he was solicited by Rev. Dr. Morse to become one of the editors of the "Panoplist." He preferred to be merely a contributor.

Dr. Morse writes again on the subject, Dec. 12, 1805 : —

"Perhaps you have something prepared, or nearly so, — your second number on Experimental Religion; if so, do forward it for the next number. I wish much for the biographical sketch of President Davies. We shall have one of Dr. Finley for this number; if we could have that of President Davies for the next, it would be very acceptable. If you can spare time, do drop me a line by post soon, and let me know what to expect from you. The 'Panoplist' continues to prosper, and is generally well spoken of.

"Yesterday the corporation elected Fisher Ames, Esq., President of the University of Cambridge. So there is an end (and on the whole a happy one) to our anxiety on that subject."

Another letter from Dr. Morse, four months later, is

specially interesting as conveying, " in confidence," the first hint as to the establishment of the *Andover Theological Seminary :* —

"CHARLESTOWN, April 8, 1806.

"MY DEAR FRIEND, — Though painfully affected with an epidemic cold, I am constrained to write you on several interesting subjects. I have deemed them of sufficient importance to justify a visit to Newburyport, that I might have a personal interview with you; but this is at present out of my power. It is, indeed, a critical and anxious period, my friend, in a great variety of respects; and we have our parts to act in the management of affairs of no small moment.

"First, let me say a word concerning the 'Panoplist.' It is, in my opinion, extremely important to the cause of evangelical truth, that this work be ably supported. It now stands high in public estimation; and you and your good father have contributed your share in raising its character. I expect there may be a shifting of subscribers at the end of this year, but, I hope, no diminution. Previous to the commencement of a new year, I wish to know whether I can calculate on a continuance of your aid, and that of Dr. Dana. Were I to see you together, with Dr. Pearson, I think we could state to you such reasons as would induce you both to say, 'We will continue and increase our aid.'

. . . "I wish to have a long conversation with you on the affairs of college; the resignation of our valuable and learned friend, Dr. Pearson; and the establishment of him at Andover in a useful and respectable station. A plan is in contemplation, at which I can only hint *in confidence*, of establishing a *Theological Academy* at Andover, and placing Dr. Pearson at the head of it.

Think on the subject, and prepare to take an active part in it.

"Our ecclesiastical affairs are in an awful state, and growing worse and worse. Is there no way in which the things that remain can be preserved and strengthened? Turn your thoughts to this subject, and request your worthy father to do the same, and to put his thoughts on paper, if he thinks proper, for the 'Panoplist,' or to be published in pamphlet.

. . . .

"Your friend and brother,

"J. MORSE."

CHAPTER VIII.

1807–1812.

ORIGINATION OF THE THEOLOGICAL SEMINARY AT ANDOVER. — PRESBYTERIAN GENERAL ASSEMBLY, 1810 AND 1812. — VISIT TO WASHINGTON AND MOUNT VERNON. — A HOUSE OF MOURNING.

AT the opening of the Theological Institution at Andover, Sept. 28, 1808, a brief account of its origin was given by Dr. Pearson. The following is an extract: —

"To arrive at its origin, it must be traced back to the pious institution, more than thirty years since founded in this place by the united liberality of two brothers, the Hon. Samuel and the Hon. John Phillips, sons of the first minister of this parish. In the constitution of their academy, they expressly declare 'that the *first* and *principal* object of their institution is the promotion of true PIETY and VIRTUE.' They have also accordingly made it the duty of the principal instructor, ' as the age and capacities of the scholars will admit, not only to instruct and establish them in the truth of Christianity, but also to inculcate upon them the great and important doctrines and duties of our holy religion.' In promotion of the same sublime object, the Hon. John Phillips farther gave, in the year 1789, the generous sum of $20,000, ' for the *virtuous* and *pious* education

6*

of youth of genius and serious disposition,' in this academy. To complete his liberality, in his last will, he
bequeathed to the academy in Exeter, of which he was
sole founder, two-thirds, and to the academy in this
town one-third, of the residue of all his estate, ' for the
benefit,' as his expression is, ' more especially of charity
scholars, such as may be of excelling genius, and of
good moral character, preferring the hopefully pious;
and such of these, who are designed to be employed in
the great and good work of the gospel ministry, having
acquired the most useful human literature in either of
these academies, or other seminaries, may be assisted in
the study of divinity (if a theological professor is not
employed in either of the two fore-mentioned academies)
under the direction of some eminent Calvinistic minister of the gospel, until such time as an able, pious, and
orthodox instructor shall, at least in part, be supported
in one or both these academies as a professor of divinity; by whom they may be taught the important principles and distinguishing tenets of our holy Christian
religion.' To this fund the Hon. William Phillips, late
of Boston, also bequeathed $4,000 for the same pious
design.

" In the special appropriation of this fund, every one
must remark the expansion of the great object of the
founders of the academy, and its intimate connection
with the theological institution now established; and,
agreeably to the principal design of the founders, and
to the express object of this fund, a considerable number of theological students, now settled in the ministry,
have been supported on this foundation while prosecuting their studies under the direction of the clergyman of this place.

" On a well-grounded expectation of liberal additions
to their theological fund, the trustees, in June, 1807, applied to the General Court to enlarge their power of
holding estate.

" Such, as we have now represented, is the connection between Phillips Academy and the Theological
Institution whose birth we this day celebrate; and
justice, as well as gratitude, requires us to recognize
the former as the radix of the latter, and as the embryo
of its future manhood.

" But, while we trace back the new institution to the
pious benevolence of men now in heaven, we cannot
fail to acknowledge the immeasurable goodness of God
in raising up others to enlarge and perfect what they
had begun."

The Hon. John Phillips, here recognized as having
laid the foundation on which the Andover Theological
Seminary was built, is the same in whose family Mr.
Dana had spent his two years at Exeter.

The desired amendment of the charter of Phillips
Academy having been obtained, the trustees were put
in possession of an " instrument making provision for
the establishment of a theological institution in Phillips
Academy, and containing the constitution of the same."
By this, the widow and the son of Hon. Samuel Phillips bound themselves " to erect two separate build-
ings for a theological institution; " and Samuel Abbot,
of Andover, gave twenty thousand dollars " as a fund
for the purpose of maintaining a professor of Christian
theology, and for the support and encouragement of
students in divinity." By these donations, the Andover Theological Seminary was founded, — in happy harmony with the wishes and intentions of the deceased

founders of Phillips Academy; who, however, could
have little imagined how tall a superstructure would
be reared on the foundations which their hands had
laid.

But a great exigency had arisen. Harvard University was at this time under influences, which, a few
years later, took the distinctive form and name of Unitarianism. It was needful that new efforts should be
made for the maintenance of the old faith.

There was, however, at this time among the Trinita-
rians, a marked division of theological sentiment. In
the first years of the present century, *Hopkinsianism*
had something of the fascinating attraction in New
England which many an *ism* has had there since. At
the very time that preparations were in progress for the
establishment of a theological institution on the Phillips foundation, at Andover, the plan of a theological
school was prominent in the counsels of some divines
of Hopkinsian proclivities. The question of a "coalition" was soon agitated.

Mr. Dana had been, three years previous (August,
1804), unanimously elected a member of the Board of
Trustees of Phillips Academy, in Andover. In reply
to their Secretary, Rev. Jonathan French, he says, —
"I have reason to doubt my sufficiency to discharge, as
I would wish, the important duties connected with its acceptance. But I would feel, too, that there is a high privilege and reward attending the taking of even a small
part in effectuating the pious and benevolent designs
which gave birth to the Institution." How unconscious
was he, at the time, of the responsibility, so long continued and so weighty, which this acceptance involved!

The letters which follow are of historic interest.
The words in italics are underscored in the original.

" Ipswich, Sept. 28, 1807.

"Dear Son, — I hoped to have seen you to-day, at your own house, but was called to attend the funeral of old Mr. Tappan; and now I know not whether I can see you before you go to Andover. I therefore enclose some minutes, made in haste, which I hoped to improve upon, and send you in better form.

"I am still in the same mind of having no coalition that shall forbid the trustees to choose all the instructors, and maintain, without interruption or mixture, the good old style of divinity. I wish, likewise, that the *plan of teaching* may be still open to improvement. Very much indeed depends on setting out right in that respect; and the case is important enough to authorize a solemn appointment of a number of divines, whether of the trust or not, to consider this subject by itself. I wish there might be time, however, for you to prepare and present a plan.

"I have had a little conversation with Judge Treadwell, who will hand you this; and I find him as unwilling for such a *mixture* as we are. Do invite him to come and see you this evening. He may be able to give you some account of Mr. Norris's wishes, and possibly to converse with him to some effect. He will converse with you, however, on the subject at large, and possibly write to Dr. Pearson (with whom you know he is much connected) or to Dr. Morse.

"Accept my love; convey much to dear Elizabeth and the children.

"I am your ever affectionate father,

"J. Dana."

MR. DANA TO MR. ABBOT OF EXETER.

"NEWBURYPORT, Oct. 3, 1807.

"MY DEAR FRIEND, — Knowing that your curiosity must be awake respecting Andover affairs, and recollecting the request you made when we parted, I sit down to acquaint you with a few particulars.

"The coalition scheme has not matured so fast as, judging from report, we were ready to believe. Nor am I certain that the worthy doctors feel altogether so sanguine as formerly in the expectation of accomplishing it. Nothing was brought before the Board on the subject; and, from some things which follow, you will draw your own conclusions whether the probability of the measure's being effected is increased or diminished.

"Mr. Abbot has chosen Mr. Woods as his professor. In taking this step, he has been governed, as he declares, not by any personal knowledge, but by information and advice communicated by Dr. Pearson, Dr. Morse, &c. It seems, likewise, that Col. Phillips and Messrs. Farrar and Newman have had personal interviews with Mr. Woods, who, as they state, has given them ample and unequivocal assurances *that he is no friend to the peculiarities of Hopkinsianism, but shall oppose them.* Being asked by one of them, whether, in case of coming to Andover, he should think it necessary to discourse on the divine agency in the production of sin, he replied, Yes, he should, and for the purpose of pointing out the error and mischief of such a sentiment. The gentlemen whom I have mentioned consider Mr. Woods as pledged. Mr. French, however, has never been satisfied. He opposed the appointment till he was overborne.

"When the appointment was announced to the Trustees, no one objected. It was probably the general apprehension that no one had a right to object. Indeed, respecting several of the Board, I have no information whether they were pleased with the appointment or the contrary. When the motions, respecting salary, &c., came forward, and there was a necessity on my part, either to act, or be singular in not acting, I expressed myself to the Trustees to this effect: I found myself in a situation extremely delicate and distressing. I acknowledged the perfect right of Mr. Abbot to make the appointment, and that, if the subsequent arrangements were so entirely *matters of course* as to imply no responsibility lying on the trustees, there would be no sufficient reason for any of them to decline proceeding; but finding that our constitution had marked out the system of doctrines which the professors were to subscribe to and teach, I was doubtful whether any of us were warranted to introduce a person to either of the professorships, concerning whose religious sentiments we had not some evidence that they accorded with the proposed system, and especially if we apprehended, and not without evidence, that, in material points, they were dissonant. This, I confessed, was my situation in the present case; and I must, therefore, be excused from acting. At the same time, I intimated to the Board that I was cordially desirous of receiving satisfaction on the points alluded to, and had, accordingly, submitted to the President a few questions, hastily penned that morning, and embracing some leading points of distinction between the old divinity and new, to which, if answers should be given in correspondence with the principles which we all profess to maintain, I should be greatly relieved. These questions I was now ready to put into the hands of any friend of Mr. Woods, that they might be communicated to him, and his written answers received. Dr. Morse readily closed with the proposal, and engaged to convey the questions to Mr. Woods, expressing his confidence that they would be answered satisfactorily. Several other gentlemen afterwards perused them, and expressed their wish that they might be answered. They are these: —

"'1. Does Mr. Woods disclaim the idea of a positive divine efficiency in the production of sin?

"'2. Does he hold that sinners are to be exhorted to use the means of grace in order to their conversion?

"'3. Does he believe, that, in regeneration, a principle of grace is communicated and received which is never afterward lost?

"'4. Does he hold the truth of the —— answer of the Assembly's Catechism; viz., The sinfulness of that state into which man fell consists in the guilt of Adam's first sin, &c.

"'5. Does he believe in the true and proper imputation of the righteousness of Christ to believers, for their justification?

"'6. Does he consider it a constituent part of Christian submission, that we be willing to be damned for the glory of God?

"'7. Does he believe that all the exercises of the unregenerate, so far as they have a moral character, are positively sinful? Is their honesty, their kindness, and awakened concern for their souls, positively wicked?'*

---

* Only the uninitiated reader will need to be informed that a *negative* answer to the *last two* questions, and an *affirmative* one to all the others, was desired, as a renunciation of Hopkinsianism.

" All circumstances considered, I have no doubt that we shall be answered ; in which case, light may arise upon our perplexed and benighted path. Reviewing the scene, and the part I felt myself called to act, you have, I doubt not, many tender and anxious thoughts about me. But interesting as the case was, and calculated to excite emotions not the most pleasant, I possessed myself. The gentlemen treated my suggestions with candor. Looking back, I feel a satisfaction in the thought of having done just so much, and no more. Still, I shall be anxious to know your opinion and feelings. If you can approve, let me know it. If otherwise, be perfectly open. Let me have your whole mind and heart on the subject at large. Advise me respecting future conduct.

" I cannot but confess to you, that, since going to Andover, I feel a sort of relief. That the prospects of our seminary are the brightest, I cannot suppose ; but an immense burden of responsibility is transferred from my shoulders to those of others, some of whom appear nowise oppressed by it. If you shall say that this is rather a selfish sort of consolation, I shall not contradict you. My solicitudes, however, will not cease ; but, having feebly endeavored to do my duty in a most interesting case, and where almost every personal consideration would have tempted me to do nothing, I desire to leave all events with him who can clear the darkest skies.

" I went to Hampton yesterday, on behalf of Mr. Webster. Mr. Appleton is feeble with the influenza, but, I hope, convalescing. Remember we have claims on you and on Mrs. Abbot. We salute you both very affectionately.   "Yours as ever,

7   "D. DANA."

MR. ABBOT'S REPLY.

"Oct. 12, 1807.

"Your obliging letter, which had been anxiously expected, was duly received, with what sensations it is difficult to say. It, however, gives me pleasure to learn that you have, with satisfaction to yourself, passed through a scene which must have been peculiarly delicate and trying; and, so far as I am possessed of the information of the circumstances, I can fully accord with you in feeling and sentiment, that you 'did just so much, and no more.' If your constitution, or the instrument which conveys Dr. Phillips' legacy, is to be any guide in this appointment, you cannot, I conceive, invest any man with the discretionary and uncontroverted power of designating the professors. To have sanctioned this unaccountable appointment, without satisfactory evidence on the score of sentiment, would have betrayed the trust reposed in you as trustees; and to sit still with the impressions which you had, while the trustees seemed precipitating into a violation of duty, must afford to you hereafter cause of self-reproach. Had you made a more decisive stand, delicately as you were situated, it might possibly have subjected you to suspicions of acting from improper motives, and lessened your influence. On the whole, I am persuaded the ground you took, and the time and manner of taking it, were fortunate. I am somewhat surprised, that nothing was said of the coalition; but do not feel relieved by the circumstance; — *timeo Danaos dona ferentes.* Can the project of union be given up? Is there not reason to apprehend that it is suspended only to be brought forward in another shape, and under circumstances more favorable to success?"

DR. MORSE TO MR. DANA.

" CHARLESTOWN, Oct. 17, 1807.

" MY DEAR FRIEND, — I have been so oppressed with engagements and company since my return from Andover, that I have not had a moment to write you. On Monday, I go to New Haven to place my two eldest sons in college. I snatch a moment, in my hurry of cares, just to say to you, that I exceedingly regret that any difference of opinion should exist among Orthodox men in regard to the contemplated *union* in the Theological Seminary at Andover. In existing circumstances, all *inferior* considerations should yield to the general good. The subject is of infinite moment. I cannot bear to contemplate the inevitable consequences of disunion. Be assured, my friend, there is *no real danger* of a predominant Hopkinsian influence, provided *we* are united, and act wisely. If we split, and they unite, they gain important advantages. I have conversed freely and fully with Mr. Woods on the questions you put into my hands. I think you would be entirely satisfied with his answers, as I am. He declines, in existing circumstances, to put his answers in writing. I pray Heaven to direct to a speedy course in which you and he may amicably settle all differences, and then I am persuaded an interview on points of doctrine would result in your satisfaction.

" Dr. Lyman, Dr. Holmes, Mr. Channing, and Mr. Bates, I learn, are decidedly for union. Dr. Dwight, and the clergy of Connecticut, and southward, and in the two western counties of this State, so far as I am informed, are for union, as is Mr. Chaplin. Be assured we unite only on *Catechism ground.* I have not time to add. Excuse haste. Let me have something for November "Panoplist." Biography (Rev.) of Dr. Tappan, &c.

"Your friend and brother,

"J. Morse."

The "differences" alluded to near the close of this last letter were not long without conciliation. They grew out of the unfriendly position which Mr. Woods, then a young man, and influenced doubtless by the theological antipathies of some with whom he was intimate, had held toward Dr. Dana of Ipswich. Nearly *fifty* years afterward, an allusion was made to the subject, too honorable to the character of all concerned to be suppressed. It occurs in a postscript to a letter dated Jan. 17, 1853.

"P.S. I have thought much of late of your good father, and of the endearing friendship which existed between us. My heart aches to think it was ever interrupted. The Lord forgive me for the mistakes I committed. It grieves me that I ever gave pain to his tender, bleeding heart. Oh that I could see him as I did once, and pour out my heart to him for a few moments, and receive the utterance of his forbearing and fatherly heart!

"LEONARD WOODS.

"Rev. DANIEL DANA, D.D."

Whatever may have been the apprehensions felt in 1807 as to the theological views of Mr. Woods, Mr. Dana in later years most earnestly desired the continuance of his connection with the seminary as a bulwark against more threatening novelties than those whose ingress had been originally dreaded.

7*

As his father's letters at this time afford, doubtless, a clue to his own sentiments, we subjoin an extract : —

" DEC. 28, 1807.

" The existing trustees will certainly consider that they are acting, not for Andover alone, not for a small section of our country, but for the whole body of ministers and Christians who wish to maintain the simple doctrine of the gospel, without the intermixture of vain philosophy. And I frankly confess that I tremble for the event of the present movements. *There is certainly an infinite distance between the two (questions),* *— whom we can hold in charity, notwithstanding diversity of opinion on many questions, and whom we ought to select for our teachers, or those whom* WE offer to the public for so great and extensive purposes? In the latter case it must be the care of considerate men to look out such persons as they sincerely believe will teach the doctrines of religion, in *all* points, in a way which best agrees with the gospel. I am not over fond of creeds ; but we know how *we* understand the gospel, and we know who, in our opinion, have obtained the clearest and most incontrovertible character in that way. I should expect my honored friend, Mr. Abbot, would proceed in that way ; and the other gentlemen of the board generally. Union is a very desirable thing, but it cannot be bought with donations."

A sequel of the letter given above is supplied (*fifty years later*) by the following extract from the commemorative discourse, by the Rev. Dr. Leonard Bacon, at the semi-centennial celebration at Andover, September, 1858.

" Eight months after the formal founding of the Seminary (4th May, 1808), another "legal instrument," entitled "The Statutes of the Associate Foundation in the Theological Institution in Andover," was communicated to the trustees. By that instrument, executed on the 21st of March preceding, the associate founders, Moses Brown, William Bartlet, and John Norris, gave each ten thousand dollars, and William Bartlet an additional amount of ten thousand dollars, constituting a fund for the support of two professors and for the aid of students, and ordained certain statutes to control the application of that endowment. It is plain, from the record, that the trustees found in the statutes of the associate founders much matter for discussion. The entire plan of a union between two parties differing in the degree of their Calvinism was to be settled by the acceptance or rejection of that instrument. The whole day was occupied with reading the instrument twice, and considering its provisions article by article; and then the meeting was adjourned from Wednesday (May 4) to the following Monday (May 9). At the adjourned meeting, beginning at two, P.M., the afternoon and evening were devoted to the discussion and consideration of the same instrument; but no conclusion was reached. The next morning, at eight o'clock, ' the discussion was resumed ; and, after mature consideration of the said instrument, and prayerful deliberation on the important subject thereof,' the offered endowment was accepted on the prescribed conditions. The vote was taken by yeas and nays, and was unanimous, with one exception. Only eight of the twelve trustees appear to have been present. Their names appear upon the record thus: ' Yeas, Nehemiah Abbot, Samuel Farrar, Jonathan French, Jedediah

Morse, John Phillips (Andover), Eliphalet Pearson, and Mark Newman. The Rev. Daniel Dana did not vote.' The now venerable Dr. Dana was a young man fifty years ago; but he was even then, as he ever has been, with unbending consistency, an Old School Presbyterian Calvinist, and not a moderate Cambridge Calvinist; then, as ever since, his Calvinism was of the sort that makes no compromises with Hopkinsian improvements in theology; then, as ever since, he was not afraid to stand, like the poet's Abdiel, alone in his unswerving allegiance to his principles."

At the time referred to in this extract, Mr. Dana was evidently in much perplexity as to the course which it became him to pursue. He preferred that there should be *no coalition* with Hopkinsianism. This was, it is thought, the preference also of the *four* trustees *not present* May 9. He sympathized fully with those who did not wish the old doctrine to be flavored with this indigenous root. But how far his dread of the possible influence of Hopkinsianism should make him active in opposing what might be a leading of Providence to some great and good result, must have given him pause. His doubts were at length removed; and he intimated, that, as he was the last to come in to the union, he would be the last to break it.

As to the result of the coalition, if either party to it were disappointed, it must have been the favorers of Hopkinsianism; for only a mild form of that doctrine showed itself in later years. *

---

* The older Hopkinsians shut the door of the kingdom pretty close. But, if severe to others, they were not less so to themselves. Later Hopkinsianism was more lenient, but still stringent.

The writer, when fresh from college, once heard a *moderate* Hopkins-

Mr. Dana had long been on terms of intimacy with Mr. Abbot, of Andover, as well as with the other founders of the institution. He writes from Andover, in 1804, "I dined yesterday with Col. Phillips, and arrived at our good friend Mr. Abbot's. The family is well, and unites in love." A letter to him from his stepmother, July 23, 1800, speaks of being "treated by Mr. and Mrs. Abbot with all the affection and kindness that I could be by the best of parents."

In his sermon (April 19, 1841) commemorative of William Bartlet, Esq., whose munificence to the Seminary had been on so grand a scale, the following reference is made to the union in 1808 between the original and the associate founders: —

"It is a singular and memorable fact, that when, about thirty-four years since, several opulent and large-hearted individuals were meditating the establishment of a theological seminary in this place, an assemblage of the same description, in a distant part of the county, were, without any mutual knowledge or communication, engaged in a design entirely similar. When the respective parties became acquainted with each other's intentions, a most interesting question arose. Would the cause of God and the interest of the churches be best promoted by a *separate*, or a *united*, organization? Each plan had its advantages, and each its difficulties. Among the *last* may be mentioned some shades of

ian instruct his newly converted hearers that "God did not bring them into the kingdom for their own sakes, but for the sake of the good which it was for them to do to others." It seemed a natural inference, that no one is bound to be very specially thankful to heaven for his own salvation. Certainly, if there were danger of too warm gratitude in any human bosom for divine benefits, such doctrine would prove an admirable refrigerant.

difference in theological views. The question received a long and ample discussion. In the issue, difficulties vanished, minor differences were merged, the spirit of union and of mutual concession prevailed, and, as the result, this theological institution rose into existence, amply endowed and powerfully sustained. The founders at Andover, having been first in maturing and arranging their plan, it was agreed that the other party should unite with them, under the appellation of ' Associate Founders.' "

Mr. Dana corresponded at this time with Dr. Morse, President Appleton, and others, in relation to Andover affairs. Some of his letters have perhaps been preserved (he kept no copies of them). In the preceding statements the writer has made use of all the material in his possession.

In these years, Unitarianism was making rapid advances in Massachusetts. A sermon, on the "Deity of Christ," was delivered by him, July 31, 1810, before the Haverhill Association, and was published at their request. A second edition was published in 1819, with additions.

A copy of this sermon, with an accompanying letter, he sent to his friend, Mr. Abbot, who, to his great grief, was now leaning to Unitarianism.

A vacancy occurring by the resignation of Rev. J. Appleton, called to the presidency of Bowdoin College, Mr. Dana was, in 1808, elected a member of the Board of Trustees of Phillips Exeter Academy.

In 1810, he went as commissioner from his Presbytery to the General Assembly of the Presbyterian Church. Here began his acquaintance and friendship with many good and eminent men whose theological views were specially congenial with his own. Writing to Mrs. Dana from Philadelphia, May 19, 1810, he says, —

" I left New York on Tuesday morning, and arrived in this city the next day before dinner. I lodged on Tuesday night at Princeton, saw the College, visited Dr. Smith (to whom I had a line of introduction from Dr. Griffin), and at five in the morning visited the tombs of the venerable Burr, Edwards, Davies, Finley, and Witherspoon. The inscriptions, which are all in Latin (though they ought not to be so), I read with many emotions of reverence and delight. . . . . On arriving in town, I waited on Mr. Alexander, who received me very cordially."

" MONDAY MORNING.

" Yesterday, I attended, morning and afternoon, at Mr. Alexander's. It was his communion; and I hope I found some comfort and quickening. His church consists of between two and three hundred. You may suppose, that, with sixty strange ministers on the spot, I have found no difficulty hitherto in being exempted from preaching. And this has been a favor. I visited Bishop White on Saturday, and had a very polite and friendly reception."

May 24, he writes, " When I wrote last I was ready to hope I should be exempted from preaching; but I have got entangled. I am to preach a sacramental lecture for Dr Green (who has treated me very politely) on Saturday evening; and a sermon for our old friend, Mr. Alexander, on Sabbath afternoon."

In 1812, he was again delegated to the General Assembly. At the close of the session, having a sister then on a visit to Washington, he proceeded thither, in company with the Rev. Mr. Codman. Those were critical times. On the second day after their arrival the sessions of Congress were with closed doors. He had, however, the pleasure of seeing, and being introduced to, a large number of the eminent men of that time. In one of his letters, he bestows considerable space on Mr. Randolph. Writing to Mrs. Dana, June 6, 1812, he says, "Though precluded from hearing the debates in Congress, I expect to enjoy, this day, the dearer pleasure of visiting the *tomb of Washington* Oh that you could be with me!"

Alluding to his return home, he says, "To this last delightful event I now look forward. Shall I once more meet you in peace; shall I again enjoy the thousand delights of home, and not wander soon from you again? May the all-gracious Being vouchsafe us a happy meeting!"

He whose heart was so tenderly alive to the endearments of his home, was soon to behold it a house of mourning. The above must have been one of his last letters to her to whom it was addressed. Twelve years of their union were not quite complete, when, with but little premonition, she was taken from him, Dec. 25, 1812.

The only record of this mournful period is contained in a letter written by him three months afterward. It is introduced here, not without hesitation; for such grief is sacred. Yet who does not feel, that, by sympathy with sorrow like this, the heart is purified?

TO MRS. D. KNAPP.

" NEWBURYPORT, March 27, 1813.

"DEAR MADAM, — I have many thanks to give for your truly kind, sympathetic, and consoling letter. It has been gratifying and comforting, not only to myself, but to many other friends of the dear, favored woman who was once mine, and of whom I was so unworthy. Next to the support which is derived directly from religion is that which comes through the medium of earthly friends. The friends of her who is gone are peculiarly dear to me now; their kind communications form a principal portion of the solace of my lonely state.

"Mrs. Dana's departure was not a little sudden. The first week after her confinement, she was remarkably comfortable; the second, not so well; but the physician was not at all alarmed. But the beginning of the third week, a fever, which for several days had been lurking about her, assumed a formidable aspect; her strength rapidly sank away; and her case became desperate, almost as soon as it appeared alarming. For forty-eight hours before she expired, she was nearly incapable of speech and thought. But before this period, and when, I believe, she was conscious of the danger of her state, she expressed to me, in a short conversation, her submission and her humble hope. At the close of the conversation, being extremely feeble, she affectionately and repeatedly kissed my hand.

"My loss, and that of my dear children, you well know, is great and inexpressible. The world knew comparatively little of her worth; nor was she anxious that it should know more. One circumstance only appears to me surprising; and that is, that she could love with such tenderness, such ardor and constancy, such an unworthy creature as myself.

"But the Lord has taken her in his own best time and way; and why should I repine? Can I ever be duly thankful that such a blessing was indulged me for twelve years? Above all I desire to bless God that I have no anxiety respecting her eternal state. I mean, I have full confidence that her spirit has found its everlasting rest, and that she is now triumphing in the presence of that Redeemer whom, while here, she loved and trusted. You know she was a sufferer, and, had she lived, would probably have continued to suffer. Her removal, therefore, was a most merciful exemption.

"When I review the scene which I have recently passed, I am frequently astonished at myself. Through the great mercy of God, I was enabled to go forth and preach to my dear people the day after the funeral; and I have been able to perform my ministerial duties with little interruption since; but my loss appears more and more real every day, and sometimes presses upon me in a way almost overwhelming. Often, when I look upon my children, my sensations are singularly acute. How shall I supply the immense loss they have sustained? How act the father's and the mother's part in one? How be suitably faithful, and yet suitably tender? How take the dear immortals by the hand, and lead them up to God and heaven?

"Let me entreat your continued and earnest prayers that this awful visitation of a sovereign and holy God may not be lost upon me; that I may neither murmur, nor despise, nor sink; that, through the blessing of God upon it, I may become a better man, a better father, a more faithful and engaged minister.

"My sister Betsey is with me, and I consider it a great favor. She cheers my solitary house, and takes the best care of my family. She thanks you for your kind remembrance, and requests you to accept her sincere love.

8

"Please to present my kind regards to Mr. Knapp. When another season shall come, you will be able, I hope, to visit Newburyport. It will afford me a sincere gratification to see you at my house. In the mean time, believe me, dear madam, with much esteem and affection,   "Yours,

                                "DANIEL DANA."

Beneath the record of her death, on the grave-stone, he placed these lines, —

> " Go, lovely mourner, to thy long-sought rest;
> Go join the songs and triumphs of the blest:
> No pain can reach thee there; no anxious fear
> Assail thy heart, or wring the bitter tear.
> Our griefs we'll banish too; soon we'll remove,
> And meet thee in the paradise above."

Two of her sisters, resident in Newburyport, lived to serene, Christian old age. Their devoted attachment to him was unchanging; the earliest, happiest recollections of his children are indissolubly associated with them and their families; and the kind and gentle attentions of those of them that survived, followed him to the latest hour of his life.

CHAPTER IX.

1813–1820.

GENERAL ASSEMBLY OF 1814. — DEATH OF MR. COOMBS. — PUBLICATIONS. — CONNECTION WITH VARIOUS SOCIETIES. — MARRIAGE. — PASTORAL LABORS. — BEREAVEMENTS.

IN 1814 he again went to the General Assembly. 'To his sister, then having charge of his household, he writes from New York : —

"I arrived in this city about eight, Saturday evening, and lodged at the City Hotel, one of those large establishments where the weary traveller can have every thing but comfort and retirement. But, being much fatigued, I slept well, and awoke greatly refreshed. I went in the morning to young Mr. Spring's, and preached for him in the forenoon. He was urgent with me to preach for him in the afternoon or evening; but in this case you have to give me the credit of saying no. . . . As to my dear families, great and small, which I have left behind, you will not be surprised to hear that my efforts to forget them are not very effectual. I expect to succeed better when I shall have plunged into the variety of business which generally occurs at Philadelphia. What I most wish is, to commit these objects of my affection and anxiety into the arms of infinite mercy."

" Philadelphia, May 25, 1814.

. . . "Mr. and Mrs. Wickes are the same kind and affectionate friends as ever. . . . Give much love to every individual of the family. To my dear Father Coombs I shall endeavor to write soon.

"Most affectionately yours,

"Daniel Dana.

" Miss Elizabeth Dana."

Sad news awaited him whilst writing the above letter. Within three days of its date, the death of Mr. Coombs took place. From the sermon commemorative of him, we subjoin a few paragraphs : —

"In the course of these imperfect observations, your minds have, I doubt not, often recurred to that beloved and venerable man whom Heaven has recently removed from us, to the unspeakable grief of his family and friends, of this Christian church and society, of the town at large, and of the friends of religion and virtue generally, wherever he was known. So deep and tender is my personal interest in the scene, that, on many accounts, it would have been a relief to be permitted to pass the subject in silence. . . .

"The friend whom we lament was the son of eminently pious parents. He himself, at a period just beyond infancy, commenced the practice of secret prayer, in which he persevered to the close of life.

"While a youth, his thirst for knowledge, and love of action, were equally conspicuous. These dispositions he gratified at once, by engaging in a maritime life, in which he continued till near the age of forty. Here, his activity, his enterprising disposition, and his punctuality in business, united with the strictest integrity, soon brought him into general notice, and engaged the unlimited confidence of all with whom he was concerned. His last voyage was performed in the year 1775, and merits particular notice. It was undertaken just before the commencement of hostilities with the mother country, for the purpose of obtaining from the island of Guadaloupe, a supply of arms and ammunition, such as he knew would be pressingly needed in the approaching contest. He succeeded beyond his most sanguine expectations. Many circumstances marked this voyage as an effort of ardent and disinterested patriotism; particularly the personal danger of the attempt, and the immediate surrender of the results of the voyage to the authorities of the town, without any stipulated recompense.

"He engaged, with all his constitutional ardor, in the cause of the Revolution; being firmly persuaded that it was the cause of justice, no less than of liberty. He promoted it by a variety of exertions and sacrifices. He was early chosen a member of one of those Committees of Safety and Correspondence, which, according to the exigencies of the times, assumed and exercised the powers of government. In this office he continued — active, influential, and useful — until the regular authority was restored.

"But it is particularly pleasant to dwell on those strong indications of *piety* by which his character was distinguished and adorned. None who knew him intimately could doubt that he was eminent in religion, and in all the dignified and amiable virtues which religion inspires.

"He was a decided friend to what have been called the *doctrines of grace;* or to those truths which dis-

8*

tinguish the gospel from every other system, and mark
it as a religion for sinners. On these doctrines, and on
these alone, he thought it safe to build his immortal
hopes. Yet he was not a high speculatist. His reading (and he read much) was principally of the experimental and practical kind. Such too was his *religion*.
It was the religion of the heart, the temper, and conduct. No man seemed to entertain a higher opinion
of the value and importance of truth; yet none was
further from the indulgence of a fierce and bigoted zeal,
or from substituting a set of barren, orthodox speculations in the place of a pious temper and practice.

" He appeared to realize no value in wealth but as it
furnished the means of alleviating distress, and of doing
good to the bodies and souls of his fellow-men. In the
most generous, yet simple and unostentatious manner
was his wealth devoted to these noble purposes. To
many he was an unknown benefactor. His humanity
and compassion were frequently conspicuous; and very
signally in that remarkable exertion to save a drowning youth which received so honorable a notice from
the Humane Society in this place. *

" He loved goodness for its own sake. Every real
Christian had a passport to his heart. He had an unusual share of the uniting, healing spirit of Christianity.
He did much, and attempted *more*, to banish those di-
visions and asperities which have operated such wide-
spread evil among us.

. . . " Yes, he is gone — mature in years, rich in faith,
rich in good works. No more will you behold, in yon-
der pew, his fixed, attentive eye. No more will you

---

* At the age of *seventy-six*, he leaped from his wharf into deep water
to save a lad from drowning.

witness his expressive, venerable countenance, alternately solemnized, melted, and cheered by the contemplation of divine truth. Ah, who shall receive his falling mantle? Who, like him, shall be at once the advocate and the ornament of genuine religion?

. . . " We who have been so *near* him; we to whom he has opened, from day to day, his inmost mind and heart; we who saw him live at the very gate of heaven,— can we doubt whether it is well with him now? No! We believe that to him to live was Christ; we have equal evidence that to die was gain."

Flavel's " Token for Mourners," and Cecil's " Friendly Visit to the House of Mourning," revised and abridged by Mr. Dana, perhaps the previous year, were in 1814 published by the then newly-formed New-England Tract Society, of which he was a zealous friend. They are now among the permanent issues of the American Tract Society. Tract No. 44 is also from his pen.

In these years, he was also actively engaged as an officer and advocate of other benevolent associations, then in their incipiency : such as the Merrimack Bible Society, of which he was Secretary; the Education Society; the Merrimack Humane Society; the Massachusetts Society for promoting Christian Knowledge, &c.

For the seven years succeeding 1813, his publications, mostly sermons and addresses, — several before the societies above named, — averaged more than three every year, besides what he contributed to periodicals. When the constitution of the Merrimack Bible Society was adopted, Jan. 17, 1810, the address which was issued, setting forth its objects, was from his pen. It would seem from the letters to him of Dr. Morse, Dr. Worcester, Dr. Griffin, and others, that he was much relied on as a contributor to the "Panoplist." In one letter, Dr. Morse says, "You need make no apology, either on account of your engagements or your eyes: I am aware of both, and feel the more obliged to you for what you do."

Some years before, he had prepared for the press a volume, entitled "Memoirs of Pious Women," abridged from the larger work of Dr. Gibbons.

No office which he held was a sinecure. At the meetings of the Trustees of the Exeter and Andover Academies he was always present; but this was doubtless a pastime in comparison with the weightier responsibilities attached to his connection with the Theological Seminary.

A pleasant reminiscence of him, as he was at this time, was given, after his decease, by the Rev. William Goodell. Writing from Constantinople, April 10, 1860, he says, —

"I have very pleasant and very distinct recollections of him from my first going to Andover Academy, in 1812, to fit for college; for he, being one of the trustees, was always present at the examinations, and his sweet countenance and his modest appearance, with his green spectacles, gave us all a pleasant impression of his character."

In these years, he was associated in good works with many eminent contemporaries. An address issued by the directors of the Education Society, soon after the inception of the enterprise, has the following names appended: "Eliphalet Pearson, Abiel Holmes, Daniel Dana, Ebenezer Porter, Joshua Bates, Brown Emerson, Asa Eaton." He was in correspondence with Dr Payson in reference to the formation of the American Bible Society.

In 1814, Dartmouth College honored him with the degree of Doctor of Divinity. Three years later, he delivered the address before the Phi Beta Kappa Society of Dartmouth College, of which they obtained a copy for the press.

On the 8th of November, 1814, he married Sarah, daughter of Joseph Emery, M.D., of Fryeburg, Me. Their union continued but four years and a half, being sundered by her death on the 8th of May, 1819. Of the eighty-eight years accorded to him by Divine Providence, but sixteen and a half were included in the marriage state.

Numerous as were the public calls made upon him in these years, he was still a most devoted pastor; and many were the pleasing testimonies given of the affectionate attachment of those for whose spiritual interests he labored with untiring zeal. At one time, he indulged himself in the grateful task of keeping a record of the generous gifts made him by individuals of his congregation. But he had also the higher joy of seeing the work of the Lord prospering. He received, in the last six years of his pastoral connection, nearly as many to the communion of the church as he had done in the twenty years that preceded.

In January, 1816, a newspaper discussion of the question, "Is Christmas Day holy time?" between himself and the Rev. James Morss ("Inquirer" and "Philo") was published in pamphlet form. Only the writers' names are suppressed: the articles of each are strongly characteristic.

In 1817, he took an active part in commencing, in Newburyport, the novel experiment of Sunday schools. The next year (Aug. 16), he delivered an address at a public meeting of the schools " under the patronage of the Newburyport Sunday School and Tract Society," at which were present eight hundred scholars.

The writer's more distinct recollections of his father commence about this time. He remembers him tenderly affectionate in his family, animated and vivacious in social intercourse, exercising a free hospitality, and especially interested in the converse of clerical strangers (some of whom were from the distant South); taking great delight withal in sacred music, which he often introduced as a supplement to the pleasures of conversation. The light of his eyes at this period was his infant son, who bore his own name. He would play with him, and sing to him, with a buoyancy of spirit perhaps never afterwards equalled.

But with these sunny recollections there rises also the image of one at times burdened with cares, with sensibilities overtasked, mind pre-occupied, thoughts absent from the scenes around. So numerous and pressing were his engagements, that, having undertaken for a while, when the Academy was closed, to superintend the classical studies of his elder son, he found but one day in the week in which he could get a leisure hour for the purpose. His pastoral duties, always arduous, were often specially trying to sensibilities like his. His large congregation included many families that had relatives at sea. If a death occurred among these absent ones, the sad necessity was usually laid on him of announcing it to the bereaved at home. One painful effect of this he saw, sometimes, and lamented, in the evident agitation which a visit from him at first excited among those who had relatives at sea.

Memory recalls the spacious church in which he

preached, as it was at that time. The pulpit adjoined the long side. Half way up the stairs to it, a door opened into a square pew, occupied by a few aged and deaf men. Below this, one or two steps above the floor of the church, was a slip in which, fronting the congregation, sat the two deacons, " whose looks adorned the venerable place." The taller of the two returns to recollection, as he sat erect, still as a statue, his high forehead indicating something of intellectual culture, his eyes modestly cast down, apparently drinking in every word of the speaker, yet not so much with any excited impulse of feeling, as with calm and holy satisfaction. By a strange misnomer, this good man, whose meek aspect was the very mirror of placid quiet and saintly benignity, was named *Moody*. By his side was good Deacon Beck.

The spacious church was always full; the congregation eminently solemn and attentive. The morning discourse, at the time referred to, was expository and extemporaneous. Some of the subjects, particularly from the 25th chapter of Matthew, the writer still recollects; but as there were no stoves in those days, during the cold months, the question, when the sermon would end, was always uppermost in the juvenile mind. By a large induction it was partially solved; the minute-hand of the clock, opposite the pulpit came to be an index of the welcome moment when " fifthly and lastly " might be expected. It was impossible not to feel aggrieved, when, as sometimes, there was a *sixthly*, and even *seventhly*.

But to hearers more susceptible of edification, these extemporaneous discourses came home with perhaps more of power and unction than any that have been

left in print. They were fresh from an excited mind
and heart, for his custom was to give up a large part of
the preceding night to their preparation. As a consequence, he was always much exhausted after the
second service on Sunday. These sermons could not
be recalled. The writer remembers, that, with some
urgency, a copy for the press of a short series of them
was desired at one time, but declined on the ground of
the impossibility of reproducing them as they had
been delivered.

In March, 1818, he was called to preach at the
funeral of his friend, Dr. Morrison. The sermon shows
how loved and venerated an associate its author had
long had in the presbytery, and what were the qualities
of the pastor and the man which could most attract
his affection.

Whilst thus responding to every call at home and
abroad, — "instant in season, out of season," abundant
in labors which heavily taxed a constitution never
strong, — more than one solemn and affecting dispensation of Divine Providence had superadded to his
pastoral cares the weighty pressure of domestic anxiety
and grief. In May, 1819, death again crossed his thresh-
old. Again were young children separated forever
from a mother's tender care. The sister, nearest to him
in age, who had once cheered his loneliness, had been
called to her rest three years before. He was left with
a family of ten children, the oldest not yet eighteen.

Still was he the devoted pastor, exhausting his time
and strength in the great work to which he was called.
Few to whom his daily life was known, would have
hesitated to apply to himself the lines he quotes in a
sermon, delivered about this time on occasion of

the early death of the Rev. Levi Hartshorn, to whom he was warmly attached, —

> " But in his duty, prompt at every call,
> He watched and wept, he prayed and felt, for all.
> And, as a bird each fond endearment tries
> To tempt her new-fledged offspring to the skies,
> He tried each art, reproved each dull delay,
> Allured to brighter worlds, and led the way."

9

CHAPTER X.

1820–1821.

ELECTION TO THE PRESIDENCY OF DARTMOUTH COLLEGE. — REMOVAL TO NEW HAMPSHIRE.

IN August, 1820, it came to his knowledge that his name was mentioned in connection with the Presidency of Dartmouth College. He immediately addressed to one of the professors of the college the following letter:

"NEWBURYPORT, Aug. 16, 1820.

"DEAR SIR, — Through a medium which claims my confidence, I have recently learned, that, in contemplating a supply of the lamented vacancy in Dartmouth College, some of the gentlemen trustees have had their attention turned to myself. In this state of things, it will not, I trust, be deemed indecorous, if, with a view to prevent the possibility of embarrassment or delay in this momentous affair, I signify my wish to decline the honor of being considered as a candidate. The reasons which govern me in this case, it is not needful, I conceive, for me to detail. It may be sufficient to state that they are, in my view, imperious and decisive.

"Let me request the favor that you will seasonably impart the substance of this communication, in what form you please, to some member or members of the reverend and honorable Board.

"I am very respectfully, dear sir,

"Your friend and servant,

"D. DANA."

This letter he sent to his friend and neighbor, Rev. Mr. Putnam of Portsmouth, a member of the Board of Trustees of the College, accompanying it with the following note : —

"NEWBURYPORT, Aug. 16, 1820.

"REV. AND DEAR SIR,—I expect to supply your desk the Sabbath after next.

"The enclosed letter to Dr. M. expresses my wish totally to decline the honor of being a candidate to fill the vacancy in college. I mention this that you may be sure to deliver the letter in season; and likewise to request, that should Dr. M. be prevented, by any casualty, from communicating my wish to the Board, you yourself would do it, either personally or by a line. Believe me as ever,

"Affectionately yours,

"DANIEL DANA."

Notwithstanding this decisive action on his part, he soon received the official announcement that he had been by the Trustees (Aug. 22, 1820) unanimously elected President of Dartmouth College.

The following is one of many letters addressed to him, urging his acceptance of the office : —

"DARTMOUTH COLLEGE, Sept. 7, 1820.

"REV. AND DEAR SIR, — Not having heard from any of our friends what is the prospect in regard to your acceptance of the appointment made by our trustees, I cannot help troubling you with a line.

"I need not tell you that our solicitude would rise to extreme distress, were we seriously apprehensive that you might decide in the negative. Oh, sir, remember the desolations of Zion here, and have compassion. The friends of the college look to you, and to you *only*, to repair the *waste places.* When you know that the voice of the trustees conspires with that of the clergy and of the public at large, and when this same voice is echoed from the tomb of our late beloved and much lamented President Brown, can you hesitate? That good man, in his last days, with almost the confidence and ardor of prophecy, declared his belief in the future prosperity and usefulness of Dartmouth College. You have, I hope, been informed of the strong manner in which he, last autumn, expressed himself in relation to a successor; and of the same decided and unwavering opinion which came from his mouth a few days before his death. 'I have,' said he, 'but one candidate, and that is Dr. Dana. Whom do they talk of for a successor? My opinion is exactly the same as when I conversed with you last fall.'

"I do pray, my dear sir, that Divine Providence may not permit you to fail of coming.

"I should be grieved if, on making the trial, you should not find yourself pleasantly situated here. I verily believe that you would find a disposition on the part of the people of the village, including all the college faculty, to render your situation comfortable and pleasant.

"We shall watch every mail and ask every friend, till we learn the decision, or rather what we may expect the decision to be.

"With great respect,
"Your obedient servant,
"R. D. M."

What is here stated as to President Brown was also true of President Appleton of Bowdoin College. Each had desired that Dr. Dana should be his successor. No stronger proof could be given of the confidence felt in him, than these concurrent last wishes of two such men. Each had brought to the office he held, not merely intellectual pre-eminence, but a dignity and elevation of character, and a singleness of purpose, rarely equalled; and to each the future welfare of the institution over which he presided was an object of the deepest solicitude. The name of Francis Brown still awakens enthusiasm among the alumni of Dartmouth. He was identified with the college during a period of unexampled trial; and to his devotion to its interests, his indomitable energy, and unfaltering faith, as much, perhaps, as to the splendid forensic efforts of Daniel Webster, was its ultimate triumph due. The State Legislature, under the influence of strong party excitement, had assumed to annul its charter, and to make the institution, under a new name, wholly dependent on itself; imposing a fine of five hundred dollars upon any one who should act as trustee, president, professor, &c., in Dartmouth College. After a five-years' struggle, most honorable to the firmness of the faculty, and to the fidelity of the students, the great body of whom adhered to the college, this radicalism was finally arrested by the successful result of an appeal to the Supreme Court of the United States.

Dr. Dana had watched, with profound interest, the progress of this remarkable struggle. No appeal could have been made to him on behalf of Dartmouth College, without enlisting his warm sympathy. The painful conflict which now agitated his mind is best presented in his own words.* "If this seminary was

---

* Farewell Sermon.

9*

endeared to me as the scene of my youthful instruction,
it was still more endeared by its own interesting character; by its early consecration to the interests of the
Redeemer and his religion; and by the important
services which, from its first existence, it had rendered
to the church and the community. Its recent afflicting
struggle for existence was viewed as giving it additional
claims to the sympathy and aid of the public, and
especially of its own sons. And the signal interpositions
of Heaven in its behalf seemed to announce it as a
favorite child of Providence; as destined to be blessed,
and to be made a blessing in future time.

"If these views of things may be naturally thought
to favor my acceptance of the appointment, other considerations arose, which seemed even more powerfully
to forbid it. To part from a people so long and so in-
expressibly endeared; to quit a scene of labors which,
though multiplied and exhausting, have been ever delightful; to leave you distressed, anxious, shepherdless,
and exposed to a variety of evils — these are thoughts
which have nearly torn my heart asunder. To enter,
at my age, and with a deep consciousness of insuffi-
ciency, on a sphere embracing new duties, new cares, new
responsibilities; a sphere demanding all my exertions,
and in which all my exertions may fail of securing success — is an undertaking from which my feelings have
a thousand times revolted.

"It was not fit, it was not lawful, in a case of such
magnitude, to resign myself to the government of mere
feeling. The very fact that my strongest sensibilities
were arrayed against the measure of a separation, imperiously forbade my trusting their decision. Amid
the agitations and conflicts of my mind, I hope I have

had but one governing object — to know the will of God — to find the path of duty."

It was determined, by both pastor and people, to submit the case to the presbytery, and abide by their decision. To this body, convened at Bradford, Sept. 26, 1820, the church sent a memorial.

The presbytery, nevertheless, gave an almost unanimous decision in favor of his transfer to the presidency of the college. On the 19th of November, 1820, he delivered his farewell sermon to his church. We select a brief passage from the introduction, and one near the close:

"This day completes twenty-six years since you were solemnly committed, by the great Head of the Church, to my pastoral care. That awful, sacred charge I received with much fear and trembling. Yet it was my fixed purpose, that, should my labors meet your continued acceptance, my life, to its latest hour, should be devoted to your service. Revolving years have but cemented and strengthened our mutual affection; nor, till a few weeks since, did it appear to me even possible that any thing but death could part us.

" But the scene is now changed. Our long and happy union must be dissolved. A separation unwelcome as unanticipated, a separation mutually and indescribably painful, must take place. . . . May God almighty bless you with a pastor far more worthy of your love than I have been, and far more successful in promoting your spiritual interests! Long after this tongue is mute in death, may the name and grace of Jesus be proclaimed from this desk, to an assembly of humble and pious worshippers; and you, and your children, and your children's children, receive within these walls a training for the immortal temple on high!

" Farewell, then, beloved people, no longer mine ; but still, and forever, dear to my heart; still to be cherished in my fondest recollections, and remembered in my latest prayers. If, through boundless mercy, I should ever reach the blest abodes, I shall eagerly look for you there. May mine be the transport of meeting many, many of you, in that better region ; and there, where no tears shall mingle with our praises, nor thought of separation imbitter our joys, may we unite in eternal hallelujahs to our common Father and Redeemer!"

Allusion is made in this sermon to his " recently impaired health." This was premonitory. Scarcely had he removed his family to Hanover, and entered on his new duties, before the crisis came to which, doubtless the wasting cares and anxieties of preceding years, and the recent severe pressure upon his sensibilities, had been silently but inevitably tending. His health gave way, and great depression of spirits accompanied his bodily languor. He took more than one long journey in the vain effort to recruit his energies. He writes to a friend of being " in a state of great and very uncommon debility, undoubtedly to be attributed to the protracted operation of distressing causes, both on mind and frame." He also states, that, whilst absent from Hanover in accordance with the advice of his physician, he still hoped to be able, after his strength was recruited, to accomplish something in the matter of soliciting aid to the funds of the college ; a work which, however uncongenial to his tastes, he found would necessarily be devolved on its president.

The winter months passed by, and there was still little or no improvement in his health. When it became known that he was agitating the question of resigning his office, many urgent requests were made to him not to decide hastily. ' He delayed only till April, and then called a meeting of the trustees, to be held early in May, for the purpose of receiving and acting upon his resignation of his office. He wished it to be considered as " absolute and final." The notification to a member of the Board with whom he was specially intimate, was accompanied by a letter in which he says, —

" You will naturally conclude that the resolution which I have taken has cost me many a struggle, and much severe distress. This is the fact. The last seven months have been with me a scene of suffering indeed. . . . I have fondly hoped that repeated journeyings would give me relief. But their effect has been only partial and temporary. Such is my *prostration* at this moment, that the *duties* of my office, and not less its *cares* and its *responsibilities*, seem a burden quite beyond my power of bearing. Had it pleased God to make me an instrument of important good to the college, I should have esteemed myself privileged indeed; but this privilege, though denied to me, awaits, I confidently hope, some more favored instrument of the divine benevolence. I earnestly pray, that, in what pertains to this great concern, the trustees may be favored with much heavenly wisdom and direction."

He now took a long journey to Ohio, visiting at Athens the brother who had been the companion of his early years. Under these favorable influences, his health began more decidedly to improve. At their meeting, July 4, the trustees of the college, by unanimous resolution, requested him to withdraw his resignation; but he declined to do so, though "gratefully acknowledging the kindness expressed in their communication." He removed his family to Ipswich, where he had taken a house for them in the immediate vicinity of his father's residence.

Many years after these events, the Rev. Dr. Lord, so long and so honorably the President of Dartmouth College, thus referred to Dr. Dana's connection with the institution : —

"He was chosen President for his well-known excellence as a scholar and theologian, and his extraordinary ministerial qualifications. He was honored, the country over, in these respects. It was not doubted that he would be equally honorable as President of the College, should his health endure.

"That he would have been, had he been able to retain his place, everybody well understood, as well from his auspicious beginning, as his distinguished qualties. He made a deep impression upon the College during the short period of his actual service.

"But his sensitive nature had received a great shock in the breaking up of his many and most endearing relations at Newburyport and the country round. He began here with health seriously impaired, and in great depression of spirit. The change of scene, of society, labor, and responsibility, was too much for his disordered frame. He sought relief by travel. But he gained little or nothing, and was driven to the conclusion that his life could probably be saved only by resignation. He could not consent to make such an office as he held a sinecure, or to see the college labor through its severe adversities without greater vigor of administration than his infirmities admitted. With great conscientiousness and magnanimity, he chose to put himself at a seeming disadvantage, rather than to risk the interests of the College upon what he judged to be the doubtful chances of his recovery.

" He left with the profound respect and sincere regret of the Trustees and Faculty. Their confidence in him was unshaken; and they never doubted, that, had he been more favorable to himself, and borne his new burdens with less solicitude, till he could regain his health, he would have been as distinguished here as elsewhere, and raised the College to a corresponding usefulness and dignity.

" Most men judge superficially and unwisely in such cases. So far as I know, the most competent judges of Dr. Dana's relations to Dartmouth, see nothing that does not redound to his honor. It is understood that he accepted the presidency with great reluctance, on account of his other responsibilities and attachments, and with distrust of his physical ability to perform its duties; that, while he performed them, it was with characteristic ability and effect; and that, when his best efforts to regain his health failed, and he saw reason to fear, that, even if his life should not be a sacrifice, his increasing infirmities would be to the disadvantage of a struggling institution, he generously, and entirely of his own accord, resigned. To my apprehension, all this is significant of great moral strength under the pressure of bodily diseases, and a memorable instance of that Christian heroism for which he has always been remarkable. ' *Maluit esse quam videri bonus.*' "

Great, indeed, to all human appearance, was the " providential adversity," by which, in one short year, he was dislodged from two such positions; one by the decision of Divine Providence, counteracting his own wishes and efforts; the other, by the constraint of his own high principles of honor. But now, in the retrospect, it appears that, even in this, the good hand of his God was upon him. In the opinion of one very competent to judge, a few more years at Newburyport, without change of scene and such respite from over-exertion as he could not there be induced to take, would, in all probability, have fatally undermined his constitution. His removal from his pastoral charge, with its severe trial to his sensibilities, did but precipitate a result perhaps inevitable. Nor is it certain that he could, in any other position, have been more happy and useful, than in that which Divine Providence assigned him for the still numerous years of his subsequent life.

CHAPTER XI.

In the fall of 1821, he was gradually gaining health, and had resumed preaching, when the church in Londonderry, with which his friend Dr. Morrison had been connected, gave him a call to become their pastor. Under the circumstances, nothing could have been more grateful to his feelings; nor could any position have been better suited to the re-invigoration of his health. He recognized the hand of Providence, and at once accepted the invitation. And now he seemed, in the way to regain something of that buoyancy of spirit to which he had been long a stranger.

In the beginning of winter, five of his new parishioners, with their fine horses and sleighs, came down to Ipswich to convey his family to Londonderry. The affair was an exhilarating novelty to his children; especially to one of them, who had never before left the sea-board, having spent the two preceding years with his grandfather at Ipswich. The first view of those high hills and the valleys between, all covered with deep snow, is even now fresh in memory. Nor are the recollections less vivid and pleasant of the unsophisticated manners and the warm-hearted hospitality of the people. In those days the " chimney-corner" was not a myth; logs of wood four feet in length were liberally piled up in the capacious fire-places; and the winter evening was a propitious time for social festivity. This

first introduction to country life was rich in pleasure
to one to whom the scene was new, and who was at
that happy age when the world seems full of sunshine
and enjoyment.

Not long after the arrival at Londonderry came the
day of installation; a great day for the whole vicinage; for not only those interested in the occasion as a
religious one, but a heterogeneous multitude besides,
were congregated, as on a muster-day, or the Fourth of
July. But, within the church, the services were listened
to with the most profound attention by a crowded auditory. The sermon was by the Rev. Samuel Dana, of
Marblehead; the other parts of service, by members of
the Londonderry Presbytery. The singing had the
advantage of the skilled leadership and magnificent
voice of Mr. Hildreth, Preceptor of Pinkerton Academy, in the East Parish village. After the installation
services, according to good old custom, the elders of
the church, and other leading heads of families, came
forward to express their welcome to the pastor.

The people were generally of Scotch-Irish descent;
and they had faithfully retained the customs which
their ancestors had brought from "the old country."
In the sacramental service, the communing members
sat at tables, and the whole congregation remained in
the church. A fast-day preceded, and a thanksgiving
service followed, each sacramental season; and the practice still lingered of giving *tokens* beforehand to those
entitled to come to the communion. Another old custom there, but a striking novelty to strangers, was,
that, at the close of service, no one presumed to leave
the church till the minister had descended from the pulpit, and passed down the aisle.

He was now in the immediate vicinity of many valued brethren, members of the Londonderry Presbytery. Twelve miles distant was Dr. John H. Church of Pelham, one of the most saintly of men, between whom and himself there was a cordial friendship. He frequently exchanged pulpits with his clerical neighbors — more frequently, indeed, than was quite to the satisfaction of some of his parishioners. His son once heard one of them say, "If the Doctor changes with Mr. ——, I think we ought to have some *boot!*"

The cordiality of the people to their new pastor is alluded to in one of his father's letters (April 6, 1822):

"It was truly affecting to learn that you find your situation 'increasingly pleasant,' the kindness of your beloved people unabated, and new discoveries so frequently made of 'worthy and amiable friends.' I expected it, for I think you have the faculty, in a good degree, of making such discoveries. I mean the faculty of loving your people, and in that way calling out whatever is amiable where you visit. By this, you will not only gratify yourself, but benefit your beloved flock in more respects than one."

About that time a stranger called on Dr. Dana of Ipswich, and told him that he was one of his son's parishioners, and that the "people of Londonderry were entirely united, and meant to make him as happy as he had been at Newburyport."

There being no suitable residence for him near the church, he was under the necessity of building a house. Deacon James Pinkerton (nephew of the founder of Pinkerton Academy, who also was the donor of liberal funds to both parishes of Londonderry) presented him with land near the church sufficient for a building-lot and garden; and the people contributed timber, and prepared and raised the frame of the house. When, upon its completion, he removed to it, he expressed to his family his thought that no other removal awaited him, except to "the house appointed for all living." No more than others was he prescient of the future.

Very pleasant friendships were formed by his children during this residence in Londonderry. There were many families that might be named, with whom social intercourse was exceedingly agreeable. Where a neighborhood included miles, and the old-fashioned hospitality substituted hours for the minutes of city calls, such intercourse had special attractions, and lived long in recollection.

With the family of his deceased friend, Dr. Morrison, his own were specially intimate. Three daughters then lived with their mother in the family mansion; another, who was married, resided in an adjoining town. The mother and two of the daughters have long since passed away; the house, the garden, the tall trees in the avenue to the road, have all disappeared; but there was a charm in the social intercourse of that family circle, the very memory of which awakens a thrill of emotion.

One of his most interesting parishioners was Deacon Bell (father of two Governors of New Hampshire), then far advanced in years, but retaining great vigor of mind.

What was then the West Parish of Londonderry (the township has since been divided) was nine miles long. The pastor devoted himself assiduously to his new charge, riding sometimes on horseback over the rough roads and steep hills, not only in summer, but also through the deep snows of winter, visiting every part of his extensive parish. He sometimes announced from the pulpit on Sunday, the district in which, often with an accompanying elder, he would make pastoral visits in the week. In summer, after two services at the church, he would ride three or four miles to preach at a schoolhouse or private residence. Many whose names had been signed to the call to him to be their pastor, were seldom or never seen at church. They had the right of voting for the minister, whose support was mainly furnished from the parish endowment; but the corresponding duty of attending on his ministrations was not, in their view, a logical sequence. The case of these caused him much solicitude. Occasionally he met a rough customer among them; but no decent person could be rude to him. In his intercourse with his congregation at large, he was quick to discover and appreciate that sterling good sense and native refinement of feeling and manners, which are sometimes found where there has been but limited opportunity for culture.

He regularly visited the district schools, encouraging the teachers, noting the progress of the pupils, and leaving sometimes a Testament, or other book, as a reward for specially good scholarship. He also made efforts to establish a parish library. He was elected a trustee of the Pinkerton Academy, in the East Parish (now Derry). He presided, and conducted the annual examinations; and the students soon discovered, as those of Andover and Exeter Academies had done long before, that he was quite at home in the classics, and skilled to ascertain whether or not they were so.

10*

A lady, truly one of the loveliest of her sex,* who at this time had occasional opportunities of hearing him from the pulpit, wrote thus of him after his decease, — from which her own was not long disjoined :

"I seem to see him at this moment as I used to see him in the sacred desk, solemn, earnest, and impressive, as no one has ever appeared to me since. Nor were his visits less interesting. He was in conversation equally eloquent; and I ever thought, after parting with him, that we ought to be a great deal wiser and better for seeing him. My sister Mary Ann and myself often proposed to take notes of his remarks ; but my intention was never executed, to my great loss."

In one of his pastoral visits he found an aged and infirm man, who appeared singularly unsusceptible of religious impression. Unwilling to leave him thus, he repeated to him the story of Death and the "three warnings," —

> "If you are lame, and deaf, and blind,
> You've had your three sufficient warnings," &c.

At the time, no impression seemed to be made upon the aged man; yet, after his death, there was found a record by himself, that this story was the first thing which effectually awakened his attention to his spiritual state.

It was his custom to sow good seed everywhere, whether the soil was genial or not. On one occasion he entered the abode of a noted termagant — one who feared not God nor regarded man. To his religious appeals she responded by avowing herself a Universal-

* Mrs. Sarah, wife of Robert McGaw, Esq., of Merrimack, and daughter of Rev. William Morrison, D.D., of Londonderry, N.H.

ist. He counselled her " not to drink poison because
it was sweet."—" I'll drink just as much as I've a mind
to," was the reply. Universalism, it would seem, was
not the only poison which she imbibed.

At this time, the temperance reformation had not
dawned : old customs were in full vigor at Londonderry. The free use of ardent spirits was thought a
needful part of hospitality: they were liberally supplied
at funerals. In the house nearest the church, a bar was
kept, and spirituous liquors sold on *Sunday*, during the
interval between morning and afternoon services.

The distress of the pastor, when these and similar
facts became known to him, was aggravated by his finding that there was need of a temperance reformation
even, to some extent, within the church. He gave
himself no rest until, single-handed, he had exhausted
every effort to bring about a better state of things.
Good men, at that time, did not fully sympathize with
him as to the evil of that free use of stimulants which
had the sanction of wide-spread and traditionary custom. Moreover, church discipline had fallen into des-
uetude. One of his best elders thought that the tares
should be permitted to grow with the wheat. All his
life he had been accustomed to a very high standard in
respect to qualifications for church-membership. His
church at Newburyport had been, from its origin,
almost ultra-puritan in its principles as to receiving accessions to the communion ; whilst, at Londonderry, the
practice in this respect had naturally been more con-
trolled by the principles of the Church of Scotland.

His father writes him, April 30, 1823, "I hope you
will be shown the true medium between remissness,
and wearing yourself out too fast. To the latter you are

perhaps, in some degree, inclinable. I hope, too, that
you will be preserved from despondency in regard to
their moral state. Whether, in the contemplation of
reforms, it may not be necessary to remember, with reference to *them*, our Lord's parables of the new cloth
and new bottles, you, I hope, will be graciously directed."

By appointment of the Governor, he delivered, in
June, 1823, the Election Sermon, before the Legislature
of New Hampshire. From this we subjoin a passage
of some length at the commencement, and one more
brief near the close.

"RESPECTED FRIENDS AND FELLOW-CITIZENS,—

"We meet, this day, on an occasion of more than
usual interest. We visit the temple of the MOST HIGH,
to acknowledge his all-governing providence, to invoke
his blessing on our State, to commit to his mercy the
selected guardians of its interests, and to search his
oracles for those great principles and maxims which
should guide all our public measures.

"The grand design of the sacred volume is to form
citizens of a *heavenly* community. Yet, while it discloses to us a world of immortal purity and joy, and
points the path by which that world may be reached,
it sheds the kindest influence on our *present* condition.
It opens the only sources of individual comfort; it re-
fines and elevates all our domestic and social enjoy-
ments; and it furnishes the lessons by which nations
may become great, wise, and happy.

"In the fourteenth chapter of the PROVERBS, and
the thirty-fourth verse, the wisest of monarchs and
of men has recorded a maxim of unrivalled sim-

plicity and beauty — a maxim in which a people and their rulers have an equal interest, and which merits to be engraven on the hearts of both.

"RIGHTEOUSNESS EXALTETH A NATION."

"In analyzing this inspired sentence, let us first ascertain the nature of that righteousness which it recommends; and then trace some of its numberless connections with the true glory and happiness of a people.

"The term *righteousness* is sometimes employed with reference to the moral and social duties, considered as distinct from those of piety. Indeed, these duties are viewed by some as occupying the whole round of human obligation. To discharge these duties, and fill up with decorum the social relations, constitutes, in their view, the sum and the perfection of human goodness. The opinion would be correct did man sustain no relation except to his fellow-man. But can this be, for a moment, admitted? Has he nothing to do with the Author of his existence? Does he sustain no relations, does he owe no duties, to his Creator, his Benefactor, and his final Judge? Unquestionably, these are his most momentous relations, and these his first duties.

"Righteousness, then, is more than mere morality. It implies a supreme regard to the Supreme of beings. It includes submission to his authority, resignation to his providence, gratitude for his goodness. In a word, it implies the entire self-devotion of the creature to his Creator and Sovereign, with an unremitting solicitude to obey his will, and approve himself to his eye. For who does not see that this is a tribute most rational, most indispensable.?

" Thus far we proceed with confidence, under the direction of reason. But here our guide forsakes us. How shall a creature, though loyal and innocent, discover, without a revelation, what are the *particulars* of that obedience which his Sovereign demands, and will accept? If he be fallen (and who can deny that *man* is this fallen creature?), inquiries of still more distressing interest arise. Is it possible that he should be restored? Is it possible that he should render to his Sovereign an acceptable obedience? If so, what must be the character of that obedience, and what its form?

" To these questions, which awakened nature can ask, but cannot answer, the Bible, and the Bible alone, furnishes an explicit and satisfying reply. It reveals a scheme of mercy, a mediator, an atonement, pardon for the guilty, restoration for the apostate and lost. As connected with this system of mercy, and as growing directly out of it, there is revealed in the Bible a *rule of human conduct* — a rule which, while it recognizes and confirms all our original obligations, superadds others which are new; carries all piety and all virtue to a far sublimer height; and, while it raises this lofty superstructure, furnishes, in the peculiar *motives* of the gospel, a foundation broad and deep enough to support it.

" That the virtue enjoined in the Scriptures is really of this novel and superior cast, may be proved by adducing a single instance. A right treatment of our *enemies* is, upon all natural principles, a perplexing problem, even in theory. And surely, none will deny, that, to the mind unenlightened and uncontrolled by the gospel, it must be the hardest of all duties in practice. The great Roman orator has made the discovery

" that we ought to hurt no man, except first provoked by
an injury." One of the sages of ancient Greece, speaking somewhat more explicitly, has enjoined us to " be
kind to our friends, and revenge ourselves on our enemies." The maxim of the gospel is, " *Love* your enemies." For the greatest of injuries, it prescribes, it admits, no return but blessings and kind offices. On
mere natural principles, these may appear *hard sayings ;*
but considered as the injunctions of that God who
loved us when we were enemies, of that Saviour who
poured his blood for our pardon, they appear stamped
with infinite reason and propriety. By the Christian,
they must be regarded as the first of duties; most imperious in their obligation, most delightful in their performance.

" While, then, righteousness implies a supreme affection and respect to God — the best and greatest of beings, the rightful Legislator of the universe — it implies a
submission of the understanding and heart to his word,
that *light shining in a dark place ;* that only infallible,
perfect, unchanging standard of human duty. It implies a regard to the law of God and the gospel of
Christ, as our rule of conduct; to the spirit and life
of the great Redeemer, as our example; and to the
divine glory, as our last end.

" This is righteousness. This constitutes the whole
moral worth, the genuine excellence, of human beings;
it comprises whatever is amiable, dignified, and happy
in individual man; and it promotes, in ways far more
numerous than can be specified, the glory and felicity
of a people.

" Righteousness, so far as it prevails, secures to a
community the inestimable blessing of conscientious

and faithful RULERS. Among a free and virtuous people, none but men of this character will ordinarily be
raised to office. The electors, acting in the fear of
God, will bestow their suffrages on those whom God
will approve. Uninfluenced by that rancorous spirit
of party which confounds and annihilates moral dis-
tinctions; insensible to the claims of the ambitious,
the obtrusive and unprincipled, they will turn their
eyes to the *faithful of the land.* Regarding the public interests as their own, they cannot fail to commit
those interests to men of substantial worth, and approved virtue. Thus, in the managers of its great
concerns, a State has the happiness of beholding those
who will refine its sentiments, and elevate the tone of
its morals. Thus the homage naturally paid to men
in high stations, becomes the tribute of the heart; a
tribute, not more consoling to the virtuous ruler, than
medicinal to the taste and manners of the community.

"But the direct influence of genuine virtue on the
character and conduct of rulers, claims a distinct consideration. It is granted, that, in ordinary cases, personal interest, regard to reputation, and even love of
place, may restrain public men from gross deviations.
But is it always thus? Do no occasions arise, on
which private interest and the public good come in
direct competition? None on which a small injustice
promises a great present advantage? None on which
the straight-forward course of integrity must be pursued, if pursued at all, at the imminent hazard, perhaps to the certain loss, of popularity and place? These
are the occasions which emphatically "try men's souls,"
and bring their principles to the test. These are the
occasions which expose the littleness and inconsistency

of ordinary virtue; while they display the beauty and majesty of that virtue which springs from piety. To the good magistrate, the presence of an observing God is more impressive than a universe of spectators; and the testimony of an approving conscience, more precious than all worldly riches and honors.

" Some politicians, and even some political writers, have maintained that virtue, though salutary to individuals, is frequently inconvenient to States; that the maxims of morality must often bend to public necessity or expediency; in short, that what is *morally wrong* may be *politically right*. Such sentiments as these deserve the severest brand of reprobation. They are an insult to the Majesty of heaven; a libel on the moral government of God; an arrogant pretence of weak and erring mortals to re-judge his judgment, to repeal his laws, to supply defects in his wisdom, and to mend the order of his universe. Nor is the good sense of these maxims less questionable than their piety. Every attempt to press them into the service of mankind, has proved wretchedly inefficient and abortive. No individual, high or low; no community, great or small; no government, monarchical or republican, was ever yet a gainer by trampling on the sacred laws of Heaven. Nor, till the throne of God is subverted, will such an event ever arise.

" What a delightful contrast to this perverse and serpentine policy is exhibited in the character of our WASHINGTON. In that mind, so keen in its sagacity, so extensive in its surveys, so rich in its resources, so profound in its wisdom, who ever detected a single particle of *cunning*? Among all his great qualities, his singular endowments of intellect and heart, nothing

11

was more conspicuous than a noble simplicity, a kind
of *crystalline purity* of character. It was this which
exalted him so far above the level of the vulgar great.
This placed him alone among the politicians of the
world. This rendered him the *ornament*, as well as
the saviour, of his country, and the wonder of his age.
This exhibits him as a model for imitation to the rulers
of every country, and of every age.

" But neither the purest motives, nor the most patri-
otic conduct, will uniformly secure general approbation.
Often has the conscientious ruler found his best intentions misrepresented, his most upright measures vilified,
and perhaps a long series of faithful public services
recompensed with neglect, or with calumny. Indeed,
such is the perverseness of human nature ; such the
fickleness of the multitude; such, proverbially, the in-
gratitude of republics, that the man who is wholly
unprepared for rewards of this species, will do wisely
to remain in the shade. And where, it may be asked,
is he who would act a different part? Where is the
man who, pained in the prospect, or smarting under
the infliction, of public reproach, will consent to wear
away life in promoting the public good? Where are
the motives to such rare and disinterested virtue? The
answer is at hand : there are no motives adequate to
sustain a virtue like this, but those supplied by religion.
In vain do we look for a character so exalted, unless it
be modelled on the Scriptures. But the man who has
been taught in this school; the man who has learned
of Him who spent his life in *overcoming evil with good*,
and who shed his blood for an insensible and thankless
world ; the man who seeks his chief reward, not in the
applause of the multitude, but in the approbation of his

conscience and his God — such a man may, without a miracle, be a *patriot*, even in the worst of times.

. . . . "If, respected Legislators, it is *righteousness* which *exalts a nation;* and if sin is reproachful and ruinous to any people, it is then in your power, by efficiently promoting the one, and discountenancing the other, to become public blessings and benefactors. Permit me to add, that this is demanded of you by your stations, by your oaths, by the honor and confidence bestowed on you, and by the influence you possess. It is the just expectation of heaven and earth concerning you.

"While we bless God for the fair inheritance of civil and religious freedom left us by our fathers, while we exult in their illustrious *example,* we contemplate, with pain and grief, many fatal symptoms of general degeneracy. In this region, once the hallowed abode of piety and virtue, the God of heaven is dishonored and provoked, his sacred name is blasphemed, his authority contemned, his sabbaths awfully and increasingly profaned. While vices of various forms stalk through the community, in defiance of fear and shame, *one vice,* whose name is *Legion,* spurns all restraint; tramples on all laws, human and divine; and devours, with unsated appetite, no small portion of the wealth and morals, of the lives and souls of the people.

"Do not evils of this magnitude challenge your attention and investigation? If the laws are defective, are you not bound to supply their defects? If, while the sons of vice are bold, the friends of order are feeble and timid; if, instead of *magistrates being a terror to evil-doers,* evil-doers are a terror to magistrates, — are you not bound, as Guardians and Fathers of the State, to ap-

ply a corrective? Especially, are you not bound, when
returning to the more private walks of life, to surround
the laws you have made with the attractive charm of
your *example;* to throw all the weight of your talents,
your exertions, your influence, and, let me add, your
prayers, into the scale of good order, good morals, and
pure religion?

"Indulge me, respected Legislators, in this freedom.
I would violate no principle of decorum. But a minister of the gospel, who could view the evils described
without an aching and a bleeding heart, would be unworthy his office. Nor could he be faithful to his most
solemn vows, if, when permitted to address those who,
under God, possess the remedy, he should pass the
subject in silence.

"Suffer me to remark further, that the high and
sacred interests of *education* prefer imperious claims to
your paternal attention and care. If, on accurate investigation, you should be fully convinced that the
system of instruction in our primary schools — the only
scenes of education for the great mass of our youth —
admits and requires great and essential improvements,
your faithful exertions will, we doubt not, correspond
with your convictions; and may it not be hoped
from the wisdom and magnanimity of the Legislature,
that it will cast a favoring eye upon the PRINCIPAL
SEAT OF LEARNING in our State? The auspicious influence of this Seminary on the literature and religion
of our country, has long been felt and acknowledged.
Your kind and fostering patronage would render this
influence still more salutary and extensive."

His father writes, June 13, 1823, "You were kindly
received; and there is ground to hope that the hints

given relative to the religious interests of the State, so candidly received, may be profitable, not only there, but elsewhere. I rejoice that *your* Governor is so respectable. I am specially glad that he so remembers the college. Your interviews with President Tyler, and your good opinion of him, must have been pleasant to you; and they give *me* pleasure.

"That 'trembling hope' you mention, respecting a number of your people, may He who is rich in mercy ripen into great rejoicing! You will, I think, be happily directed, and see in the issue, precious fruit of your anxieties and labors.

"It had occurred to me, that you must feel very sensibly the loss of Mrs. Phillips, and of Mr. John Phillips, whom long acquaintance must have endeared to you. The *public* loss in the latter is extensively lamented."

In these years, as in many subsequent ones, the interests of the Theological Seminary at Andover occupied a large place in his thoughts. Dr. Porter writes him as follows: —

"ANDOVER, Oct. 18, 1821.

"MY DEAR SIR, — I presume you feel the importance of the business on which you are to act as committee, and report to the trustees next Tuesday. But recent circumstances show it to be more important than any of us had apprehended, that the thing be finished in some way soon. Our good fathers at Newburyport are distressed. On Monday, I attended there the funeral of dear Betsey Bartlet, and saw Father B. He enquired *anxiously*, 'Will Dr. Dana be at Andover next week?' Mr. Bannister came in to show Mr. B. a letter which Mr. Brown had dictated to the

11*

Trustees, and another to Dr. M., expressing his full conviction, that Dr. M.'s resignation should be accepted, and that he ought not to think of staying in *any department.* I just hint things to show you why your presence here next Monday, as early as you can come, is indispensable. If you must go into a division of duties in the present untoward posture of affairs, it will be a severe tax on your wisdom and patience.

" Affectionately yours,

" E. Porter.

" Do come *seasonably.*"

In 1824, he delivered, by appointment, the annual sermon, before the Convention of Congregational and Presbyterian Ministers of New Hampshire. His subject was the Atonement. This sermon created some stir in the theological world. The reason of this will appear from the following passages, bearing on a theory which was then attracting much attention in New England : —

"If what has been advanced on this great subject be true, it directly follows that every system of religion which denies the atonement, must be radically defective and erroneous. It equally follows, that every system of *atonement* which omits or rejects the great principle of *substitution* must be, at least, extremely questionable.

" A scheme which represents the atonement as an *exhibition,* or *display ;* a *symbolical transaction* merely; which rejects or omits the Saviour's *substitution ;* which denies that his sufferings were *vicarious ;* and of course denies that they constituted a *proper satisfaction* for the sins of men — such a scheme is new to most Christians, and needs to be well examined before it is embraced.   .   .   .

" It is a serious question whether the theory in view does not comprise a *virtual denial* of the *atonement* itself. It leaves us the name; but what does it leave of the reality? An *exhibition* is not an atonement. A *display* is not an atonement. A mere *symbolical transaction* is not an atonement. To employ either of these terms in such a sense, is a *catachresis* of the harshest kind. If, as we have seen, the principles of substitution, of vicarious suffering, and a proper satisfaction to the violated law and justice of God are all essential to constitute the nature of atonement for sin; does it not follow, of course, that a theory of atonement which rejects these principles, virtually abandons the doctrine it professes to maintain?

" But, it is asked, If Christ was a substitute, for whom was he substituted? If he made a proper satisfaction for sin, did he satisfy for the sins of all, or of a part only? From some real difficulties attending these questions, occasion has apparently been taken to deny both his substitution and his satisfaction altogether. But surely, my hearers, this is a most dangerous principle. Would it not lead us to discard the whole system of revealed truth? If the Bible contains doctrines hard to be understood, and even apparently at variance with each other, should we not still receive them with implicit assent, humbly waiting for that world of superior light, in which they will blaze upon the mind in all their lustre, and in all their harmony?

" Much difficulty would at once vanish from the subject, should we consider the atonement, rather in reference to the law and justice of God, than to the numbers of mankind to be finally saved by it. And this is the proper mode of considering it. So far as we can perceive, all that the Saviour has rendered, of obedience and suffering, must have been rendered, though but a single sinner of the human family were to have been saved. Nor have we reason to doubt, that, had it pleased the Supreme Being to save the whole human race, what Christ has done and suffered would have been amply sufficient for the end. If these principles be admitted, the atonement may be considered without respect to numbers. It may be viewed as a kind provision of the Father of mercies for his perishing human family; as opening the door of mercy and of hope to a dying world.

"If the question still recur, For whom did Christ die as a substitute? — we reply, that, whatever difficulties meet us here, some things are perfectly plain. That he died for all the elect none will deny. Nor can it be doubted that his death had a special reference to them. At the same time, we have an equal warrant to affirm that he died for all that should believe on his name, to the end of time. Nor need we hesitate to add, that such is the effect of his intervention and death, that a free and sincere offer of mercy is made, wherever the gospel comes, to every sinner that breathes the air. If any perish now, they perish by closing on themselves the door of hope, which Heaven has opened. They perish, not because no Saviour, no atonement, has been provided, but because the Saviour and his atonement are rejected. . . .

"My respected hearers, it is with heart-felt reluctance and pain that I have mingled so much of controversy in the discussion of the subject of the atonement; a subject never designed, surely, to perplex our minds with the subtleties of debate, but rather to overwhelm every human heart with a tide of grateful admiration and love. But an imperious sense of duty has constrained me. Should I have *increased* the darkness in which the subject has been involved, I should be unhappy indeed; nor less unhappy, to have infringed on the sacred principles of Christian meekness and decorum. My simple wish has been to bear testimony to a doctrine which I verily believe to be the *article of a standing or falling church ;* the article of a standing or falling *religion.* And were this the last act of my life, I should wish it to be substantially the same. My humble attempt I submit to the candid judgment of my hearers; especially of my brethren in the holy ministry; but, most of all, to the patronage and blessing of our common and glorious Lord."

This sermon gave great satisfaction to one class of theologians — and very little to another. Its views were ably sustained by the Philadelphia "Christian Advocate." A notice of it, deemed specially unfair, appeared in the New-Haven "Christian Spectator." It is to this that Dr. Porter refers in the following letter. Contrary to his supposition, however, the secret transpired, that the article in question had originated, not at New Haven, but with a coterie of students (or, perhaps, recent graduates) of the Andover Seminary.

"ANDOVER, Feb. 7, 1825.

"MY DEAR SIR, — Some weeks since, I wrote to Pres. Day and Prof. Goodrich that I was much disturbed by the manner in which the 'Spectator' had treated you; and that my first impressions on reading their notice of your letter, was that I could not continue my patronage of the work. I assured them, however, though I did not resolve on this course, that, in my opinion, they were ruining the magazine in this quarter, if they had not already done it. This state of my own mind I had no intention of stating to you, till my thoughts this evening incidentally turned to our relations with you, and the propriety of your knowing in what manner I had regarded that flippant and puerile performance.

"I am especially desirous, for public reasons as well as my own gratification, that you should preach a Sabbath in our chapel. I am *winter-bound,* and we are all out of question as to exchange, except Brother Woods. But we could certainly send a good preacher to your pulpit, such, say, as Mr. Hallock, if none of us could come. I want to see you an evening, or rather a whole Sabbath. Please drop me a line.

"Yours ever,

"E. PORTER."

Half a year before this, Dr. Woods had thus written him:—

"Dr. Richards and Dr. Hill of Virginia, have lately been to see us. Dr. Hill has been an ardent friend to our institution, but was near being alienated by Dr. Murdock's sermon. He came on purpose to get his mind relieved as to the state of the Seminary, which was the subject of his chief solicitude. He went away with gladness of heart, all his apprehensions as to a general danger of the Institution having been removed.

"Dr. Porter gave him your sermon. He said he could not express the pleasure he had in seeing such a sermon from a Trustee of our Seminary."

The next year, he delivered a discourse before the New-Hampshire Colonization Society, which was also printed.

During his residence at Londonderry, the visit of Lafayette to this country occurred. He was appointed to deliver an address of welcome. This, with a consideration not always shown for the comfort of the "Nation's Guest," he pre-determined should be very brief. The occasion happily recalled to him the visit of Washington to New England, when his father had officiated as chaplain at the collation at Ipswich — as he did now at the dinner at Londonderry.

In the winter of 1825-6, when he had become much discouraged and disheartened, seeing but little fruit of his labors, an overture was made to him to remove to Portsmouth, and take charge of a church to be constituted there. This he declined. Soon after, information reached him that the Second Presbyterian Church in Newburyport was about to give him an invitation to become their pastor. It seemed the voice of Providence, recalling him to a more hopeful field of labor, and to the endeared associations of a large portion of his life. The following letter from a highly valued relative, conveyed to him the first intimation of what was in prospect.

"NEWBURYPORT, Feb. 11, 1826.

. . . "I have been informed, from good authority, that it is the intention of the Society where Mr. Ford was settled, to invite you to become their pastor; Mr. Ford having given notice that he shall leave in April. Be assured, my dear brother, we should esteem it a great privilege to have you so near us; it would rejoice many of your old parishioners to have you so near us, even to hear you occasionally, probably some of them statedly. Capt. Wills this day informed me he should become one of the number. I cannot but hope you will again be located among us. It will not be exactly like returning to the House and people endeared to you by many pleasant associations, but you will see the faces of many who attended on your ministrations with pleasure and profit; with many, too, who will have the pleasure of hearing you occasionally.

"I trust, should such be the result, that you would see no cause to regret the exchange. Mr. Williams and yourself might be helpers of each other in the great and good work of promoting the spiritual interests of affectionate people; there need be no jealousy nor discord, either between ministers or people, but each should strive to promote the interests of the other, as one common faith will be inculcated, and I trust the most affectionate and kind offices reciprocated, your own personal happiness promoted, and the great Redeemer's kingdom strengthened and increased.

"Your people at Londonderry might be more willing that you should return to this town, rather than any other, as they must well know your attachments here were strong, and that your own comfort might be promoted. Your children would no doubt be pleased to return to the place of their juvenile pastimes, and again to associate with those who were their earliest friends. No meeting has yet been called of the church and society, but the disposition of the people (so far as I can learn) favors the invitation. Mrs. Wheelwright and children desire their affectionate regards to you and family.

"I am your affectionate brother,

"E. WHEELWRIGHT."

The call to Newburyport was accepted. He preached his farewell sermon at Londonderry, May 7, 1826.

A "Sketch of the Londonderry Church," by one of his successors there, being already in print, the following extract is perhaps admissible: —

" It was during Dr. Dana's ministry that the temperance movement began. His spirit was grieved by the customs and habits of the people in respect to the use of intoxicating drinks. He saw great need of reform, and labored hard to effect one. Spirit was sold, and drank on the Sabbath by members of the church. This was a common practice; nor was it then considered disreputable. Indeed, one is said to have remarked, " I do not see how I can worship God acceptably when I feel *so very thirsty.*" On a Sabbath preceding a State fast, Dr. Dana urged his hearers to give him a full house on that occasion, as he had for them a special message from the Lord. Fast-day came, and the house was very well filled to listen to the message. It was a plain, searching discourse on temperance. Though much opposition and disaffection were excited by his decided treatment of this evil, yet great and permanent good was the final result of his efforts."

When a few years had passed by, the seed which he had sown in discouragement and grief yielded a rich and joyful harvest. No place became more distinguished for the change in its habits as to temperance, than Londonderry. Religion was revived, and large accessions were made to the church, of those into whose hearts the impression of his preaching and of his character had silently and deeply sunk. In subsequent years, his visits to Londonderry (where, after a time, his eldest daughter resided) were exceedingly pleasant.

12

CHAPTER XII.

1826–1837.

ON the 24th of May, 1826, he was installed Pastor
of the Second Presbyterian Church in Newburyport.
The Rev. Samuel P. Williams, his successor in the
First Presbyterian Church, delivered the installation
sermon. A few weeks later (July 15), he thus writes
to his son, then a student in Dartmouth College : —

"We begin to feel somewhat more settled and at
home : in one particular, at least, I seem to have gotten
back to former times. I have scarely a moment that I
can call my own ; and begin to think that I must, if
possible, devise some means of securing some portion
of my time to the great purpose of study. Hitherto,
my people appear candid and kind. The congregation,
since I came, has been rather increasing. It numbers
probably from one hundred and thirty to one hundred
and forty families. The sermons delivered the Sabbath
after my installation, have been requested for the press ;
and I have acceded to the proposal, though to this
moment I have done nothing toward preparing them.
Yesterday afternoon, I made a beginning with a Bible-

134

class of young ladies. The number likely to attend is probably thirty at least; and I have a hope that the attempt will be blessed to some purpose of spiritual good. I have some prospect, likewise, of a Bible-class of young men."

He was now surrounded by friends, old and new. One of the earlier signs of recuperated vigor in his church, was the erection of a lecture-room.

In June, 1826, he preached the ordination sermon of the Rev. Daniel Fitz, settled, as colleague pastor, with the Rev. Dr. Joseph Dana, over the South Church in Ipswich. Near the close is the following address to the people : —

"MY DEAR FRIENDS OF THIS CHRISTIAN CHURCH AND SOCIETY, — Permit one who drew his first breath among you, and who has followed you through life to this moment, with affectionate solicitude, to mingle his feelings with yours on this joyous day. But how can my tongue give utterance to all which my full heart prompts? Let me simply lead you up, in admiring gratitude, to the Eternal Source of all good. Adore, with me, my friends, that wonderful mercy of Heaven which has watched over you in days that are past; which has preserved your union in such a degree unbroken; which has prepared this young man for you, and prepared you for him; which has opened, not only your hearts harmoniously to receive him, but your treasures to give him a liberal support; which has preserved your aged Pastor, who has so long preached to you the word of life, so long been honored with your esteem, and happy in your affection, to witness the solemnities of this joyful day; to receive a fellow-

laborer whom he cordially approves, and whom he can
cheerfully entrust with a people so beloved; and thus
to hope, that, in closing life, he will leave you, not a
divided people, to be scattered to the winds, or to become the prey of ruinous delusions, but a united
church and congregation, listening to the same gospel
which has been preached in this house from the first,
and which has conducted so many of your fathers to
glory. And now, my friends, for all this signal and
surprising goodness, *what will you render?* Will you
not pour out your full souls in love and gratitude to
the glorious Author of every blessing? Will you not,
in opening your hearts, this day, to receive a beloved
young pastor, open them to receive the gospel he
preaches, and the Saviour he brings to you? Will you
not, by united, importunate, persevering supplications,
bring down a shower of divine influences upon yourselves and your families, upon this church and this congregation? What strength and animation would this
give to the heart of your young pastor. What a cheer-
ing and heavenly light would it shed on the closing
years of your aged minister."

Attending the General Assembly in 1827, he writes
his eldest daughter: . . . "I was much gratified in attending the anniversaries (at New York). Some of the
speeches were truly excellent; and it was remarked of
them generally that they partook more of a *practical*
cast than usual. On the Sabbath, I preached in the
morning for Dr. McAuley, and in the afternoon for Dr.
Matthews.

"I spent a night at Princeton, where I lodged at
Mr. Bayard's, and paid short visits at Dr. Alexander's
and Dr. Miller's.

"The business of the Assembly is various and complicated. . . . My mind is much occupied with a variety of objects. I usually rise by five in the morning, and rarely retire much before eleven at evening."

Describing his journey to Ohio, where he paid a pleasant visit to his brother and to his eldest son, he says, "I arrived on Saturday afternoon at Cumberland, where I spent the Sabbath. It was a communion season. The minister of the place was a Lutheran; and we had, at the feast of love, Lutherans, German Reformed (so called), Episcopalians, and Presbyterians, all holding communion with one another, and with their common Saviour. I took some part in the sacramental exercises (at which five ministers were present; one, an Episcopalian, past sixty years of age), and preached in the afternoon. I need not tell you that the season was delightful."

To his second daughter he writes, from Philadelphia, —

"My dear Jane, — . . . In the Assembly we have many ministers, both of piety and talents. I have renewed many former acquaintances and friendships, and formed some new ones. As to Mr. and Mrs. Wickes, they are the same kind and excellent friends that I have ever found them. Every thing is done to promote my comfort, and to make me forget that I am not literally at home. Dr. Alexander dined with us yesterday. I have always found him an entertaining man. But yesterday we spent more than an hour in talking about President Davies, who, you know, is a great favorite of mine, and of whose preaching, life, manners, &c., the doctor could tell me much, having preached for several

12*

years in the same region, and intimately known many of President Davies' hearers and friends."

In November, of this year, occured the peaceful death of his venerable father, Joseph Dana, D.D., of Ipswich. "On the Sabbath, but one, previous to the last Sabbath of his life, he preached a discourse which he had recently written; and, on the very last Sabbath of his life, attended public worship three times, and performed a part in the public services. In his last sickness, which was short and severe, he was calm and resigned; and, on the morning of the 16th, aged eighty-five years and three days, and having been *sixty-four* years in the ministry, he sweetly fell asleep in Jesus." *

The year of 1831 was marked by very extensive religious awakening. Writing, July 19, to his eldest daughter, resident at Londonderry, Dr. Dana says, —

"Our protracted meeting, was, on the whole, very well conducted. There is much reason to conclude that precious blessings have followed: a seriousness more extensive than was ever yet known in the place, appears to prevail.

"You will help us to be thankful for all the mercy we have seen, and you will pray that the good work may be continued and extended. I long to hear that you have a good faithful preacher among you, in whom your people will be likely to unite."

On the last day of December, 1831, a united meeting was held in Newburyport, to give thanks for the spiritual blessings which had crowned the year. In a note to his sermon on that occasion, he pointedly refers to the

* Funeral sermon by Rev. Robert Crowell. " Oh, he was a saint!" was the recent exclamation of an old resident of Ipswich, when Dr. J. Dana's name was mentioned.

views in theology then recently advanced at New Haven. Long before those views had much attracted public notice, they had been with him a frequent topic of conversation.

Two letters, of the same date, both from theological professors, were elicited by this sermon.

" YALE COLLEGE, Feb. 6, 1832.

" REVEREND AND DEAR SIR, — I thank you for your sermon, with the accompanying note, received a few days since. I have not time to enter into the subject extensively, and will only say a few things. In some of the important facts or doctrines, at least in their general form, I suppose we do not differ; such as the entire depravity of man by nature, the necessity of divine influence to renew the heart, that the depravity of man consists in a sinful disposition, &c. But the points of difference seem to be two; viz., *whence comes this sinful disposition, and what is it ?* " &c., &c.

The writer says, in conclusion, " Be assured that I have no unpleasant feelings on the subject towards you, and am, with sincere respect and affection,

" Your friend and brother,

" N. W. TAYLOR."

" ANDOVER, Feb. 6, 1832.

" MY DEAR BROTHER, — I have read your sermon with more than ordinary pleasure, and think it wholly suited to the occasion, and the times. The views expressed are, in my view, agreeable to the word of God. The error opposed in your first note seems to me to be of very bad tendency. The considerations which you suggest I think generally weighty and conclusive. I

should not think of making any objection to any of
them; though I should doubt a little how far it might
be expedient to urge one or two of them. I am glad
you have preached and published such a sermon; and
it would give me much satisfaction to know that your
brethren all around you accord with the sentiments
of the sermon.

"I am as strongly impressed as you are with the
danger of the new speculations, and am determined,
with openness and decision, though with all the prudence I can command, to oppose them.

. . . "Your affectionate brother,

"L. WOODS."

Writing to one of his family, in 1832, he speaks of a
visit which he had recently paid to Londonderry, and
says, "My old people received me very cordially. I
preached three times on the Sabbath, and for Mr. Parker on Monday." He had the happiness of finding
many now united with the church who were not so
when he was with them. "The interview (he says)
which I had with numbers was refreshing and delightful."

Another letter, written the next year, speaks of the
very pleasant visit which, with a daughter accompanying him, he had paid to Hanover, on occasion of deliver-
ing the address before the Alumni of Dartmouth College.

In August, 1834, having been invited by a committee
of citizens of Ipswich, he delivered a discourse at the
two-hundreth anniversary of the incorporation of the
town. The occasion was one of great interest. The
Hon. Rufus Choate, also a native of Ipswich, likewise
delivered an address.

In reference to some financial troubles in his church, he writes his third daughter, then visiting at Londonderry : —

"My dear Susan, — I wrote Mr. Anderson, the other day, respecting the affairs of the society, *prematurely*, though agreeably, as I thought, to existing appearances. I have now the satisfaction of saying to you, my dear child, that the aspect of things is since quite changed. The salary has been raised by subscription (the best way at present), and with great ease and apparent cordiality. My friends and people seem in good spirits; and every one, almost, seems to wonder at the heartlessness which prevailed for several days. Let us give our thanks to God, who can turn all the past to good, and order things in the best manner for the future.

"I am sorry to have given trouble to you and the other friends. It is not pleasant to feel ourselves dependent on our fellow-creatures. But it is good, very good, to feel a constant and unlimited dependence on God. Give him, my dear child, *all your heart*, and you are made forever. With love, much love to all, I am as ever,

"Your very affectionate father,
"Daniel Dana."

The year 1834 was greatly distinguished by revivals of religion in Newburyport and many other places. He writes to his daughter at Londonderry, March 12:

"My dear Mary, . . . It is indeed a remarkable time in this place. The Lord has done great things for

us, for which we are glad. The work of mercy has taken
hold of very considerable numbers whom *nobody would*
have thought of, — the careless, the vicious, the abandoned, scoffers, infidels, and even atheists. Many of
these *hopeless ones* are thought to give decisive evidence
of a deep and thorough *renovation.* Should *some* of
them disappoint expectation, it would certainly be less
wonderful than if the greater part should hold out."

In December of this year, he was called to mourn the
death of his eldest son, Joseph Dana, Esq., who had
been for some time in the practice of law, at Athens,
Ohio. Two years later, his youngest son, Samuel, died,
at the age of seventeen.

In these years he performed much parochial duty
among the people of his first charge, who were
long without a pastor. In one of his letters he says
(June 3, 1835), "Long as the days are, my great *desid-
eratum* is time." In his address to the congregation,
at the ordination of Rev. J. F. Stearns, Sept. 16,
1835, he says, — " If, in the late and long season of your
bereavement, it has been delightful to give you my
sympathy and my feeble aid, I have a much increased
delight in mingling with you in the joys of this day."

In October, 1836, he preached at Hampstead, N.H.,
the sermon at the installation of Rev. John M. C. Bartley. To those who have marked the course of things
in New England during the last thirty years, the extract that follows will not seem too long.

"If the *matter* of preaching is transcendently important, there is no small importance attached to its
manner. If, as ministers of Christ, we are indispensably bound to preach the truth, and the whole truth,
we are not less bound to preach it in its native sim-

plicity, its force, its dignity, its majesty. We should exhibit it, not only unpolluted by human mixtures, and undisguised by metaphysical subtleties, but unsullied by meretricious ornaments, and undepraved by degrading associations.

"There is a *style* which is level to every understanding; above no one, and below no one; lucid and transparent; and, like the crystal of a watch, attracting the attention, not to itself, but to what is underneath. This is the style which the preacher should seek and cultivate. A style which attracts attention to itself, and excites the admiration of a multitude of injudicious hearers, is almost certainly faulty, and the very style which a minister should avoid.

" And there is a mode of composition which tells us that the preacher is filled with his subject; too much absorbed in great things to have attention for little things; intent, not on the applause of his hearers, but their benefit; *serious in a serious cause,* and anxious to make others serious too. Such was the manner of Baxter and Howe and Flavel, and a host of other British preachers, whose memory ages have not effaced, but embalmed; whose writings are most prized by those who know them best, and, when once perused, will be sure to be perused again and again. The same may be said of no small number of American ministers, who have long since departed from earth, but who still survive in their writings — writings full of gospel truth, and of plain, powerful appeals to the understanding, the conscience, and the heart; writings which did such abundant execution in their day, and which ought never to be forgotten or neglected.

" But we have fallen on other times, and other modes

of religious instruction. And it is worthy of a serious
inquiry, whether what we fondly think we have gained
in accuracy and refinement, we have not lost in solid
power and usefulness; whether many of our modern
sermons are not fitted rather for show than use; rather
for display than execution; rather to amuse a mind at
ease, than to answer the inquiries of the anxious, or to
harrow up the feelings of the insensible.

" Who that reflects seriously can but be startled at
the fact, that a great portion of the reading of the
present day is confined to works of imagination. Fic-
titious writings, which once constituted the amusement
of youth, now constitute the *business*, not only of the
young, but of *children grown gray.* Thus it is easily
seen, that, if our community are far too much disposed to serious thought on the realities of eternity,
the evil has found a sure and effectual antidote. One
consequence of this state of things — a consequence perfectly natural — is an eager and extensive demand for
sermons of the same imaginative character; sermons
which please the fancy, which gratify the love of novelty, the love of amusement, the love of excitement,
the love of every thing, in short, but of truth and
piety. It is painful to think that this demand has been
but too well met; and that we have too many sermons
about as amusing as novels, and about as much calculated to pain the conscience with a sense of guilt, and
warm the heart with the love of God.

" Do not many sermons of the present day treat their
hearers absolutely too much like children, by dealing
almost continually in *illustration ?* They contain a
few truths, and those often not of the most interesting
kind; for great, fundamental, vital truths, like the rays

of the sun, are sufficiently seen by their own light : but what is wanting in solid, sober instruction, is amply supplied by labored illustrations. The consequence often is, and very naturally, that the illustrations are remembered, while the truths themselves, thus gilded, not to say stifled and concealed, are overlooked, neglected, or forgotten.

"There is a *cloudy, misty* way of preaching, borrowed from the German school, or from some of its humble pupils, which promises much, and performs but little. Words apparently select and sufficiently elegant are not wanting; but the thoughts are too feeble and ill-defined to make their way through the darkness. What is unintelligible appears to some profound : the superficial admire, perhaps; while those who attend the sanctuary in search of gospel instruction, grieve while they stay, and retire bitterly disappointed.

" There begins to prevail, in some parts of our country, a style of preaching — it is painful to call it vulgar, and yet it cannot be denied that it makes a near approach to vulgarity. It affects to treat the most sacred themes, and the most awful truths of religion, with perfect familiarity. Those exhibitions of divine majesty and wrath which have appalled and shaken the souls of the holiest of men, it can approach with unhallowed boldness. That ETERNAL NAME which fills all heaven with reverence, and all hell with terror, it can pronounce with irreverent lightness. It can even expatiate on the torments of the world of despair, and on the danger of those who hang over it, without either awe or compassion. In the mean time, it speaks of religion itself in terms the most superficial and delusive. The great and pervading *change* which it involves, it

13

fritters down to a simple *resolution ;* while, addressing
itself to the mere selfishness of human nature, to its
hopes and its fears, it builds this resolution on a foundation of sand.

"I am compelled by a kind of necessity to notice
another abuse of the sacred desk. The time is remembered by most who hear me, when every thing
which indicated or excited levity of mind, every thing
in the shape of jest or merriment, was by general consent banished from the sanctuary. What was ludi-
crous was deemed profane. But times have changed,
and sentiments and tastes have changed with them.
In the opinion of many, our religious anniversaries
have scarcely received their proper seasoning, till some
shrewd jest has relaxed the muscles of the audience.
Not only so, the pulpit (will it be believed?) the pulpit is employed by some who bear the name of Christian preachers, as a place from which to retail merry
stories and favorite jokes. Thus immortal beings are
led to trifle with their Maker, while in his immediate
presence; to trifle with heaven, and with hell. Thus
they lose, not to say murder, the precious moments
which will stamp their eternity. Thus numbers resort
to the house of God, as they attend the ball-room or
the theatre, for *amusement ;* and return disappointed if
the favorite gratification happens to be denied.

"I have thus glanced at some of the novelties in
preaching, some of the strange perversions of the pulpit, to which our times have given birth. I have done
it from an imperious sense of duty, and with undis-
sembled, inexpressible pain — a pain, I frankly confess,
not unmingled, in some instances, with indignation. I
will not insult the understandings of my hearers by

inquiring whether, by these changes in the style of preaching, the pulpit has gained any thing; whether religion has gained any thing; whether sabbaths have become more solemn, sermons more impressive, hearers more serious, and churches replenished with greater numbers of solid and devoted Christians? Nor may I pause to inquire whether, if the cause of religion is at the present time unusually depressed; if Christians are more languid, and the impenitent more bold than ordinary; or if, in short, error, infidelity, atheism itself, with the most appalling forms of licentiousness and vice and crime, threaten to overwhelm the land, and to sweep away every thing precious and sacred from our country — the *cause* of these enormous evils is not to be traced in part to the sanctuary, and even to the pulpit? I am arrested at present by the fact that the abuses mentioned exist, prevail, and too probably increase; and by another fact more wonderful still, that some of the most prominent and alarming of these abuses have received hitherto but little rebuke.

"Yes; it is evident and undeniable; a false, a perverted, and most pernicious taste respecting preaching, prevails, and is apparently still extending in our country. Hearers of the gospel, in multitudes, are at length absolutely disgusted with the solemn and dignified exhibition of its doctrines; with the simple, unadorned, faithful, serious, pungent declaration of its truths. It is, they think, a worn-out and hopeless experiment. "Give us," they loudly and imperiously demand, SOMETHING NEW, — something more attractive, more amusing, more exciting, more consonant to the improvements in science and philosophy, and to the taste and spirit of an enlightened age." What is most of all astonishing and humbling is, that some real Christians, instead of breasting the torrent, seem to be absolutely carried away with it, and to give their influence to a cause which, in proportion to its prevalence, must banish real Christianity from our country and the world.

And now, who does not see that the Christian minister who would be faithful, has a part to act, which demands all his fortitude, all his courage, all his immovability of resolution? He is bound to adhere, not only to the truths of the gospel, but to the gospel method of defending and inculcating those truths. He must come to the Scriptures to learn not only *what* to preach, but *how* to preach. He will gladly accept, indeed, whatever aid in defending and elucidating the Scriptures may be derived from ancient learning and modern science; from history and philosophy and polite literature; from observation and experience. But he will beware of depraving the pure and sublime religion of Jesus by any human mixtures; by the subtleties of metaphysics, by sickly sentimentalities, or by affected refinements of style. Still less will he consent to degrade it by irreverent familiarities, or wretched attempts at wit and humor. And though, in this resistance to the taste and the demands of a corrupt age, he may encounter a torrent of fashion and of obloquy; though he may meet the opposition of some, the scorn of others, and the affected pity of a third class; though friends and enemies may unite their efforts to turn him from his path — *none of these things will move him.* Anxious only for the smile of his Saviour, and fearing nothing but his frown, and leaning on his almighty arm, he will boldly stand his ground. Strong in conscious integrity, he will dare obey his conscience and his God, and calmly leave it to time, to truth, and to the judgment of the great day, to vindicate his course.

"Ministers of the present day are frequently perplexed in regard to some of the *measures recently adopted for the promotion of religion.* I have now more immediate reference to those *protracted meetings* to which many have looked as the principal, if not the only means of religious revivals. It needs not be doubted that the plan of these meetings originated in a sincere and ardent desire to promote the salvation of sinners and the increase of the church. Nor does a partiality in their favor necessarily infer an idolatrous dependence on their efficacy, or a sinful neglect of the other means of grace appointed by heaven. Nor can it, I think, be denied, that, in a variety of instances, these meetings have been evidently crowned by the blessing of God and the saving influences of his Spirit. As little can it be questioned that many, even of the pious, have placed an unwarrantable confidence in these measures, and have looked to them too exclusively as instruments of conversion; while, in the mean time, the precious appointment and privileges of the Sabbath have been too much undervalued and neglected. It is equally evident, that, by many, the success of these measures has been greatly overrated; and, that, in various instances, they have brought numbers into the church who have subsequently proved themselves to be either hypocrites or apostates. Who, indeed, can think it strange, that, in those cases where a complicated and powerful machinery has been set to work on the passions of human beings, great numbers should be deceived, and mistake the excitements of natural feeling for the operations of divine grace. We are called to notice with pain and grief the

13*

remarkable languor and deadness in religion by which these seasons have been frequently followed, and the awful withdrawal of the divine Spirit from most of our churches, of which there is now such melancholy and conclusive evidence. Let the churches, then, humble themselves in the dust before a justly offended God; let them meekly accept his righteous rebukes; let them search out, and mourn, and confess and forsake their errors and their sins. *Corrected by their own wickedness, reproved by their own backsliding, let them know and see that it is an evil thing and bitter, that they have forsaken the Lord their God.* Let them remember, too, that while he may, in *sovereignty*, bless *human means and efforts* sincerely directed to the promotion of his cause, he has pledged his *truth and faithfulness* to prosper *his own appointments.* What judicious Christian can doubt that the present aspects of the time and the Church significantly and loudly demand a return to these neglected appointments? Should the churches turn a deaf ear to the call; should they, in the face of all the instruction and all the reproof which they have received, prefer measures of human invention to the ordinances of heaven; should they, in seeking to rise from their depression, turn from the Sabbath and the ministry, which God has appointed, to other means and other instruments, the experiment may prove as abortive as it is unwise and preposterous. And in this case, faithful ministers will have a most arduous part to act, and all their wisdom, their firmness, and independence may be but sufficient to meet the exigencies of so alarming a crisis.

"I will touch but a single topic farther, and that as briefly as possible. At the present era, when men move rather in masses than as individuals, and when a variety of objects are pursued through the medium of associations, frequent and strong claims must, of course, be made on ministers of the gospel. Of the objects in view, some are of vast and universally acknowledged moment; for they aim at spreading the light of divine knowledge and the blessings of salvation through our country and through the world. Others are calculated to unite all benevolent hearts, as they are directed to the removal or alleviation of some of the principal forms and sources of human suffering. A third class may be somewhat *Utopian* in their character, and, if they excite a smile, may well be suffered to pass without opposition. A fourth class may be more questionable; as, though they may present interests of vital importance and dear to humanity, they may be embarrassed with serious difficulties. The evils to be removed may be political, as well as moral: they may be inwrought in the framework of society, of government, laws, and civil institutions; and their sudden and violent removal might induce general convulsion, misrule, and ruin.

"In a case so distressing as this, to whom shall the Christian minister resort for instruction, but to his Saviour? That Saviour was wholly devoted to the preaching of his gospel — a gospel which offers salvation to all, and claims a sovereign control over all; a gospel which, wherever it goes, sheds a most salutary influence on rulers and subjects, on the rich and poor, on the elevated and the depressed, on laws and liberty, on every interest of man. But he let civil institutions alone. He addressed men as individuals, and he designed, through individuals, to bless communities, by cherishing among them every thing excellent, and removing, ultimately, every form of evil.

"St. Paul pursued the same course. When he wrote his celebrated letter to the converts at Rome, the empire was the seat of the most absolute and cruel despotism. But he inculcated no sedition; he preached no revolutionary doctrines. 'Let every soul,' said he, 'be subject to the higher powers;' and this, when the highest of those powers, the Emperor, was a monster of cruelty, oppression, and every vice. And when, among those to whom he wrote his epistles, *slavery* existed, and in its most repulsive forms, he made it his great object to preach — courageously, tenderly to preach — both to masters and slaves, that gospel which was the grand instrument of softening the ferocity of the one, and healing the lacerated spirits of the other.

"Surely, these examples may be imitated with perfect safety by ministers of the present day. In the fondness of speculation, we may have discovered better forms of government and better laws than those we now possess. Yet, rather than become preachers of politics, it were preferable, perhaps, that we should treasure up our discoveries for our own private use. And if the evils of slavery, and the sufferings of the slaves, are enormous (and who can deny it? who can doubt it? where is the heart of sensibility that does not *feel* it?) let us beware, lest, by an injudicious and violent interference, we exasperate those evils and those sufferings. If we have confessedly no power over the masters but that of moral suasion, let that moral suasion consist of something different from exasperating menaces and bitter invectives. If the cause of African liberty and emancipation is a sacred cause, let it not be polluted by impatience, by intolerance, by recklessness, by expedients which obstruct rather than promote its advancement. If the evils to be removed, being deeply seated, and intertwined with a thousand interests, demand the calm deliberation of the wisest, let not excitement and passion attempt the hopeless work.

"I know that to some, the moderation now recommended may seem to be the very thing we do not want. But I am equally assured, that, without it, our peace, our Government, our union, are lost. And the cause of freedom, of African freedom, is lost too. A civil war, and, worse, a *servile* war, the most terrible of all wars, may be at our very doors. Of such a war, the issue is but too easily seen. And how lamentable would it be, should that race, already so deeply injured, find itself reduced, through the injudicious interference of its professed friends, to the dire dilemma of a more cruel bondage, or absolute extermination!

"Let us, then, as ministers of the gospel of peace, as friends of our country and of the African race, have the courage, in this season of excitement, to be calm. Let us resolutely and mildly adhere to our proper calling and our proper work. Let us go on *preaching the gospel;* that gospel which is destined to regenerate the world, to remove all its sins, all its oppressions, and all its miseries; that gospel which is the best friend of liberty and of man; that gospel which accomplishes its work, not like the earthquake or the tornado, but like *leaven;* by a process noiseless, gradual, yet effectual, and ultimately complete and universal. Let us not be precipitated into measures from which our conscience and our best judgment revolt. If, in this course, we are assailed with reproach and denunciation, let us meekly and patiently bear it. Let *none of these things move us.* Let us be solicitous only to know and do our duty, and let us cast every other care on the Master we serve."

In January, 1837, he delivered, by appointment, the annual election sermon before the Governor, Council, and Legislature of Massachusetts. His text was, "And the leaves of the tree were for the healing of the nations." Shortly after, he received a letter from the Hon. Edward Everett, then Governor, expressing his thanks for "the sound and seasonable sentiments contained in it." He adds, "Happy would it be for our beloved country and Commonwealth, could their councils be directed, and the people generally be guided, by the principles maintained in this excellent discourse."

CHAPTER XIII.

1837–1844.

Division of the Presbyterian Church. — Suffering from his Eyes. — Anniversary at Exeter. — Letters to Professor Stuart. — Fiftieth Anniversary of his Ordination.

In respect to the division of the Presbyterian Church, growing out of the proceedings of the General Assemblies of 1837 and 1838, Dr. Dana's views can be stated in his own words. The year previous to the disruption, he had addressed to the moderator of the assembly the letter which follows: —

"Newburyport, Mass., May 18, 1836.

"To the Moderator of the General Assembly.

"Reverend and dear Sir,—If thus to address myself to one whom I cannot know, and to whom I may very probably be unknown, require an apology, that apology must be found in the nature and the pressing circumstances of the case.

"The Presbyterian Church in our country has come to a great crisis. Both its friends and its enemies look to the present meeting of the General Assembly with a solicitude hitherto unparalleled. On its decisions may depend, under God, the continuance and prosperity of the Church, or its disruption and ruin. The idea of influencing those decisions might well seem, in me, the extreme of arrogance. Yet I hope I shall at least be pardoned, if my mind, pressed as it is with almost overwhelming anxieties, seeks a momentary relief in pouring a few of its thoughts into yours.

"The subject is altogether too ample for any thing which might claim the name of a discussion. I shall attempt nothing but a very few suggestions, and these expressed as briefly as possible. Still, these suggestions will touch, however imperfectly, both the *cause* and the *removal* of the present most serious and alarming evils.

"Instead of *cause*, I know that *causes* might seem the most appropriate term. Yet, various as may be the sources of our present danger, is there not an important sense in which they all meet in one? I allude to that *tendency to extremes* which seems more or less apparent in every part of our church. In other words, I refer to the want of that dignified moderation, that Christian meekness and forbearance, that mutual deference, that calmness and candor in deliberation, that caution and impartiality in decision, and that combined wisdom and energy in action, which once constituted the glory, the strength, and safety of our church.

"May I be permitted, with the modesty which becomes me, yet with the fidelity which the occasion demands, to ask, Has not the Church, of late, lost much, very much, of its distinctive character? Instead of standing up as the *example* and the *reproof* of an excited, disordered community, is it not itself a lamentable spectacle of excitement and discord? In looking over the records of some of its judicial tribunals, do we find the dignity, the meekness, the mild and heavenly spirit, of the gospel — or the reverse? Who would not wish that many things which these records contain might be blotted from existence; might at least be obliterated from the minds of men? But the wish comes too late: they are written in the tablets of eternity; and they have gone through the length and breadth of the land, to the dishonor of religion, to the grief of the pious, and the triumph of the ungodly.

"That our church has vast interests to be preserved, and vast evils to be removed, who can doubt? And who can doubt as to the instrumentalities by which these objects will be accomplished, if accomplished at all? Decision, zeal, and energy are all needful; but decision, zeal, and energy are all, by themselves, insufficient. They may be just as powerful to ruin a cause as to aid it. And surely we need, we greatly need, in the present crisis, the spirit of *wisdom*, the spirit of *humility*, the spirit of *prayer*, and the spirit of *love*.

"It cannot be denied, that, within the pale of our church, some collisions have arisen, even in respect to important doctrines of the gospel; but may not these collisions be traced, in some instances, to a different understanding and use of terms, and, in others, to conflicting theories of philosophy? Ought there not, in each of these cases, to be much mutual candor and forbearance? Shall even real differences of religious opinion be needlessly exaggerated? Shall they give rise to angry debates; to endless crimination and re-crimination? Are not those the best friends of truth, who defend it in the spirit of love, and by its own appropriate weapons?

"As for the charge of *heresy*, it is a most serious affair. Nothing but *plain, palpable opposition to fundamental*

14

truth can justify it. If the supposed heretic has contended, not so much with a doctrine of the gospel, or of
the creed, as with a phantom of his own creation,
should he not have the benefit of his own mistake? If
what he has plainly denied at one time, he has as plainly affirmed or admitted at another, should he not have
the benefit of his own inconsistency? Desperate rem-
edies belong only to desperate diseases. To amputate
a limb supposed to be unsound is confessedly a short
and easy process. But will not the good surgeon be
more gratified, and will not his skill be more apparent,
if, by any means, he can restore and save it?

"Emphatically, at the present time, *Zion spreadeth
forth her hands.* Shall there be *none to comfort her!*
Our church bleeds with deep, reiterated, and (may I
not add?) self-inflicted wounds; but *is there no balm
in Gilead?* Is there no resource in heaven? Is there
not in prayer, in faith, in Christian love, in the much-
enduring and healing spirit of the gospel, a species of
omnipotence? Will there not be found, in the present
assembly, a great and dignified majority who will un-
weariedly pray and labor for its peace ; and who, while
valiant for the truth, will as readily (to use the words
of Baxter) *be martyrs for love as for any article of
the creed?* I firmly believe there will; and I confidently hope, against all disheartening appearances, that
*darkness will be made light before them, and crooked
things straight.* God himself will approve and prosper their efforts ; and the blessings of the Church
and of its glorious Head will be their high reward.

"I again implore your pardon, reverend and dear sir,
for the liberty I have taken in thus disburdening my
full heart. Although I have addressed you as Modera-

tor of the Assembly, it is far from my wish that these free and unstudied effusions should be communicated to the body. Should my views meet your approbation, you may submit them to any brother whom you please. The letter is at your entire disposal. I would not for worlds, even in this feeble way, give a mistaken or unhallowed touch to the ark of God; but to contribute the smallest particle of aid to the sacred cause of *truth and love* (and the cause is one and the same) would give me inexpressible satisfaction.

"With sentiments of respect, I subscribe myself, reverend and dear sir,

"Yours in the bonds of the gospel,

"DANIEL DANA."

The following extract from the records of the Newburyport Presbytery exhibits his position in 1838: —

"The Presbytery of Newburyport met by adjournment in the chapel of the First Presbyterian Church on Wednesday, Nov. 14.

"The following resolutions, presented by Rev. Dr. Dana, were unanimously adopted; viz.: —

"*Resolved*, That this presbytery cannot contemplate the disordered and divided condition of the Presbyterian Church in these United States but with profound regret and grief.

"*Resolved*, That, without impeaching the conduct of its commissioners of the present year in withdrawing from the assembly which held its session in the Seventh Presbyterian Church in Philadelphia, and joining the other body, this presbytery holds itself not bound to pursue the course indicated by the said act of its commissioners.

"*Resolved*, That, in the present perplexed state of things, this presbytery is not prepared to declare its adhesion to either of the two bodies claiming the name and the rights of the General Assembly of the Presbyterian Church in these United States. Being unable to act with satisfaction and with a clear conscience, it solemnly asserts the right of not acting at all.

"*Resolved*, That if, in the exercise of this privilege of deliberation and delay, this presbytery shall incur censure or excision, it will prepare, with Christian meekness and magnanimity, to meet the consequences; while it will solemnly appeal to that higher tribunal at which all erroneous judgments of the Church itself will be reviewed and reversed."

TO REV. JOHN M. C. BARTLEY.

"NEWBURYPORT, May 13, 1839.

. . . "The views of Judge Gibson appear to me both more enlarged and more discriminating than those of Judge Rogers: I presume they are generally just; and I am particularly pleased with the determination of the judges to interpose their jurisdiction no further than the nature and necessity of the case seem absolutely to require. The main point on which Judge Gibson has failed to satisfy me, is the connection of the formation of the rejected synods with the *plan of union*. If that plan can properly be considered as giving them birth and being, then, with the abrogation of that plan, they cease of course to be a part of the Presbyterian body, and the whole matter is settled. But here my mind is still somewhat perplexed.

"What will be the effect of the decision of the

judges we shall soon see. I cannot but hope that it will induce the contending parties to come together with feelings somewhat less exasperated, and to devise coolly and deliberately the means and terms of an *amicable separation ;* for this is the most favorable issue of difficulties which can now be anticipated.

" What course Mr. H. will take I can only conjecture. I am however pretty clearly of opinion, that, if he is guided by the views of his presbytery as expressed at their late meeting, he will join neither of the assemblies. . . .

" Very affectionately yours,

"DANIEL DANA."

TO REV. MR. BARTLEY, PHILADELPHIA.

" NEWBURYPORT, May 21, 1839.

" MY DEAR SON, — I owe you many thanks for your kind and excellent letter. It touched on the very topics on which I wished to be informed, and the information it conveys is generally very gratifying. Your letter was the more interesting, as it gives me all the intelligence from Philadelphia which I have as yet received. The " Presbyterian," which generally arrives here on Saturday evening, has not arrived yet.

" I rejoice in the excellent spirit manifested by Dr. Green and other leading men. I have often thought that the good doctor has been most undeservedly and cruelly reproached, and cannot but hope that his last days will yet be some of his brightest and happiest. From what you state of the views and feelings of some of the most influential men, I cannot but hope that an end is now to be put to the deplorable collisions which have already existed too long. What a fine opportu-

14*

nity is now given for the contending parties to lay
aside all bitterness, to devise and adjust equitable terms
of separation, and to part in peace. In this case the
matter will at once be taken out of the civil court,
and the Presbyterian Church will cease to be the subject of unhallowed reproach and profane ridicule.

" I rejoice in the plan you mention of an address to
the churches on *doctrinal purity.* It could not have
been committed to any one more properly than Dr.
Alexander. From his head and heart I shall anticipate
something very excellent and impressive.

" The commissioner of the Newburyport Presbytery, it seems, is with the New School Assembly. I
confess I had some hope that we should escape this
last mortification. You know that I opposed the appointment from first to last. Other brethren thought
it might tend to aid in a friendly and equitable adjustment of existing difficulties. With this view, professedly and expressly, the appointment was made. As
to the mode of promoting the object, some discretion
was allowed to the commissioner. Should Mr. H.
make himself, properly speaking, a member of the New
School Assembly, and act with them throughout as a
partisan, he will not only transcend his powers, but
oppose his instructions. After all I shall not be much
surprised, if, by some act of the other assembly, direct
or indirect, our presbytery shall be excluded from their
connection.

" Should Dr. Green have published his history of
the Presbyterian Church, I would wish you to procure
it for me ; otherwise, I should wish for Dr. Hodge's
first number. If you could conveniently procure me a
set of the Presbyterian Tracts (bound) I should be
pleased.

" Wishing you the divine protection and blessing at all times, and a safe and auspicious return,

" I am yours, most affectionately,

" DANIEL DANA."

There was at this time a Presbytery of Newburyport. It had been formed from the Londonderry Presbytery in 1826. It was never flourishing as to numbers; and, in 1847, after having stood alone for several years, it was re-united to the Presbytery of Londonderry, whose connection with the Old School Assembly had been continued without interruption. Dr. Dana was thus brought again into the ecclesiastical connection to which he naturally belonged.

In 1838, a slight accident to one of his eyes resulted in his being for many weeks confined to a room made totally dark. This was a severe trial to him. " My time is so short," he would say. The activity of his mind, which he could not repress, doubtless prolonged the privation. It was at this time that the half-century connection of his friend Dr. Abbot with the Exeter Academy was celebrated. The presence of Daniel Webster, and of not a few gentlemen of distinction besides who had been school-boys at Exeter, gave *éclat* to the occasion. His absence was deeply regretted : a letter dictated by him was read to the assembly. Mr. Webster called on him on his return from Exeter, and cheered his seclusion with many pleasant anecdotes and reminiscences. One was, that, when at school at Exeter, Dr. Abbot once sent him home to his boarding-house with instructions to *wash his hands*, with the added recommendation to him to " use plenty of soap ! "

It was at one of the Exeter anniversaries that Mr.

Webster, following him in the choice of bread at table (of which two kinds were offered) said, " I will take the same with Dr. Dana : it is generally *safe to follow* Dr. Dana." The remark had special point if it was on this same occasion (the date is not remembered) that a clergyman present, zealous on a subject which has agitated New England for thirty years, said pretty earnestly, " But, Dr. Dana, what shall we *do* about slavery, — what shall we DO ? " He replied by quoting Father Moody's pithy saying, " When we do not know what to do, we must be careful *not to do we know not what!* "

Dr. Abbot's regret at the absence of his friend was warmly expressed. He writes, " I had anticipated the presence and aid of my early and much-loved friend, whose countenance and cordial sympathy I have from early life so often experienced, and which on this occasion would have been peculiarly grateful."

In 1839, he published in pamphlet form, " Letters to the Rev. Professor Stuart," comprising remarks on his " Essay on Sin," in the American Biblical Repository for April and July, 1839. Although the longest of his publications, it seems, from the date appended to it, to have occupied him but a short time in the preparation. It attracted much attention; and some copies of it found their way across the Atlantic. A quotation from it occurs in one of the notes to Dr. John Pye Smith's " Scripture and Geology." The subject of these letters, and the spirit in which they were written, sufficiently appear in the following passages from the first and last pages : —

" I begin by repeating my thanks for your kind and candid reception of my first letter, plain and uncere-

monious as it was. This kindness of yours combines
with a thousand other considerations to inculcate a
similar spirit on myself. Indeed, every feeling of my
heart recoils from the thought of unkindness to a
Christian brother, long loved and valued; while fidelity
to the truth bids me treat his statements and reasonings
with the utmost freedom.

"The object of your essay seems to be to disprove
and explode the doctrine of *original sin,* or of *native
depravity,* taking these terms in their ordinarily received and well-understood sense. It is true, that
you occasionally employ expressions, which, taken by
themselves, might be viewed as not materially exceptionable by the friends of the doctrine in question ;
but I appreciate too highly your independence and
integrity to suspect that you intend to be equivocal.
There is an affluence in the English language which
supplies appropriate terms for all our ideas ; and of this
affluence you are amply possessed. When you intimate
an opinion that the whole debate may be resolved into
a difference in *terminology,* I can only express my surprise ; or rather, I can only avow a surprise which it is
out of my power to express.

"If, in the remarks I shall offer on your theory, I shall
make it appear that the philosophic principle on which
it is built is erroneous ; that the celebrated author
whose support it claims gives it no support at all ;
that the theory itself is in conflict with the Scriptures ;
that it is inconsistent with your own repeated admis-
sions and statements ; and, finally, that it stands opposed to your publicly avowed opinions, — you will
doubtless admit that it should be abandoned. On the
points thus indicated, I will venture no confident prom-

ises.   All I ask is to be favored, in this discussion, with
the candid attention and the critical scrutiny of yourself and of my readers at large." . . .

"I cannot conclude without adverting to one point
in your essay which has not yet been touched.   You
seem to apprehend that the great evil in the Church, at
this day, is an intolerance of error, an extreme sensitiveness to every departure from truth.   But others
are of a different opinion.   They think that a ' wide-
spread and increasing indifference to sound doctrine
is the present great sin of the Christian Church.'   And
you yourself, I think, will not be backward to admit
that ' there can be no surer sign of degeneracy than
the *peaceable progress of error.*'   For myself, I have no
disposition to defend any arbitrary methods of sup-
pressing heresy.   It is the *truth* which, in this case, is
the sufferer.   Yet if there is not, in this age, an unusual
and alarming insensibility to the progress of error, and
to the duty of opposing it; if many Christians have
not too much forgotten their obligation to ' contend
earnestly for the faith once delivered to the saints,' —
then I am utterly unacquainted with the signs of the
times.

"I have thus, my dear sir, given utterance to some
of the many thoughts occasioned by the perusal of
your ' Essay on Sin.'   If these letters are pervaded by a
style of plainness and freedom which may seem not
quite congenial to your character and station, my apology must be found in the deeply interesting nature of
the subject, and the imperious demands of truth.   Nor
has it escaped me, that I address one who obviously
holds the freest expression of thoughts and feelings to
be no crime.   Never did I more sincerely deprecate a

belligerent spirit in the Church than at the present moment. Never did I cherish a more ardent desire to live in peace with all who love the Redeemer and his cause. But peace itself, if purchased at the expense of essential truth, is too dearly bought.

"Humbly commending what I have written to your candor, and that of the Christian public, and, above all, to the patronage and blessing of the great Head of the Church, I subscribe myself,

"Very affectionately and sincerely,

"Your friend and brother,

"DANIEL DANA.

"NEWBURYPORT, Aug. 20, 1839."

The following, from a professor in a theological seminary, is one of many letters expressing thanks to him for this publication : —

"REV. DR. DANA : *Dear Sir*, — I have received, some time since, your very excellent pamphlet containing a series of letters to Professor Stuart, for which I most sincerely thank you; and for the production of which I would have thanked you, even though you had forgotten me in your kind distribution.

"I have read your pamphlet with very great satisfaction, and fully assent to its entire and important truth. I think it clear and kind; brief, yet full; easily understood; and altogether unanswerable, if the Bible is to be umpire. I think, moreover, that the time, the occasion, the spirit, and ability, and, above all, the great importance of the truths involved, will recommend the book to the best feelings of all who love truth more than theory, or gospel more than theology."

In June, 1841, he writes to his daughter at Londonderry, —

"How can I ever forget the delightful visit I had with you about this time last year? It was a gratification indeed, and the remembrance is as pleasant as it is always fresh.

"I transmitted, some days since, to Mr. Anderson, my sermon on Mr. Bartlet. Perhaps you were surprised that I should undertake so formidable a task. But the circumstances were somewhat urgent. What principally reconciled me to the task, was the opportunity it gave me to bear my emphatic testimony in favor of preserving in purity the genuine principles of the Seminary; and I hope I may now say, that, should it ever swerve from its original design, I have washed my hands of the guilt."

Writing one of his daughters, he says, —

"My time passed very pleasantly at Dorchester. After the second service, Mrs. Codman took me to Mr. Withington's. The mother of our friend *Leonard* is certainly one of the best of women; and probably he is indebted to her for much of his genius and good feeling.

· · · "You have, probably before this, seen some portions of the Lyceum lecture of which you speak. My account of Newburyport has little to recommend it save its *truth;* and to this, I hope, it has some valid claims."

March, 1842. "We have been much pestered here, the past winter, with Mr. Miller's doctrines, and their incompetent, but very presumptuous preachers. Much excitement has been occasioned, which we hope will in most cases prove transient. Other sources of uneasiness arise in some of our churches. Mr. Campbell has had his full share with the disorganizers. But I hope and believe he will weather the storm."

In 1844, he was gratified with a letter from a friend of his early years who was near the close of a long life of eminent usefulness — the Rev. Dr. Charles Coffin, for many years President of Greenville College, Tenn.

Dr. Coffin says, "Your expressions of esteem and attachment, and best wishes for time and eternity, are most cordially reciprocated. Your ministerial course, as to ecclesiastical connection, and some of the more exciting topics of the day, I have been able, with no small pleasure, to trace."

The 19th of November, 1844, completed fifty years since his ordination. Without his knowledge, it was determined beforehand by his friends that it should not pass unnoticed. An invitation was given him, too cordial to be declined, to deliver a discourse on that day in the church in which had been his earliest ministry. From the printed copy we subjoin several extracts : —

. . . .
" Fifty years since, standing on this spot, I received in sacred charge, and with a trembling heart, a beloved people. Little did I then think that my unworthy life would be prolonged to its present date, or that aught but death could terminate that endearing connection. Twenty-four years since, the event, so unanticipated and so painful, took place. I gave you my parting, and, as I supposed, my final, benediction. Little did I imagine that the scene would ever be renewed, or that any thing analogous would ever arise. But your affectionate invitation, coming to my heart

15

with all the force of a command, brings me again before you this day.

"A multitude of thoughts and feelings excited by the occasion must be suppressed; for they are absolutely unutterable. It shall be my humble aim to employ the present hour, deeply interesting as it is to myself and to most of my hearers, in a manner which may be profitable to all.

" Suffer me, then, in opening my heart to those beloved friends to whom, in *former* and more *recent* time, I have preached the gospel — for both classes are now before me — suffer me to appropriate the address of the apostle in the text. For, pre-eminent as he was in every natural, acquired, and supernatural gift, he only speaks *here* the language of every sincere minister, though of the humblest talents and station. All such can truly say to those whom they have served in the gospel '*Now we live, if ye stand fast in the Lord.*'

"You see, then, my friends, what constitutes the *crowning joy and felicity of ministers:* It is *the pious steadfastness of their Christian hearers.*

"Let us meditate a while on this momentous truth, and open our minds and hearts to its influence.

. . . "Indulged as I have been, beloved hearers, to accomplish half a century of ministerial service, chiefly in this place ; and called, this day, to utter some of my last words, I may be expected, perhaps, to take, at least, a momentary review of the past.

" I was first invited to officiate in this congregation in the spring of 1794. Here I found a church which had been gathered about a half-century previous, and this, with a professed view to cultivate great purity in the truths and ordinances of God. Heaven had signally

smiled on the design; and under the successive ministrations of two distinguished pastors, the church and
congregation had attained an unusually flourishing
state. Recently, indeed, their numbers had been somewhat diminished by a secession, which, being not small
from the first, speedily increased to a large and respectable society. My ordination proceeded with a degree
of harmony, but not to universal satisfaction; and the
worthy members who dissented retired the following
year, and formed the church and congregation to which
I have had the honor to minister for the last eighteen
years. My own flock, however, still remained large,
and furnished ample employment for all my powers of
both body and mind. To me, my labors, though arduous, were delightful; and to the honor of my heavenly Master, I would acknowledge, that they were not
wholly unblest. Without any signal revival of religion,
the church received gradual, but not inconsiderable,
accessions; and these accessions were rather increased
in the closing years of my connection. When invited
to a new and distant scene of action,* I felt it a duty
to submit the question of compliance to the judgment
and advice of others. When, in obedience to that
judgment and advice, I forced myself away from a
people most tenderly beloved, the scene was heart-
rending. And such was my prostration of bodily, as
well as mental power, that, for a time, the hope of future
action and usefulness almost deserted me. That my
heart was not separated, my friends are all well aware;
nor has it been a small delight, since my return to this
place, occasionally to revisit their pulpit, and to mingle
my sympathies in the scenes of their sickness and sorrow.

* The presidency of Dartmouth College.

It has likewise been a source of heart-felt satisfaction, that, with each of the highly esteemed ministers who have succeeded me, I have maintained a sincere and unbroken friendship. I have rejoiced in their prosperity, and have been gratified in lending, as occasion has presented, my feeble aid in lightening some portion of their labors.

"I am deeply sensible, too, to the privilege of ministering to the Christian society now under my care. Their small numbers have seemed well to comport with my own increased years and infirmities. The minister who duly estimates the exigencies of his people, and the responsibilities of his office, can never want employment. In my last connection, I have found friends firm and faithful; friends who have aided me by their efforts, and prayed blessings down upon my feeble labors; and here, too, adored be the goodness and the grace of God! I can speak of the spiritual children he has given me. In the season of quickened attention with which this place was blessed about thirteen years since, a number not small was gathered into my church. Nor, before that favored period, nor since, have my efforts among my present charge seemed to be wholly unrewarded.

. . . "Among the privileges allotted me in this place, I ought to mention the solid friendship which I have enjoyed with some of its best inhabitants, without regard to Society limits. Their conversation has often been instructive to me, their kindness animating, their sympathy consoling. Indeed, from every description of citizens, I have received all the attention and respect I could desire, and far more than I have deserved. So multiplied are the tokens of regard and affection which have thronged around me of late, that my heart must be composed of strange materials, if its liveliest sensibilities have not been awakened.

"With the ministers of the place generally, I have lived in an interchange of kind offices which has been rarely interrupted; while from those with whom circumstances have particularly connected me, I have derived much aid and support in the discharge of my ministerial functions.

. . . "Let me only add a few closing words to the members of those two beloved societies to which so great a portion of my ministerial life and labors has been devoted.

"And let me call you, my dear friends, to unite with me in gratefully adoring the mercy of God, that he should be pleased to intrust me with the ministry of the gospel, and permit me to execute it during the unusual period of fifty years. To preach the unsearchable riches of my Saviour, I have truly preferred to the very highest of earthly honors. To be continued in the gospel vineyard, when most of my fellow-laborers, and nearly all my contemporaries, are gone, is a great and distinguishing mercy.

"If any good has resulted from my ministry; if the cause of Christ and his truth has, in any degree, been served; if, in my unworthy hands, the gospel has instrumentally saved immortal souls from ruin, or quickened and comforted the children of God; ascribe, I entreat you, all the glory, now and forever, to the riches of sovereign and almighty grace.

"Let me entreat you, likewise, to join your prayers with mine, that the defects and sins of my life and ministry (ah, they are great and numberless!) may be

15*

graciously pardoned; and that, through the precious
blood shed for the *priesthood* as well as for the congregation, my very imperfect and stained services may
find acceptance, and myself be permitted to appear
with comfort before my final Judge. *The Lord grant
that we all may find mercy of the Lord in that day!*"

Our space admits but one of the hymns composed
for the occasion, that by the Hon. George Lunt : —

" Our fathers' God, we bless thy name,
　Whose promise stands in words of light,
That still, from age to age the same,
　Thine own are precious in thy sight.

Our days, like bubbles down the stream,
　Dissolving, float and melt away;
And life we call a fleeting dream,
　As worldly hopes and thoughts decay.

But when a servant of thy house
　The nobler work of life has done,
And round his venerated brows
　The crown appears already won;

'Tis then our souls adore the Lord
　For every bright example given,
To bind us closer to his Word,
　And fix our wandering hearts on heaven.

And thus, to-day, within thy courts,
　Thy people's grateful songs ascend,
That Israel's mighty God supports,
　Nor leaves his chosen to the end.

And spared, through long descending days,
　Be this thy ancient servant blest,
To guide our souls to seek thy grace,
　And find with him the promised rest."

The " Newburyport Watchtower" of Nov. 22, 1844,
thus notices the occasion : —

" The exercises at the First Presbyterian Church on the fiftieth anniversary of the ordination of the Rev. Dr. Dana as pastor of that church and society, held on the 19th inst., were deeply solemn and impressive. Few men are permitted to labor in the "vineyard of the Lord" through the long period of half a century; and fewer still maintain for that space of time, through "evil and good report," such steadfastness in the faith, and such an exemplary and consistent life, as this venerable divine has exhibited.

"His words of counsel and admonition come to us with the weight of authority; his voice, so full of tenderness and love, awakens the deepest emotions of the heart; and long will the solemn and affectionate warnings of that day animate us in our struggles after holiness of life.

. . . " The most devout and reverent attention was given by the large audience during all the services.

" In the evening, the friends of Dr. Dana, in testimony of their unabated affection and esteem, made him a donation visit. We had the pleasure of mingling in the happy throng that came to pay their respects to one ' so venerated and so loved;' and never have we passed an evening more agreeably."

The author of the "History of Newbury" thus chronicles the day: —

"Nov. 19. This afternoon, the Rev. Daniel Dana preached to a numerous audience, in the church in Federal Street, a sermon in commemoration of his having been ordained the pastor of that church and congregation a half century before.

" In the evening, his house was literally crowded with those of all ages, who gladly came to show their

respect for the good and eminent man, who, for a half
century, had devoted himself with untiring zeal to his
Master's great business. Drawing towards the close of
his labors, nothing could have been more gratifying to
him, than to witness the respect and good will of the
few who had listened to his earliest instructions, mingled with the many who had been favored by his later
ministrations. It was, indeed, a cheerful and happy
meeting."

Several pleasant letters were elicited by the occasion. A gentleman who had obtained distinction as a
public journalist, writes, "I have never forgotten, that,
from the age of seven to that of twelve years, when
poverty and sickness bore heavily upon me, and promised to be my only inheritance in life, I was indebted
to you for much of kindly sympathy and generous aid.
The first books which I ever read were received from
your library. . . . That I have not often acknowledged to you the kindness then shown to a child of
sorrow and pain, is not because I had forgotten or was
ungrateful for it, but because I knew that such generous devotion was but the ordinary, even tenor of your
whole life."

Col. Samuel Swett of Boston, the son of his early
friend, Dr. John Barnard Swett, writes, "The occasion
carries me back to my earliest days, and the ever-
changing scenes of a long and variable life, during
the whole of which your kindness and friendship have
fringed the darkest clouds which have hung over me
with a heavenly and benignant light, and added a
new zest to the rosy hours when they visited me again
in their turn. Two of my reminiscences recur to me
here so importunately, that they will not permit me to

proceed until they have been recorded. Your Millot's History, and Addison's Evidences of revealed religion, which you kindly bestowed on me when I entered college — and your horse which you kindly loaned me to ride to Cambridge, &c. . . .

FROM DR. ABBOT.

" EXETER, Jan. 16, 1845.

"My dear Friend, — I received with surprise and great pleasure your half-century sermon, which you had the goodness to send me; and for which, and for many other excellent discourses, I most cordially thank you, I could hardly realize that fifty-six years had passed away since we united together harmoniously, and, as I trust, affectionately, as instructors of youth; and, although since separated, and somewhat divided in our course of instruction, never, I trust, in affection. How similar the termination of our career! Nothing could have given me more sincere gratification, than the recital of the events and circumstances at the close of your half-century services. Next to the approbation of our Father in heaven, at the close of so long a period of active and public service, is the cordial approbation of numerous friends and a discerning public.

" Your labors for the public good, I trust, are not yet over; mine have already terminated, and with them the ability to perform them. How long I may be continued here, a useless life, I cheerfully submit to Him who gave it; and in grateful remembrance of his past goodness, and in humble trust and assurance of again joining my friends in the services of a better world. In the mean time, I am, most affectionately yours,

" B. Abbot."

CHAPTER XIV.

1845–1853.

PORTRAIT. — LIFE AT .HOME. — PERSONAL TRAITS. — RESIGNATION OF THE PASTORAL OFFICE. — MINISTRY AT LARGE. — ORDINATION AT BELLEVILLE. — SERMON. — DANIEL WEBSTER. — REMONSTRANCE ADDRESSED TO THE TRUSTEES AT ANDOVER.

WHEN about seventy years of age, he had been with difficulty persuaded, chiefly by the urgency of his youngest daughter, to sit for his portrait. The artist had at first an unpromising time ; but, one day, an allusion (either by a happy accident, or by design) to the British poets, kindled that pleasant light in the eye, which was, to some extent, transferred, presenting him as he was when in his lighter conversational moods. It served to remind his children of the happy times when he had read to them from his favorite authors — the more striking passages, perhaps, of "Gertrude of Wyoming" (although he mourned over Campbell as having "begun in the spirit and ended in the flesh ") or something from Cowper, or Mark Antony over the dead body of Cæsar, where, at the line —

" Through this the *well-beloved* Brutus stabbed " —

his voice inevitably faltered, so intense was his feeling of the passage.

178

His literary tastes befriended him through life, relieving often his over-wrought mind and sensibilities, and giving ever new zest to his conversation, which was affluent and sparkling, even in old age. He retained in his later years the ardor and enthusiasm, and something of the imaginative temperament, which are usually more characteristic of the earlier period of life. His sensibilities were always acute. In the public reading of the Scriptures, pathetic passages would often overpower his feelings.

A single reading by him of any thing that particularly pleased him, would often leave a lasting impression. The tones still linger in the ear with which he once repeated —

> " Give me again my hollow tree,
> A crust of bread, and — *liberty!* "

"O, world! thy slippery turns," and many other favorite quotations of his from Shakspeare, vividly recall his manner of uttering them.

His earnestness in the pulpit was too real to be boisterous. So, too, were his sympathies intensely real. It was this which made his visits to the afflicted so highly prized. In the sick-chamber, at the communion service, in public and family devotion, the depth and tenderness of his sensibilities, and the fervor of his religious emotions, were specially manifest. He performed none of the offices of religion in a perfunctory way. At the same time, his sermons were not so much above the tone of his ordinary conversation as is often the case. They were none of them oratorical efforts, in distinction from the clear and forcible expression of sentiments and convictions deeply felt.

What made his conversation so interesting was, that whilst he took no interest in common gossip, he was animated and enthusiastic on every topic of a more elevated character. Classical allusions, fine sentiments, pleasant anecdotes, humorous sayings, all had place in the ample storehouse of a retentive memory. He could, too, without abruptness or formality, give a religious turn to conversation.

His study was always a delightful place. It would be difficult to describe the associations which his children had with it from their earliest years. It was to them a hallowed spot, not wholly of this world. A sacred serenity seemed to dwell there. It was pleasant to see him there in his old age, surrounded by his books. Long, long will it be, before that venerable form can fade from memory.

It is remarkable how Providence cared for him, where he had not much cared for himself. He had always been singularly indifferent to pecuniary interests. They were crowded out of his thoughts by higher and more congenial themes. His tastes were simple : the only luxury that he could not deny himself, was books. On these he expended, from first to last, an amount, which, judiciously invested, would have been almost a competence for old age. He was sensitive to the moral relations of money : he could not live in debt, and he must have something to give to every worthy object ; but, beyond this, he seemed to be, in his freedom from worldly anxieties, like the bird that Luther describes, as " tucking his head under his wing, and going to sleep, leaving God to think for him."

But this exemption from worldly care could not last always. To one of his sons, who had, years before, ineffectually endeavored to direct his attention to worldly interests, he at length acknowledged that his mind was oppressed with the thought of a dependent family, and no provision made for the future. The reply given was, " Well, father, as you have all your life gone on the principle of *trusting Providence in these matters, without much use of means,* I think Providence will make a special effort in your behalf." The words, uttered at random, as far as any definite foresight was concerned, nevertheless proved true prophecy.

For a year or two previous to his resignation of the pastoral office, his mind was evidently oppressed with many anxieties. The wounding thought had doubtless occurred, that, however attached to him his church at large might be, some few, at least, were perhaps saying in their hearts,

" Superfluous lags the veteran on the stage."

But one day he came down from his study with a light in his eye, and a chastened sensibility in his whole countenance, which at once attracted his daughter's attention. He had just received a most affectionate letter from a widowed sister, telling him that he must not be anxious about himself or his family; that she had made some provision, in case of her death, which she now determined should be for his immediate benefit, &c. Such an expression of human and divine kindness affected him deeply.

The amount ultimately secured to his daughters from this source, exceeded what, by a pinching frugality, he might have laid up in the course of his life, had his principles and feelings as to this world's interests been precisely the reverse of what they were.

16

By a sort of miracle, moreover, the only investment
he ever made proved, after thirty years' interval, to be
not thrown away. To a brother, of kindred elevation
of character, and equally *unworldly* with himself, he
had transmitted a sum of money (received by inheritance) to be invested in Ohio lands. At the time,
land on the present site of Cincinnati was in the mar-
ket; but the professor of languages, more skilled in
Homer and Horace than in the chances of land speculation, preferred a beautiful valley on the Hocking River,
— a "Rasselas" Valley, as he himself named it. The
investment was a most eligible one — with the single
drawback, that the whole world beside was likely to be
colonized before settlers would find their way over the
heights that enclosed the Rasselas Valley. Nevertheless, the era dawned when "every valley should be exalted, and every mountain and hill be made low;" and,
as railways advanced, something, at last, came from the
Ohio lands.

In the later years of his life, as munificently as if he
had a fortune to leave his family, he gave away to
individuals and to public libraries the books which had
so drained his purse. Beyond the more simple needs of
life, he seemed to attach no value to money except as
a means of doing good. At the last meeting which he
ever attended of the American Board of Foreign Mis-
sions, he subscribed an amount which was nearly
half his year's income at the time. When, upon this,
a gentle remonstrance came to him from the house-
keeping department, he turned it off very lightly, saying that he wished to give a last testimony to the
greatness of the cause.

He was singularly remote from some traits popularly

ascribed to New England. The reverse of shrewd in money matters, he was, moreover, so inexpert with the penknife, that (unlike his usual conservatism) he hailed as a welcome relief the radical innovation of metallic pens; which he used exclusively in his later years.

Whether these facts bear any testimony to his *ancestry*, need not be discussed, especially as in relation to that subject he himself never evinced much interest. Perhaps his very firm faith in the descent of all from Adam, and in the consequences to all of that descent, had something to do with his indifference as to questions of ancestry.

In the warmth of his patriotism, he was often in advance of the sympathies of those around him. When he came from the post-office with the announcement, "Good news!" his daughters were sometimes disappointed to find that it only related to the prospects of his favorite candidate for the presidency, or some similar matter of public concern.

It was his constant habit to rise very early, resort to his wood-shed for exercise, and then return to his study in time, when the days were shortest, to improve the first sufficient daylight for reading. When some new work that interested him was in hand, — such, for instance, as Good's "Book of Nature," — he would be in fine spirits at the breakfast-table; where, however, the morning-paper must still be glanced over before any thing else could be attended to. The lengthening of the days was always pleasant to him, his hours for reading and writing being limited to daylight.

Very pleasant recollections have his family of his great enjoyment of sacred music. The hymns, "There is a fountain;" "Oh! could I speak the matchless worth;" "Jesus, lover of my soul;" "Guide me, O thou great Jehovah;" and others that might be named, — are delightfully associated in their memories with the tones of his voice.

In the autumn of 1845, he came to the determination to resign his pastoral charge. This conclusion was reached only after long-continued mental conflict. To preach the gospel of Christ was still his delight, nor was he weary of pastoral cares and labors; but other burdens had been, of late, superadded to these legitimate ones. There had existed for a long time some dissen-. sion among his church-members, in respect to one of their number, whose business relations had attracted severe remark. This, by the agency of a few individuals, had been made the occasion of much worrying annoyance to himself. He was now in his seventy-fifth year. Maturely weighing all the considerations in the case, he became satisfied that Divine Providence had at length affixed the term to his pastoral office. His decision, once taken, was understood to be unalterable. The action in the case, of the church and of the presbytery, was honorable to him and to themselves.

His brother at Marblehead writes him at this time (Nov. 10, 1845), —

"Most heartily can I sympathize with you, my dear brother, in the trial which such an event, under almost any circumstances, must necessarily from the nature of the case occasion, especially to a mind so sensitive as your's; yet I trust that on the whole you will find (as it is with me) no cause to regret it, at your time of life; and, after having labored in the vineyard for such an unusual length of years, it must be a great relief to you to be released from the weight of care and responsibility belonging to the pastoral office, which is always sufficiently exhausting, and particularly in our day. The retrospect of your ministerial life and services must be attended with much consolation, and furnish abundant cause for thankfulness and rejoicing; and, now, what should prevent your passing the remainder of your life — which I pray may still be greatly prolonged — in peace and comfort. I am persuaded that in some way or other it will be made useful, and productive of much good, to the church and world. Providence has most kindly made some provision for your support; for this I cannot feel sufficiently grateful: and you have not only good children to cheer and bless you, but also troops of other friends who will not fail to be steadfast and faithful to the end. Above all, He whom you have served so long and with so much success, will assuredly never leave nor forsake you."

These kind wishes and predictions met a signal and speedy fulfilment. Just two days after they were penned — one week after the dissolution of his pastoral connection — the following paper was circulated: —

"We, the subscribers, entertaining the sincerest respect for the Rev. Dr. Dana, who for more than fifty years has labored with fidelity and success in the Christian ministry, chiefly in this town, and desirous of retaining his influence and services for the community of which we form a part, agree to pay the sums annexed to our names towards his support for the year to come in the capacity of a *minister at large;* expecting him to perform such labors, not otherwise provided for, as in his judgment shall be deemed useful, and consistent with his health and strength.

"NEWBURYPORT, Nov. 12, 1845."

16*

To this paper were appended the names, with liberal subscriptions, of a large number of the most respectable inhabitants of Newburyport.   ·

His daughter writes: "One evening, Dr. H. C. P. came in to inform him, that a large number of his friends desired him to take the office of *minister at large;* that he, Dr. P., had devoted that day to going from house to house obtaining subscriptions; and, he added, "it has been the *happiest* day of my life." Every one had entertained the proposal with such cordial pleasure, that but two or three days now were needed to complete the roll-call, that none of his warm friends should be wounded by being left out. This token of continued attachment from his fellow-citizens was very gratifying to him, and he immediately entered on the duties of the newly created office; duties which he was left to define and fulfil at his own discretion."

The following notices appeared in the Newburyport papers: —

"Through the generous liberality of a portion of our benevolent fellow-citizens, we have the pleasure to inform the members of our community, that the valuable services of the Rev. Dr. Dana, as minister at large, have been secured to them for the coming year. The spirit with which this enterprise was undertaken, and the hearty reception it met with on the part of the public, may be judged of from the fact of its accomplishment in a day." — *Watchtower.*

"MINISTRY AT LARGE. — We have been much gratified to hear that the spontaneous liberality of a portion of our citizens has engaged the services of the Rev. Dr. Dana (whose connection with the Harris-street

Society has recently, at his request, been dissolved) as a minister at large in this town. The readiness with which this proposition was adopted by our citizens speaks well for their kind and liberal feelings, as well as for the estimation in which Dr. Dana is held among them; for we learn from the gentleman who took about the paper for this purpose, that he obtained the sum of four hundred and fifty dollars in a single day, without effort (almost every one to whom he presented the subject having promptly appended their names); and that a large number of the friends of the doctor were not called upon, it not having been necessary." — *Herald.*

The following is from a letter to Dr. Abbot: —

"NEWBURYPORT, Dec. 6. 1845.

" MY DEAR FRIEND, — Nothing could be more gratifying to me than your letter, and I thank you for it from my inmost heart. For myself, I have sometimes thought that age has not materially impaired or chilled my social feelings; and your letter gives me a delightful demonstration that with you the case is the same. To have your sympathy in my trials, greatly alleviates them — not to say makes me almost willing to bear them. . . . To the last, the affection of the great body of my church and people continued unchanged; and they were deterred from opposing my dismission, chiefly by my own earnest request, and by a consciousness that my release from such a condition of turmoil had become absolutely necessary.

" I ought to add, that Providence has overruled the unkindness of a few — a very few — opposers, to elicit, from numbers of the most respectable inhabitants of the town, tokens of regard and affection, such as, otherwise, I should not have known, nor even suspected, to exist.

"My new sphere of duties is, as yet, somewhat undefined. The subscribers for my support have declared it to be their first object to detain me in the place; and, with great delicacy, they have manifested their wish that I should choose my own mode of employment. This imposes on me a task of some difficulty. To divest myself of the habit of preaching on the Sabbath will be neither easy nor pleasant: but, doubtless, I shall be called to much visiting among the sick, the ignorant, &c.; and this is a task to which, so far as health and strength shall permit, I shall most willingly give myself.

. . . "Believe me, with every sentiment of friendship and affection,

"Most truly yours,

"DANIEL DANA."

He speaks, in one part of the above letter, of the great "relief" which the dissolution of his pastoral relation had given him; but adds, "I ought to confess, with much gratitude to God, that my ministerial life has been, on the whole, a favored and happy one."

The sense of "relief" was soon very apparent. He was now again buoyant in spirit, as, with a temperament like his, was impossible amid the disquietudes of preceding years. He had always been the friend and comforter of the poor and distressed; so that the sphere of his labors, as minister at large, was a very congenial one. He would often now at night appear much fatigued (for a lax construction of duty was never possible to him); but his spirit was cheerful.

Nor was he at all left to " divest himself of the habit of preaching on the Sabbath." Constant calls were made upon him to officiate in the neighboring pulpits; and he also preached, at stated times, at the almshouse. As long as health and strength permitted, his voice was still heard in what had been the great labor and pleasure of his life, — " testifying the gospel of the grace of God."

One of the journalists of the day says, of his becoming minister at large, —

" This was a spontaneous expression of deep respect and sincere affection, and testifies equally of his eminent services, and of their appreciation by the community. It was left to his own judgment to determine upon the duties of this station, and to perform such labors, not otherwise provided for, as should be consistent with his health and strength. He is now, therefore, the minister of the whole town, and not of a particular church. Although the freshness and strength of youth and manhood have departed, and the infirmities incident to advanced life now prevent the active performance of those labors which were pleasant in earlier years, he still retains the clear judgment and lofty intellectuality which distinguished him in other days. Not yet lost is the rich and glowing eloquence which once thrilled the heart of the hearer, as it proclaimed to him the high and holy messages of heaven. May a kind Providence grant that many long years shall elapse before this community shall be deprived of the presence of its venerated counsellor and friend, and the benefits which flow from his wisdom and piety! "

This arrangement, after continuing some years, gradually declined, as his strength was less adequate to its fatigues. " Yet " (his daughter says) " he always, as his strength and engagements admitted, continued to preach at the alms-house. He sometimes selected large parcels of tracts, and, at the close of sermons, invited each one of the inmates to come forward and receive one. He used great freedom in addressing them. His warnings were solemn, his persuasions very earnest — irresistible, I sometimes thought."

Writing to one of his daughters, he says, " Though I have no *charge*, I have almost no leisure." Again, April, 1846 : " I have preached on various Sabbaths at the poor-house ; have given some aid to Mr. Stearns and Mr. Campbell, and especially to Mr. Dimmick, who has been confined for several Sabbaths. The last five Sabbaths I have devoted to the people of Mr. March, who is sick."

On the 30th of September, 1846, he was called to preach the sermon at the funeral of the Rev. John C. March, the beloved pastor of the church in Belleville. He had been much with Mr. March in his last illness, and sympathised deeply with those who mourned his early departure. Many will vividly recall that rural burial-place, and the sun sinking in full-orbed radiance beneath the horizon — emblem of the close of a good man's life. In 1847, he prefixed a brief memoir to a small volume containing four sermons by Mr. March.

To his daughter and son-in-law (Rev. E. R. Tucker), then in Ohio, he writes, July, 1847, " You will naturally conceive that Elizabeth and myself are somewhat solitary ; but we live in great peace. I have no parish, but have thence no want of employment. My Sabbaths are, almost without exception, occupied in preaching for ministerial brethren who are absent or indisposed. In this way, I come into contact with a much greater variety of character than most ministers do. And I sometimes indulge the hope, that, through the divine blessing, I may be accomplishing more good than if my connection with my people had not been dissolved."

An incident illustrating his principles occurred in 1847. A candidate for the ministry, just from the Andover Seminary, was called to the church at Belleville. The Ordaining Council were generally satisfied with the theological views elicited at the examination. He was not so. The Rev. Mr. Eells (his successor in the Second Presbyterian Church) withdrew from the council. A newspaper discussion of the matter occurring soon after between Mr. Eells and Mr. Stearns, in which his position was referred to, he thus stated it himself: —

"The case was to me difficult and perplexing in no common degree. The Society in which I had cherished a deep and affectionate interest, were well united in favor of the candidate, and confidently expected his ordination. Its failure might have been fatal to their peace. The young gentleman himself appeared intelligent, amiable, and hopefully pious. He brought with him, probably, the instructions he had received; and he could not reasonably be expected to *have more understanding than all his teachers.*

"In these peculiar circumstances, I adopted what may be thought a peculiar expedient. I proposed to the council, that, before ordination, the candidate should pledge himself to a *serious and prayerful reexamination* of the questionable points; and I engaged in this case to withdraw my objection. This course appeared to me to be kind and faithful to the candidate, and not unfaithful to the cause of truth. It might accomplish the very end in view. It would certainly have involved a testimony of the council against the errors which were disclosed by the examination."

The "Christian Register" (Unitarian) made some comments on this, which are, perhaps, admissible here : —

"Towards Dr. Dana personally, we feel no other sentiments than those of sincere esteem and respect. We look upon him as one of the best representatives of piety formed under the old regimen, and wish there were many more like him. The goodness of his heart appears above the dogmas of his understanding, in expressing his belief that the young candidate, whom he regarded as unsound in the faith, was, nevertheless, in his estimation, "intelligent, amiable, and hopefully pious." With Dr. Dana's uncompromising hostility to the new school theology, and to whatsoever in his opinion is contrary to the form of sound words, he unites great tenderness of spirit. Undoubtedly there is no one of the numerous individuals concerned who has felt sincerer or deeper grief than himself for the step he felt obliged to take ; and for our own part, though we do not actually know that Dr. Dana would be ready to concede piety to those who, like ourelves, have gone. so far beyond his standard of orthodoxy, we should, nevertheless, feel surer of his charity than that of not a few New School men whom we could name.

"There is, in the letter, one sentence in which the doctor's uncompromising hostility to error is very apparent : we mean no disrespect if we should call it a manifestation of a little "original sin," or, more familiarly, of the old Adam. It is in his allusion to Andover, in which he says, " the young gentleman brought with him the instructions he received, and he could not reasonably be expected *to have more understanding than all his teachers.*" Those who know, that, since Dr. Woods has ceased to be an active professor, the old school theology has all died out of Andover, will appreciate the keenness of Dr. Dana's sarcasm. And yet if Professor Stuart or Professor Park, or any others of the present Faculty, were to die, we believe that no man in or out of New England, would be more ready to acknowledge their piety, or more sincerely hope he should meet them in heaven."

The unknown writer of the above was not wrong in his judgment of Dr. Dana's character, and of the motives and spirit of his course in defence of the old divinity. Those who knew him intimately, knew that his zeal was not that of the polemic or of the partisan. When his position in the New England of late times became, necessarily, one of antagonism to new theories which he considered as infringing upon divine truth, he accepted the position, with all its disquietudes, as a simple matter of duty. One proof of the purity and elevation of his principles was, that the question of *numbers* never weighed with him in the least. It made no difference as to his course (whatever it might as to his feelings), whether he had a majority with him, or was left to stand alone.

The extract above given, from "The Register" of Feb. 5, 1848, bears a singular relation, in point of time, as well as in other respects, to the following memorandum : —

17

"March 1, 1848. — Yesterday, father returned from Andover, where he had had two interviews with Professor Stuart, who was ill and in low spirits. The Professor received him very affectionately, and, in the course of the interview, said to him, that, if he had ever wounded his feelings in any way, he regretted it sincerely. Father assured him that his feelings of kindness toward him had never been interrupted in the least. At the second interview, after praying with him, my father, saying that he, too, was drawing near the grave, asked for himself a remembrance in Professor Stuart's prayers; to which he replied, 'I should be very ungrateful if I did not pray for you.' My father was much affected by this interview."

On the proposed list of lecturers before the Newburyport Lyceum, in 1848, was the name of one of distinguished ability; but whose teachings were unsound in the extreme. Doubtless, regarding this as one of the prevalent and most fatal methods of undermining religious faith, Dr. Dana publicly took ground against it. After referring to the lecturer's *pantheistic* doctrines, and quoting his exceedingly irreverent language as to our Saviour, he says, —

"Judge, now, my friends, whether, with these facts full before me, I had sufficient reason to enter a *caveat* against a lecturer of this description. Was it bigotry or fanaticism? or was it such a regard for the cause of truth, and for your best interests, as a minister not recreant to the claims of his office, might naturally be expected to feel?

"It has given me, I repeat it, inexpressible pain to speak reproachfully of an individual who has once sustained the character of a Christian minister, and who is now regarded by numbers as a sprightly and attractive writer; but the demands of truth, of piety, and of real benevolence, seemed imperious and decisive. I have likewise the melancholy satisfaction of not having treated him so disrespectfully as he has treated the Saviour. Nor would I overlook the wonderful and instructive example of that Saviour, who spent his dying breath in supplicating for his enemies, 'Father, forgive them; for they know not what they do.'"

In 1849, he acceded to the wish of several friends, in the publication of a sermon, prepared some years before. We give an extended extract from this, as better representing the *general spirit* of his preaching. than many of those printed discourses, the subject of which was dictated by the occasion.

From the text, Rev. v. 9, "*And they sung a new song,*" after presenting the song itself as "a hymn of praise to the divine Redeemer," he thus discourses:—

"Further: the redeemed, while celebrating the glories of their Saviour, celebrate with peculiar emphasis his *sufferings and death.* These constitute the *burden* of their everlasting song. 'Thou art worthy,' say they, 'to take the book, and to open the seals thereof; for thou wast slain, and hast *redeemed* us to God, by thy *blood,* out of every kindred and tongue and people and nation; and hast made us unto our God kings and priests: and we shall reign on the earth. Here the sufferings and death of Christ have a *prominence* which strikingly illustrates their infinite moment and worth. They are acknowledged by the redeemed as the grand procuring cause of their salvation, as the source of all their blessings, and joys, and honors, in time and eternity. In their Saviour's blood, they have a real *redemption ;* redemption from sin, and all its dreadful consequences; redemption to God, and to immortal glory. They do not regard the death of Christ, as it has been too often regarded, merely as an example of submission, or as a seal of the truth of his doctrines, or as a mere exhibition of God's regard for his law, or as placing sinners within the reach of pardon.

"But they regard it as a proper atonement for sin, and the meritorious price of all spiritual and eternal blessings for his people. Such is the doctrine uniformly and most explicitly taught throughout the Sacred Scriptures. Such is the foundation on which the pious of every age have reposed with confidence for time and for eternity. Deny the atonement, and you blot out the grand peculiarity of the gospel, you blot out the sun from the spiritual heavens, and you tear from the bosom of the Christian his dearest hope. Deny the atonement, and you restore to death its sting, and to the grave its baleful victory. Deny the atonement, and you rob the Saviour of his highest glory; while you strike a note of harshest discord with the eternal song of the redeemed.

"But why is this song styled in the text a *new* song?

"We reply, first, Because there was a period when it was literally new to heaven itself. The Church, under the ancient dispensation, celebrated the glories of God the Creator. They gave him honor for all his wonders of power and mercy wrought in their behalf. Especially did they celebrate in strains of rapture the deliverance of his church from Egypt,—the type of a more glorious redemption from the bondage of sin and Satan. And all the pious of ancient time looked forward to the day of the Messiah with humble faith and joyful anticipation. From the redemption he was to accomplish, they derived all their comfort in life, their support in death, and their hope of immortal glory. But they could not celebrate this great work as actually finished ; nor, before the advent of Christ, could even the Church triumphant celebrate the price of its ransom and its glory as actually paid. But when the Son of God appeared in flesh ; and when, having expired on the cross as a sacrifice, he re-ascended to heaven, clothed with all his mediatorial offices and glories, — then a new scene commenced ; a new lustre gladdened the regions of immortal light; new raptures of joy were poured into the hearts of its blest inhabitants. They beheld in the midst of them the Friend, the Saviour, who had recently died, in unutterable agony, for their redemption. They beheld, even in his glorified body, the signatures of those sufferings, perhaps the scars of those wounds, to which they traced their immortal salvation. Hence their new anthems of praise. Hence their *new song*, — a song unheard, even in heaven before : " Worthy is the Lamb that was slain. " " Thou hast redeemed us to God by thy blood."

" Again : it is called a *new* song, on account of its *transcendent excellence.* Such, sometimes, is the import and force of the term employed. When the Psalmist exclaims, in a rapture of devotion, " Oh, sing unto the Lord a new song," he calls for a strain of praise more grand and sublime than any which had been known before, — praise which might correspond with the new and transcendent display of divine glory and goodness. The song of the redeemed far tran-

17*

scends in excellence all other songs. It converses with the brightest glories of the Deity. It celebrates the most sublime and stupendous of all his works, mysteries into which angels desire to look, a scheme of redemption which employed the counsels of Heaven from eternity; and which, in its gradual development, displays such unsearchable riches of wisdom and power, such matchless combinations of majesty and condescension, truth and mercy, purity and love, as are calculated to pour a flood of rapture into the astonished mind, and to call forth all its faculties, and all its affections, to their highest possible exercise.

"In a word, it may well be called a *new* song, as it will never become *old;* never lose its attractions; never cease to supply, to the most enlarged and exalted minds, materials for delightful contemplation. There are few themes, my hearers, which are absolutely inexhaustible. Most of the subjects of our contemplation, as they lose their novelty, lose, likewise, their attractions. Some subjects which have attracted, and even surprised us for a while, have, on a more familiar acquaintance, left us no ground of wonder, excepting our former admiration. Far different in all these respects is the subject of redemption. To the transient and superficial observer, it exhibits little to surprise, or to interest; but to the careful, devoted student, it discloses unsuspected beauties and unknown wonders. Every accession of knowledge imparts new delight, and excites new astonishment; and he who has penetrated farthest into the mysteries of this divine theme is most convinced that it is absolutely exhaustless; that it contains new mysteries, not only undiscovered, but, by finite minds, absolutely undiscoverable. Yes:

in the love of Jesus, there is a height and a depth, a length and a breadth, calculated to afford everlasting employment to the ever expanding, ever active mind of man; calculated to call forth an admiration forever fresh, and a song forever new. . . .

"And with what *emotions* do they sing this new song?

"Doubtless the language of mortals is very inadequate to express them. Nor can we even form a *conception* on the subject, which will not fall far short of the reality. Still we may be assured that the spirit which animates the new song is a spirit of the profoundest *humility* and *self-abasement.* For what were those who chant it, once, but rebels against their God, and ingrates to their Saviour? And rebels and ingrates they would have continued forever, — wretched by their own depravity, doubly wretched by their Maker's frown, — but for his own sovereign and astonishing mercy. This they feel; and this they can never forget. They felt and confessed it while on earth; but, ·in heaven, their views of their unworthiness are vastly strengthened and enlarged. The glories of a present Deity dart on their minds new convictions of the malignity and odiousness of sin. And when they recollect how low they were originally sunk in guilt; how long they resisted the call of heavenly mercy; and what poor returns they rendered, even after their conversion, to the Saviour who redeemed them by his blood, and conquered their hearts by his power, — how deep, how overwhelming, must be their abasement! With what ardor must they breathe out the confession, that, *not by works of righteousness which they have done,* but according to the riches of heavenly mercy, they are saved! With what overwhelming sensibility must they exclaim, '*Not unto us, not unto us, but to thy name, be glory!*'

"Hence we remark, that in proportion to their self-abasement, will be their *love and gratitude to their Saviour.* All their views of the guilt in which they were originally involved, of the depravity by which they were enchained, of the wrath to which they stood exposed, of the awful, endless ruin which they deserved, and of the astonishing deliverance which they have experienced, will but enhance their sense of their Saviour's love. And when they contemplate the astonishing forms in which that love has been expressed; when they behold in his sacred body, now glorified, the memorials of the sufferings which he endured for them, —the prints of the nails, and the spear,—with what a tide of grateful emotions must they be overwelmed! How must they pour out their very hearts in the song, *Worthy is the Lamb that was slain! Thou hast redeemed us to God by thy blood!* To thee, bleeding Saviour, we owe all our salvation and all our bliss. Thy dying agonies have redeemed us from eternal death. To thy cross are we indebted for these spotless robes of righteousness, these palms of victory, these crowns of unfading glory, these rivers of immortal delight.

"In fine, the redeemed sing the new song with unutterable emotions of exulting *joy.* If, while on earth, it was delightful to celebrate their Redeemer's praise; if they esteemed those the brightest and most privileged moments of life, in which they could pour their hearts in gratitude to an unseen and distant Saviour, —what must it be to find themselves in his immediate presence; to behold him *face to face;* to perceive, yes, to *see* him, listening with infinite condescension and complacency to their songs of praise? If the distant and trembling hope of heavenly blessedness was once so transporting, what must its actual and full possession be? To look back on unutterable woes escaped; to experience an overflowing fulness of present delight; and to know, with undoubting certainty, that this delight will experience neither interruption nor end, — what varied sources of happiness are here! But these are not the only sources of happiness to the glorified saint. He enters, with a sacred and generous sympathy, into the joys and felicities of his fellow-heirs of salvation. He is transported to find himself in the midst of an immense assembly in which every heart glows with exalted affection to his Redeemer, and every tongue is employed in celebrating his glory. Above all is he transported to see that once humbled and suffering Redeemer re-invested with his heavenly felicities; wearing those peculiar and immortal honors which his death has purchased; receiving the humblest, loftiest ascriptions of praise, not only from his ransomed people, but from angels and archangels, and from the whole creation of God.

. . . "The subject reminds us of the transcendent excellence of the religion of the gospel, and its perfect adaptation to our race. Surely the spirit which animates the songs and felicities of the blest above, must constitute the essential, the vital spirit of religion. And what is this but genuine *humility?* Those beatified souls that behold and enjoy the unveiled glories of the Deity, sink proportionably low in self-abasement. This is their happiness. This is their heaven. Take

from them their overwhelming sense of obligation for
redeeming mercy, and the happiness of glorified saints
would be far inferior to that of angels. But we know
from the infallible Word that it will be far superior.
The remembrance of their original guilt and ruin, and
of that unutterable love by which they have been redeemed, is ever fresh in their bosoms. It gives a
sweetness to their songs, an elevation to their joys,
which angels cannot reach; and, while it exalts them
in bliss, it sinks them low in humility. This is the
spirit of heaven; and this, be it remembered, is the
grand essential *preparation* for heaven. None who
are destitute of a tender, grateful, abasing sense of the
Saviour's condescending, dying love, can join in the
everlasting song of the redeemed. None who possess
it can possibly fail of attaining this sublime felicity.

"The same humility which prepares for heaven, and
which characterizes the felicity of heaven, is the source
of the best enjoyment on earth. It is this which gives
a zest to every present comfort, while it gently extracts
the sting from every affliction. Feeling that, as sinners, we have forfeited the mercy of Heaven, we receive the bounties of Providence with tender and delightful gratitude. Conscious that, as sinners, we merit
only frowns and wrath, we bear the common trials of
life, and even its severest calamities, with uncomplain-
ing submission.

"Who does not know that the neglect and reproach
which we often receive from fellow-creatures are acu-
minated chiefly by our own unsubdued pride? The
proud man is a kind of *sensitive-plant*, shrinking from
every touch, chilled and shrivelled by every wind that
blows; while the humble man finds shelter and com-

fort in his own calm and undisturbed spirit. While the one, too, groans under the self-imposed burden of resentment for every real or fancied injury, the other effectually eludes the trouble by cherishing a meek and forgiving spirit.

"So true is it, that that religion which trains us for heaven is our best friend while we remain below. It puts a crown on all our comforts. It facilitates the exercise of our best and most difficult virtues. It removes, or it greatly mitigates, our afflictions. The man who lives daily on the promises, feasts daily on the bread of heaven. The man who, with his Saviour, can pray for his enemies, '*Father, forgive them; for they know not what they do*,' — this man is but a single remove from his Saviour's presence in glory."

In another part of this discourse, he says, —

"I cannot persuade myself to leave this delightful subject, without offering a word on the dignity and importance of *sacred music*, considered as a part of the worship of God in the earthly sanctuary. We have seen that glorified saints above celebrate the praises of their God and Redeemer in a song. Thus they express their emotions of impassioned gratitude and holy love. This is their unceasing employment, their sublime felicity. Nor is there any employment on earth in which we make so near an approach to the work and bliss of heaven, as that in which we sing, with pious fervor and delight, the praises of God; for here we concentrate all the powers of our nature, our spiritual faculties and our bodily organs, in the same service, and that of the noblest kind. The excellent President Edwards informs us, that, in a great revival of religion in Northampton, the pious people spent much time in *singing ;* and that they found the employment remarkably efficacious to excite their religious affections, and to bring down something of heaven to earth. Nor can it be denied, that there is that in sacred music which is peculiarly fitted to solemnize and elevate the mind, to disenchain it from earthly objects, and to rouse all its best and holiest affections into vigorous exercise. If such is the high office of sacred music, it ought surely to be considered as something very different from a mere gratification of sense, or a mere amusement of the fancy. To regard it in this light, is to degrade it. It is irreverent, not to say profane ; for it is to pervert a divine ordinance to the purpose of mere unhallowed gratification. Never let it be forgotten, that, when we engage in sacred music, we professedly place ourselves in the immediate presence of the Deity. We make a particular and solemn address to that awful Being with whom is the breath of our life, and the destiny of our immortal souls. Nothing can be more evident than that, in such circumstances, the utmost reverence is indispensably incumbent. If, as all must acknowledge, an air of thoughtlessness and levity, while we are engaged in *prayer*, is a species of impiety, why should it be thought less so when we are engaged in praise ? Who that contemplates the profound solemnity and awe which pervades the worship of glorified saints and angels in heaven, can avoid being pained at the irreverence manifested in some private circles, and even in some Christian assemblies, while praise is sung to the eternal and omnipresent Jehovah ? Is it not likewise to be regretted, that the performance of this interesting part of divine worship should be confined, as it too generally is, to a very small portion of the assembly? Why should it be so? Is not singing the praises of God a divine ordinance? Has the Christian Church fewer materials and incentives for praise than were possessed by the Jewish Church? If a very small portion in our assemblies are *constitutionally* debarred from an active part in this work, shall the great majority, who have no such disqualification, remain silent? Grant that accuracy and grace of performance are desirable, shall all be excluded who do not completely rise to this standard? Or shall a change in the tunes employed be so exceedingly frequent as to constrain nearly the whole congregation to be mere silent hearers?

" It is likewise important that the music employed in the worship of God, should possess a character and style adapted to this high and sacred purpose. It is needless to say that such is not the description of all music. Nor can it be denied that a considerable portion of the tunes, which, for many years, have been employed in our congregations, are destitute of most of the attributes which should recommend them to the service of the sanctuary. Far from being fraught with that dignity, simplicity, and tenderness which are fitted to excite and to express the best emotions of the soul, they have tended rather to dissipate serious thought, to chill the ardor of devotion, to disgust cultivated minds, and to gratify only the frivolous and the gay. They may fill the ear, and they may gratify a vagrant fancy; but they starve the mind. It is, however, consoling to reflect that tunes of this description are, in many instances, sinking into merited disregard; and that a taste — perhaps I may say a *demand* — for

18

music of a dignified and impressive character is diffusing itself in various regions of our country.

"Is it not desirable, too, that, with a change so auspicious in the *matter* of our psalmody, there should be a correspondent improvement in the style of execution? — an improvement which shall render the music of our public assemblies what it ought to be, — one of the most solemn, impressive, delightful, and edifying parts of the whole service. It is a sad and humbling evidence of the earthliness of our minds, that we are so capable of celebrating, with little emotion, the glories of the Deity, and the wonders of his creating power and providential goodness. Still more humbling is it to reflect, that those mysteries of redeeming love which fill angelic minds with admiration, and glorified saints with rapture, should so often leave our hearts insensible and cold. Oh! when shall it be otherwise? When shall we see a whole assembly animated with the spirit of pure devotion, and pouring the fervor of their inmost hearts into the songs of Zion? When shall the praises of the earthly sanctuary afford an emblem and anticipation of the songs and felicities of heaven?"

When the speech of the Hon. Daniel Webster, in the United States Senate, March 7, 1850, had alienated from him the popular majority in New England, Dr. Dana joined with a large number of the most respectable citizens of Newburyport in addressing a letter to Mr. Webster, warmly approving his course. "We honor especially" (say they) "the courageous patriotism which pervades it; recalling to a due sense of their constitutional obligations the North as well as the South." To this letter, Mr. Webster gave a printed reply. His high regard for Dr. Dana had been often expressed. The last indication of it, probably, was the address on the cover of the speech of March 7: "My dear Dr. Dana, will you accept this as a testimonial of my great respect and my most affectionate regard." The handwriting of the great statesman appears in a similar but more extended note, accompanying a copy of his speech at Philadelphia, in 1846.

After Mr. Webster's death, Dr. Dana, writing to Mr. J. H. Williams (son of his first successor at Newburyport), who had favored him with an account of the celebration at New York, in 1855, of Mr. Webster's birthday, says —

"As to the reproach poured on Mr. Webster in the closing part of his life, I have ever thought it most grossly unmerited. I never could perceive that it was occasioned by any thing else than his inalienable attachment to the Constitution, and his conscientious, invincible determination to do his duty."

In April, 1851, he delivered at Bedford, N.H., a sermon before the Londonderry Presbytery, from Matt. ix. 15, which was published at their request. In it he says, —

"I advert, with inexpressible reluctance, to a practice which increasingly prevails in our cities, and from which I pray God that our country congregations may keep themselves pure. I refer to the custom of *sitting in prayer ;* a custom sanctioned neither by piety nor decorum; a custom which would almost seem to say that we have worshipped our Maker with too much reverence in former time, and may now approach, on terms of greater familiarity, the High and Holy One whom prostrate angels adore. Many pious persons have, doubtless, been insensibly betrayed into the habit. But it must be hoped, that, on consideration, they will abandon it; or, at least, that their example will prove as little contagious as possible."

To his daughter in Ohio, he writes : —

"NEWBURYPORT, Aug. 26, 1852.

"MY DEAR DAUGHTER, . . . While I feel it to be no small self-denial, that we can enjoy your company so little, I am afflicted, too, on *your* account, that you are so far removed from the friends you most love; but I have observed with much satisfaction, that you seem, in a good measure, reconciled to the disposing will of God in the case. Indeed, my dear child, you are doubtless convinced, that, without an absolute submission to the will of Heaven, we have no adequate source of real enjoyment. And you have found, too, I trust, that this spirit of resignation can reconcile us to many things which would otherwise be scarcely tolerable, and can furnish, by *itself*, an unfailing source of satisfaction.

. . . "I go to Andover next week; but almost with the feeblest possible hope of accomplishing any thing which I wish.

"Your very affectionate father,

"D. DANA.

"Mrs. LYDIA C. TUCKER."

In 1853, he published his "Remonstrance, addressed to the Trustees of Phillips Academy, on the state of the Theological Seminary under their care." It had been presented to the Board of Trustees in September, 1849. Its publication is prefaced with the following observations : —

"It is with a reluctance not to be expressed, that the writer gives publicity to the following Remonstrance. Nothing, probably, would have reconciled him to the measure, but the decided opinion and advice of ministerial brethren of the highest respectability, who have thought that he owed it to himself, to the religious public, and to the cause of God, and his truth.

"In the sacred Seminary brought to view, he has ever felt the profoundest interest. To witness its best prosperity, and, in his humble way, to promote it, has been his delight. These objects have been, and are still, very near his heart. Should any suggest an *inconsistency* between these avowals of feeling, and the present publication, he has a brief and simple reply. He has been able to discover no more natural and efficacious method of promoting the prosperity of the Seminary, than steadily and vigorously to befriend the great *principles* on which it was established, the known *designs* of its noble founders, and the *sublime objects* to which they devoted their aims. If there is a mode of accomplishing the object more direct and unequivocal than this, let it be pointed out.

"To his brethren of the Board of Trustees, he has aimed to manifest all due respect; and this is still his aim. He hopes he has never departed from this line. While painfully constrained to say that their course, for some years, has been to him mysterious and inexplicable, he has never denied that they have been governed by their own convictions of duty. While freely remarking on the tendency of their measures, he has never impeached, nor has he wished to impeach, the purity of their motives.

"Nor does he intimate that his Remonstrance has

18*

been treated by them with entire neglect. But since the report upon it, made and accepted after a period of two years from the time of its presentation, was, in his view, entirely unsatisfactory, and since his suggestions have been followed by no correspondent action on their part, he has felt himself justified in this form of appeal to the Christian community."

The following passages exhibit the scope of the Remonstrance : —

" To the Board of Trustees of Phillips Academy:

"My respected Brethren, — Having been honored for forty-five years with a seat in your Board, I have ever appreciated highly the importance of the place. Since the annexation of the Theological Seminary to the academic establishment, my responsibilities as a trustee have appeared to me as greatly enhanced. With the venerable founders of the Seminary I was intimately acquainted ; I knew their favorite objects and designs ; I have carefully pondered their constitution and statutes ; and I have watched, with deep solicitude, the course of things in the institution from its first inception to the present time. These circumstances, it will perhaps be conceded, authorize me to address you on the subject at large, with a degree of plainness and freedom ; and this I shall now attempt.

" The questions which for years have pressed with inexpressible weight on my mind are such as these : Has the Seminary answered the just expectations of the public and the churches ? Has it fairly carried out its own distinctive and avowed principles ? Does it bear the very stamp which its founders designed to fix upon it ? Does it exercise the precise influence which they intended it should exercise ?

"These are questions, my brethren, of vital importance, and of profound interest. They merit, as you
will readily admit, the most solicitous attention from
us all. To assist your minds, as far as in my power,
in forming a just judgment in the case, I will simply
remind you, in the first place, of some leading provisions of the constitution and statutes.

"The constitution provides that every professor in
the Seminary shall be a man of sound and orthodox
principles, according to the system of doctrines de-
nominated the Westminster Assembly's Shorter Catechism. Every professor must, on the day of his inaugu-
ration, publicly make and subscribe a solemn declaration of his faith in divine revelation, and in the
doctrines of the Assembly's Catechism. He must solemnly promise to defend and inculcate the Christian
faith, as thus expressed, in opposition to all contrary
doctrines and heresies. He must repeat the declaration and promise at the close of every five years; and
should he refuse this, or should he teach or embrace any
of the proscribed heresies or errors, he shall be forth-
with removed from office.

"Such, as you well know, are the provisions of the
constitution. The associate statutes are in perfect
accordance. They provide, indeed, an additional
creed, but a creed in entire harmony with the catechism, and no-wise designed to supersede or invalidate
it.

"Such was the design of the venerable founders of
the Seminary — a design, not only easily understood,
but impossible to be misunderstood. If there are
words in the English language which can make any
thing plain, the founders have made plain and unde-

212   REMONSTRANCE.

niable their intention, that the doctrines of the Assembly's Catechism, which they viewed as the doctrines of the Bible — that these, and no other doctrines, should be maintained, defended, and propagated through the instrumentality of their seminary.

"Our duty, then, as trustees, is made plain, as with a sunbeam; and if, through our faithful care, the doctrines stated have been uniformly maintained, and distinctly taught, in the seminary, and, through its alumni, given in their purity to the churches, then has our duty been performed. If these objects have failed of accomplishment, *we*, too, have failed, in duty, or in success; and the great object of the Seminary is lost.

"Here a wide field of inquiry is opened. This inquiry shall be limited, at present, to the latter stages of the seminary. Has the orthodox character, which, for many of its first years, it maintained, been subsequently preserved? Have the preachers whom in recent time it has sent forth, been signalized and acknowledged as champions of the doctrines of the cross? Have their sermons embraced the great principles of the creed of the seminary? Have they presented distinct and lucid exhibitions of human depravity, of regeneration, of the atonement, of justification by faith, of the nature of experimental and saving religion? That numbers have thus preached is cheerfully conceded: but they are in the minority; and this minority has been still decreasing from year to year.

. . . "And now, my brethren, are we prepared to give account to God of our stewardship? Here is a seminary committed to our hands, most richly endowed, solemnly consecrated, from the first, to the defence and the diffusion of sacred truth, of the doctrines of the gospel, of the great Reformation, of New England in its best days, of the excellent Westminster Summary. Have we been faithful, and are we now faithful, to the precious and sacred deposit? Were its founders now present, would they acknowledge our fidelity in the execution of their plans and wishes?

. . . "I have addressed you, my honored brethren, on subjects of the greatest moment, and with a freedom and explicitness which those subjects demand. If, in any act of my life, I have deeply felt my responsibility to my final Judge, and earnestly supplicated his guidance, it is in this. In one point, I am confident you will do me justice. If the convictions I have uttered are real and sincere, they could not have been warrantably suppressed. They could nót have been suppressed without a guilty treachery. However, then, they may be received, I think I can never regret to have imparted them. The act may bring down upon me reproach from professors and students; it may expose me to public odium; it may greatly imbitter the closing years, or rather days, of my life ; it may possibly lose me *your* friendship, my brethren : still, I can never regret it ; for I have carefully counted the cost. In the cause of my Saviour and his truth, I am willing to suffer, and, I humbly hope, willing to die. Compared with these objects, peace, comfort, reputation, life itself, ought to be trifles with me.

"And now, having performed what has long appeared to me a most solemn and imperious duty, I shall, from this moment, feel my heart lightened of a burden which has oppressed it for many an anxious and painful year. Should you give to my suggestions a kind and candid consideration, I shall be gratified and grateful. Should I be denied this privilege, I can only refer these momentous affairs to the period when we must stand together before the bar of God. I have honestly endeavored to view the whole scene in the light of eternity. It is my earnest prayer that you, too, my brethren, may view it in the same awful and instructive light."

The following, from a distinguished clergyman, is one of several similar letters received at this time : —

" Rev. Dr. Dana. *Dear Brother*, — I have this moment risen from the perusal of your Remonstrance addressed to the Trustees of Phillips Academy; and I cannot refrain from expressing to you my hearty thanks for your courage and fidelity in making it, as I have to God for giving you the disposition and ability to do it. You have done well, in my judgment, in consenting to its publication; and I cannot but believe that it will be of salutary tendency. Having had my theological education at Andover, I have always felt deeply interested in its character and prosperity; and I feel bound to add, that I have, for a considerable time, been constrained to believe that the Seminary has been sliding from its original foundations.

. . . "May that great Being whose truth you have vindicated add his effectual blessing, and restore the Seminary to its original soundness and usefulness! which is the sincere desire and humble prayer of, dear sir,

"Your friend and brother in the Lord."

In these later years of his life, few were left in New England who could sympathize with his sensitiveness to theological change. His solicitudes as to Andover seemed, to the multitude, exaggerated, if not morbid.

The long concentration of his mind on these topics did, indeed, give them a prominence in his thoughts and conversation, which those only could understand, who, placing spiritual above secular interests, felt, also, something of his own impassioned attachment to the older, and (as he judged) the simple scriptural forms of divine truth. There were not wanting, however, defenders, as well as assailants, of the Remonstrance.

In the circle of his most interested and congenial correspondents, in these years, were his son-in-law, Rev. J. M. C. Bartley, and Rev. J. M. Whiton, both of the Presbytery of Londonderry. An able and interesting letter, addressed to him, was published in 1852, by Rev. President Lord of Dartmouth College.

Only those can fully appreciate his relations to the Seminary at Andover, who bear in mind his early intimacy with its founders and its original professors, and the part he had himself borne in its organization. He could not but know their theological views, and his own — their expectations and his, as to the doctrinal position which the institution was designed to hold. A change had taken place in that position — a change, hailed by some as improvement, mourned over by others as defection. He who, in his youth, had stood alone in declining to act, when action seemed like countenancing the milder aberrations of Hopkinsianism — how could he fail to utter, in his old age, his "remonstrance" against what he considered plain departure from the creed which the founders had prescribed?

Those who have traced in these pages his entire course, will perhaps concur in the remark of one well qualified to judge; "He was consistent as few men are, through his whole life."

CHAPTER XV.

1854–1859.

His Last Years. — Celebration at Newburyport. — His Last Publication. — Resignation of
his Seat in the Andover Board. — Centennial
at First Presbyterian Church. — Installation at Second Presbyterian Church. — State
of Health. — Interview with the Presbytery.
— His Death.

The Fourth of July, 1854, was a great day in Newburyport. A call had previously been issued to her
sons and daughters resident abroad to join with those
at home in a grand celebration. The invitation was
largely responded to; half the States in the Union —
nearly all the principal cities — were represented in
the assemblage. The grand procession, including a
floral procession, the decorations of the streets, the
exercises at the church, the dinner (for two thousand
persons), were all an admirable success. Liberal scope
was given in the arrangements to native ingenuity and
taste, nor was there wanting to the occasion an ample
supply of native oratory and poetry. In the pamphlet
which preserves the record of that interesting day, the
reporter says, —

"But no circumstance excited more attention than
the appearance of the venerable Dr. Dana, now more
than fourscore years old, to pronounce the benediction.
216

The eyes of hundreds, who themselves had grown gray and old since last they listened to him, were fixed upon his thin form, and placid, intelligent countenance; and hundreds hung upon his words, probably to be heard no more by most of them this side the grave, who felt they were amply repaid for all the trouble and cost of their visit, in the reception of his solemn blessing."

At the dinner, he spoke at some length in response to a toast given to the "memory of Rufus King, for many years a resident of Newburyport," &c. He said, "At the distance of more than seventy years, I have as vivid an impression of his person, his air, his voice, his affluence of ideas and language, as if these were affairs of yesterday."

After sketching the political course of Mr. King, he closed by saying, "I can form, then, no kinder wish for my country, than that in each of its future Presidents it may find, not a Washington, — the wish would be extravagant — the age of miracles has ceased — but one who will follow in the same path. Let me wish, too, that every such follower of Washington may have the vigorous and efficient support of a Rufus King."

A pleasing incident occurred in the early part of the day. He was passing down Federal Street, in order to see the procession from the house of a friend, and was near the parsonage (now private property) in which he had spent his earlier years in Newburyport, when the gentleman occupying it begged him to walk in; and he was standing in the door-way when the procession passed. The effect upon many former residents, of thus seeing him where in their childhood

19

they had been accustomed to see him, was indicated by prolonged and hearty cheers.

Kind and touching allusions were also made to him by the Rev. George Wildes (the orator of the day), Hon. Caleb Cushing, and other speakers; and the private interviews sought with him by many whom he had known in their younger days, were to him exceedingly pleasant and refreshing. One toast offered (not in his presence) by a gentleman of Unitarian creed, might tempt even a Puritan to smile: "REV. DR. DANA — His actions speak louder than words; for while he attempts to convince us of original sin, he shows by his life that he is free from it."

Not long after this, an engraving from the portrait taken several years before, elicited some notices which convey a pretty correct impression of his personal appearance. The following is from the Boston "Evening Transcript":

"The expanse of forehead is very striking in this venerable face. Beneath, are those eyes of mild yet animated intelligence; those amiable but highly intellectual features; that truly spiritual expression which overspreads the whole, and betokens a life devoted to the things not seen; and the head is nobly surmounted by that "crown of glory," becoming one who, at the decline of protracted life, is found in the way of righteousness; for this venerable clergyman is now considerably advanced beyond the long period of fourscore years, but retains a degree of physical, as well as mental activity, which encourages his many friends to hope he may be long spared as a living object of their veneration and love."

A Newburyport paper contained the following: —

"None who are familiar with the features of this truly venerable 'man of God' can fail to recognize the 'speaking likeness' presented in the engraving. None, we feel assured, who have listened to his pious counsels in youth, and known of his faithful 'walk with God,' will omit the opportunity of securing a memento of one whose name and works will ever be held in grateful remembrance in the church and the world. Dr. Dana still lives, active, at an advanced age, in his Master's work, honored and revered by Christians of every name.

"He is one of the few remaining ties that connect us with the better characteristics of the past. With a mind richly stored with the treasures of the English classics, and skilled in accurate criticism, he is still one of the best and most reliable authorities in all that pertains to its nicer shades of interpretation and analysis. Profound and acute as a theological and polemical writer, his mind still lights up with 'its wonted fires,' in any insidious attacks upon the essential doctrines of his faith. Identified with the domestic joys and sorrows of nearly three generations, ripe for the Master's presence, a kind Providence still permits the blessings of his counsels and his prayers to the descendants of those who have long since preceded him in the pathway to 'glory, honor, and immortality.'"

The correspondent of a Western paper describes him as he was in 1855:

"It was my privilege to be somewhat intimate in his family during the summer of 1855. He was then in full possession of his ordinary faculties of mind. Perhaps his intellect may have lost some of its vigor for deep

and original thinking; and there probably was less vivacity of imagination and manner than he had once possessed; but I could not see that his memory or judgment were at all impaired. I heard him preach twice,
with as much method and coherency as any one. His
sight had for some time been so much injured that he
could not read; but he repeated the portion of Scripture
and the hymns that a full service required, with ease
and fluency."

The same writer speaks of "his kind and loving
spirit, his simple faith, his soul without guile."

For the last ten years of his life he was much
harassed with cough. In the autumn of 1852, he had
suffered a further privation as to the use of his eyes.
His daughter states that, "when the first snow of the
season commenced, one morning, as the large, thick
flakes came down, and he perceived that he was to
have a day uninterrupted by visitors, with his native
joyousness he exulted at the prospect. He wrote letters — he read — but the next day he found that he had
over-tasked his eyes; and from that time he was able
to use them scarcely at all. This was a sore affliction
to one of whom it had been justly said, that his native
activity was so great that he was never unhappy when
fully employed. But it was borne with the usual un-
complaining patience. He could still listen to reading,
sometimes three or four hours in the day; he dictated
letters, also articles for the 'Panoplist,' and other periodicals. As the 'Annals of the American Pulpit' came
out, he listened to them with the greatest avidity.
Though enfeebled at times by disease, he usually sat
up all day, rising early in the morning, as had been his
life-long custom."

In 1855, he contributed, at the request of the author, an Introduction to "The Theology of New England." In this he says, —

"What is the influence which German theology has exercised for years, and is now exercising, on the theology of our own country? On this subject, we need not adopt a strain of indiscriminate reproof. The history, geography, and chronology of the Scriptures, their criticism, literature, and antiquities, — all have their importance and use. In these departments, the German religionists have exhibited indefatigable activity, and amassed immense stores of knowledge. Of these accumulations, religious students may safely and wisely avail themselves. Yet if, in these pursuits, their minds should be insensibly drawn away from the great and distinguishing *doctrines* of Scripture, or should receive perverse or indistinct impressions of them, the evil would be immense. The largest acquisitions of such knowledge would but ill compensate for the want or loss of the essential and saving truths of God's word.

"The attribute of Scripture which pre-eminently stamps its value and importance is its inspiration. Here lies the basis of all the instruction, the hope and comfort which it imparts. To renounce this precious attribute is to give up ourselves to endless doubt and blank despair; while to have our faith in it shaken or impaired is to want the first and most essential qualification of Christian instructors. Surely no one will contend that our young men, destined to the ministry, and subjected to the influences we have described, are in no danger of contamination."

After specifying other divergences of the new from the old theology, he proceeds: "The subject of man's

19*

ability and *inability* has been much discussed. Questions on this subject are much less likely to be decided by philosophic reasoning, than by common sense and the Bible.

"Still there are truths in the case, the force of which most candid minds will admit. That all human beings are under immediate and everlasting obligations to repent of their sins, to obey the law, and receive the gospel; that there is no obstacle in the way, but such as arises from their own obstinacy and wickedness; and that their perdition, if they finally perish, will be of their own procuring — these are unquestionable facts.

"It is equally unquestionable that sinners lie wholly at the mercy of God; that he holds their salvation and perdition in his own sovereign hand; and that all their efforts to save themselves will be utterly abortive without divine and omnipotent aid.

"Between these two classes of propositions there may be seeming discrepancies; but they are only seeming. All truths are reconcilable with all other truths. What appears to our frail minds to be discordant may be quite otherwise in the eye of an omniscient God. And we ourselves, in a future state, may see clear and satisfying light, where now we behold only impenetrable darkness.

"The propensity of the present day seems to be to magnify human power. Thoughts are sported on this subject, obviously irreconcilable with Scripture and common sense. This is undoubtedly a serious evil; for though these views seemingly tend to excite men to action, their real tendency is to lull them into sloth and security. Let a man believe that his salvation is fully, and in every sense, in his own power, and he will delay the disagreeable task to a more convenient season. He will become proud, self-sufficient, and careless. It is worth a serious inquiry, whether that recklessness as to religion and the soul, and even that laxity in principles and morals, which so lamentably prevail in our day, are not attributable to extravagant views of human power and sufficiency.

"On the topic thus briefly discussed, there arise some reflections too important to be neglected or forgotten. The error in question respecting human ability was, in former times, inculcated by ministers of great seriousness and fidelity, — men who, in their private speculations, cherished sound and Scriptural views on many gospel subjects; and who, in their public instructions, uttered many things suited to alarm the fears, and awaken the consciences, of the impenitent. But the case is otherwise now. The modern theology is superficial and unimpressive. It contains little which tends either to awaken the consciences or alarm the fears of the irreligious. Of course, the error in question is left unqualified and unchecked, to produce its disastrous effects on the minds of men, and lead them insensibly in the path to ruin.

. . . "The writer of this Introduction is aware that, by his present and former communications to the public, he may incur the suspicion of severity towards his Christian and ministerial brethren. But he pleads innocence. On this point, he can appeal to his own conscience, and he hopes also to his omniscient Judge. At no period has he felt more anxious to live and die in peace with every human being. Yet feeling that his final account is near, he is anxious to spend his last breath in defending the truth of God, and in opposing the errors which threaten its subversion. Conscious that he is liable to error, he knows that the same liability attends his valued brethren who differ from him in judgment. Nor is it impossible that, when he shall have retired from the stage, they may remember his warnings with regret that they have not been regarded."

This was his last public utterance on the subject so near his heart. It is dated "Newburyport, Nov. 19, 1855." He was then in his eighty-fifth year.

In 1856, he was once more called to feel the pang of domestic affliction. His youngest daughter, Sarah, wife of Mr. I. W. Wheelwright, died, after a lingering illness, on the twenty-seventh day of April. After her decease, his affection toward her children seemed, if possible, more tender than before.

This year, he resigned his seat in the Board of Trustees at Andover. His letter of resignation, dated Aug. 2, 1856, concludes thus: —

"It now remains, that, having feebly but honestly performed a sacred duty to the living and the dead, I should remit these vast concerns to your cool and conscientious deliberation, and to the disposal of an all-governing and all-wise Providence.

"In parting with the Seminary, I shall by no means lose my deep interest in its prosperity and its usefulness. It shall have my latest prayers. May light from Heaven directly dawn on the minds of its guardians, its instructors, and its students! May it prove a rich and lasting blessing to the church and the community!

"With much personal consideration and respect,

"I am, my dear brethren, yours,

"DANIEL DANA."

Later in the same month, whilst on his way to Boston, he had a fall at the railroad depot in Ipswich, occasioning some injury to his head, attended with temporary loss of memory. This created some alarm; but before the most distant member of his family could reach him, he was convalescing; and, a few days later, his buoyancy of spirit was such as to call forth expressions of surprise. He said that he felt something of the elasticity consequent on recovery from sickness. He was cheered, too, by a brief visit from a daughter of his eldest brother — (who had deceased, in honored old age, some years before.) The other members of his father's family, and most of the children of his younger brother at Marblehead, had usually been not remote from him; and no small enjoyment did he derive from this vicinage; but the family of the brother who had been his companion in college, he could see only at long intervals.

There was doubtless another cause of his cheerfulness at this time. His resignation of his connection with the Andover Seminary could not but be attended with a sense of relief — which some of his children shared. One of them, indeed, whose visits often synchronized with the annual gathering at Andover (when the affairs of the Seminary were wont to fill a large place in the conversation), had once gravely proposed memorializing the trustees to change their anniversary to the dead of winter. But now a more effectual relief was secured by his resignation; and the graver tone of his conversation was delightfully qualified by anecdotes, reminiscences, classical allusions, and that genial flow of soul which was always his when his spirit was not oppressed. He gave from memory at this time the jocose lines of Erasmus ("Nonne meministi, quod saepe dixisti," &c.) with perfect fluency; and brought out, from his stores of anecdote, things new as well as old.

After all, he was doubtless somewhat indebted to Andover. With less incitement to activity, his mental powers could scarcely have retained so prolonged vigor. It is but just to add, that, where he was personally known, his principles were held in honor by many who differed widely from his opinions. The Secretary of the Andover Board, writing him the year previous (Aug. 24, 1855), says, "On an examination of the Report of the Committee, you will find no unkind word; and I am very sure there is no unkind feeling in the breast of any one of the trustees. On the contrary, so far as I know, they cherish a very profound respect for you, though they may not be able to adopt all your views." When, at the semi-centennial celebration at Andover, in 1858, the orator compared him to "the poet's Abdiel," it was a tribute from an unexpected quarter.

About this time, he repeated to two of his daughters, who were visiting him, a long and beautiful poem from memory. The life of Dr. Mason interested him deeply. On some days, three of his daughters took part in reading to him; as a listener, he "tired them all out."

On the twenty-eighth of November of this year, the First Presbyterian Church in Newburyport, with which had been his earliest pastoral connection, celebrated the one hundredth year since the erection of the church edifice. In the morning, a sermon, rich in historical interest, was delivered by the pastor, Rev. A. G. Vermilye. The following is from a newspaper report of the afternoon services: —

"In the afternoon, the house was again filled, at two o'clock, to listen to the counsels and remarks of four successive pastors of the church, who occupied the pulpit, and who had come to unite again in a new consecration of the sanctuary so dear to them all. Rev. Dr. Dana was the first speaker. Sixty-two years ago, this eminent and devoted servant of Christ was solemnly ordained to the pastoral care of this church. Under his ministry, the church rapidly increased, the congregation became large and influential, and soon attained a vigor and influence unsurpassed by any church in the vicinity. The most eminent ministers in the country were often in its pulpit; the voices of Dr. Dwight, President Appleton, Dr. Griffin, Dr. Payson, Dr. Porter, Professors Stuart and Woods, Dr. Codman, and many other faithful ministers, chained the attention and penetrated the hearts of multitudes. It has often been remarked by strangers, that, in no congregation, during the ministry of Dr. Dana, had they ever witnessed more serious attention, or united in more solemn and impressive services.

"Dr. Dana's remarks were heard with most respectful attention. They were directed to the simple point of the duty of his audience as *hearers of the gospel.* Such a theme was fitting indeed for one, who, standing on the outposts of life, could look back upon the sixty years in which he had uttered the warnings of the gospel, and proclaimed its messages of pardon. This revered and beloved minister is still among us, still engaged in offices of Christian love, still, we rejoice to say, a preacher of righteousness in the great congregation. Long may his light continue to shine, and his loved and venerated form be seen in our streets, and in the house of God!"

A month later (Dec. 30, 1856), he delivered the charge at the installation of Rev. H. R. Timlow as pastor of the Second Presbyterian Church, with which had been his latest pastoral connection. In this he chiefly availed himself of some former preparation.

With respect to the state of his health after this, his daughter writes, —

"During the winter of 1856–7, he attended church quite regularly, enjoying the ministrations of his young friend and successor, Mr. Timlow. In the spring, though feeble, and so pale that the sight of him in the pulpit was an affecting one, yet no persuasions could induce him to remain at home. His eyes had now become less sensitive to light, and no longer needed the green glasses which had so long concealed them. Both pastor and people loved to see their aged friend in his place, and to have him take part in the communion service. The first Sabbath in July, 1857, he was there as usual, and dined, as was his custom, with his niece, Mrs. C. (who lived opposite the church), in order to attend the afternoon service. Feeling very feeble, he would have returned home; but, as Mr. Vermilye was to preach, he did not like to seem to neglect him. Returning home in a state of great exhaustion, it was with difficulty that he could be supported into the house, and up to his room. He could scarcely speak. For two or three weeks, he was confined chiefly to his room and bed.

"In the summer of 1857, he made farewell visits to two daughters, resident in New Hampshire, and also to relatives and friends in and around Boston.

"His cough had been for years at times distressing, but he bore it with great patience. When not suffering in this way, he enjoyed hearing reading. "The Words of Jesus," and Dr. Alexander's "Consolation," gave him much pleasure.

"His conversation was still often vivacious. Speaking one day of the alterations needlessly and wantonly made in hymns, he said, 'What absurdities those critics commit, who are forever attempting to alter hymns! For instance, in that verse of Addison, "Through all eternity — But oh!" they have got it, "For oh!" as though eternity were to be used for the very thing it was unfit for. At another time, he objected to the line, 'A heaven of joy, because of love!' and preferred, 'A heaven of joy, a heaven of love.' 'Poetry,' he said, 'does not reason.' He said that was a fine remark of Daniel Webster, on a verse of Dr. Watts, 'And sit and sing herself away;' he thought it had allusion to the swan, whose dying notes are sweetest. The change, 'Till called to rise and soar away,' he condemned as a great impertinence.

"One day, he wished that the clock, which was out of order, should be attended to. On my asking if he had any objection to defer it for a few days, he answered, 'None at all, only that which a certain king gave. I believe that was about a clock; he said he would have nothing about him that *would lie.*'"

The Rev. Mr. Timlow (writing after his decease) says, —

"He always occupied the pulpit with me. Often after service, he would take me by the hand, and with paternal tenderness encourage me. He showed me too much deference. I was conscious of not deserving it; but his desire was to relieve me from all feeling as to his interference as an ex-pastor. And this he did. As

20

I went out among my people, some would say, ' What
a good friend you have in Dr. Dana!'"

The latest visits of the writer of this narrative to his
father were among the pleasantest ever enjoyed. That
of 1858 was delayed till near the end of November.
At this time, he rose early, and was with his family at
breakfast, and sometimes at dinner; but the greater
part of the day he kept his bed. His cough was sometimes harassing; but, with this exception, he was free
from pain, although evidently much reduced in strength.
He seemed now to have got beyond all earthly care.
Even Andover had ceased from troubling. His mind
was still clear and bright, and his eyesight was sufficient to make him observant of any change in the
countenance of those with whom he conversed.

He was now in his eighty-eighth year. Two notes,
dictated about this time, show his undiminished vigor
of mind, warmth of affection, and delicacy of style.
The first was addressed to friends lately bereaved; the
second to a highly esteemed relative.

"MY DEAR AFFLICTED FRIENDS, — I feel myself im-
pelled to express a tender sympathy in your recent bereavement. I have cherished a very tender affection
for your deceased parents, and, if their children were favored children, it is not improper for me to say that
the parents were favored too. The loss of such friends
carries us forward to the world where 'adieus and fare-
wells are a sound unknown.' Let us feel that such
calls are sent in Fatherly love; fitted, as they are to
uproot us from the present world, and lead us to Him
for the future.

"Believe me very affectionately yours,

"D. DANA."

TO W. W., ESQ.

" NEWBURYPORT, Jan. 5, 1859.

" MY DEAR SIR, — The late manifestation of your generous kindness does not permit me to be wholly silent, while it forbids me to speak in such terms as would wound your delicacy. I can only wish and pray that it may be richly rewarded by the Giver of all good.

" But the occasion gives me leave to touch a topic which I doubt not will be delightful to your heart. I refer to your mother, so dear to us all, and so much the ornament of her sex. It so happened, that, many years since, I took two journeys in quick succession : one to Maine, the other to Dartmouth College. In both these journeys, she was my companion ; and, though I thought I was intimate with her, the intimacy was much increased. I found her possessed of a remarkable mind ; and from that period to the time when Providence took the treasure from us, my estimate of her worth was greatly heightened. For excellence of disposition, and dignity of manners, and universal benevolence, she was very highly distinguished. If to be surrounded with friends here, whom we tenderly love, and whom it is improving to love, why should it not be correspondently gratifying to have such friends in heaven ? Nor can I form a kinder wish than that we may meet her in that world where all that is excellent is raised to the highest pitch, and freed from every imperfection.

" Believe me with great esteem and affection,

" Yours,

" D. DANA."

His daughter writes, " One day, repeating part of a hymn, he said, ' That line is a very fine one — ' *His love can ne'er be told ;'* the music is so exactly adapted, as if striving to reach the sentiment.' He then sang, ' His love, his love, his love can ne'er be told.'

"He enjoyed very much his Thanksgiving visit from W. and F., and often looked back to it with pleasure. He said to me of F., ' She is a lovely one!'

"In April, the Presbytery of Londonderry met in Newburyport. Two of its members called, and asked whether I thought him able to receive a visit from the members in attendance. I referred it to him, suggesting that there would be probably eight or ten. He said he should be happy to see them. The next day (April 27), he was feeble, and unable to sit up after breakfast. He was preparing to rise, but had leaned back on the pillows, when the members of Presbytery, nineteen in number (including corresponding members), were announced. Receiving them at the door, I heard only the last words of his welcome, — ' and take chairs, gentlemen ; that is, if you can find them.' Mr. Savage addressed him in behalf of the Presbytery, congratulating him upon his continued tranquillity and Christian cheerfulness, and then alluded to a time when they had stood side by side at Andover (perhaps thirty) years before. At this, he said, in his way of gentle earnestness, ' Indeed! you surprise me — I could not have thought that it had been so long.' After the address, Mr. Allen prayed, or rather gave praise to God. The ministers and elders (three of the former were his successors in the pastoral office) were standing around, many of them looking at him with fixed and intense interest ; he, with his pale, spiritual face, joining in the prayer, and then evidently seeking to identify many of them. As it closed, he spoke :

" Brethren, I thank you; I feel as if I would like to take each of you by the hand. As they in turn came forward, he had an appropriate word for each."

The scene was described by those present as "truly sublime and affecting." The Presbytery, on returning to their place of meeting, adopted the following resolutions: —

" *Whereas,* the Presbytery of Londonderry had the precious privilege, this morning, of visiting their venerated father in the ministry, the Rev. Dr. Dana, in his chamber, to which he is confined by increasing infirmity, and of taking his hand, probably for the last time as a body; and

" *Whereas,* by that interview, we were reminded of his devotion to *the faith once delivered to the saints,* and of his bold and repeated protests against the incoming of a false theology, therefore, —

" *Resolved,* That we express our conviction of the important service he has thereby rendered the cause of truth and of Christ; and, also,

" *Resolved,* That while we regret the decay of the natural vigor of one whose whole life and character give such weight to the position he assumed, and to the testimony he has borne, we are incited, by his example, to cleave the more tenaciously to those tenets, the defence of which has endeared him to us all, and will always endear to us his memory."

Early in June, the writer of these lines visited him for the last time. He was in a most delightful frame of mind. The nervous system being completely in repose, all the amenity of his nature seemed more conspicuous than ever. The stream of life, now no longer

20*

troubled, was flowing smoothly and sweetly on toward the peaceful shore.

A little incident showed the quickness of his memory. On his son's telling him that he had just come from the General Assembly at Indianapolis, and that his chief inducement to attend had been the fact of his father's having gone to the Assembly nearly half a century before, he instantly said, " Yes, I attended the General Assembly in 1810, 1812, and 1814."

At the parting, having named very affectionately his son's wife (always much beloved by him), he said, " Commend me to her in the kindest terms that language supplies." These words, spoken, not with the halting utterance of old age, but with perfect fluency, distinctness, and sweetness, were the last which his son ever heard from his lips.

His daughter states that " he now turned from other reading chiefly to the Bible, and to the hymns of his favorite Watts, and of other writers. Baxter's hymn, beginning, —

> " Lord, it belongs not to my care,
> Whether to die or live,"

he dwelt upon with great pleasure. Once, when I read to him, at his selection, the fourteenth chapter of the Gospel of John, he exclaimed, at verse 27, ' Beautiful ! '

" On the 21st of July (three days before he entered his eighty-ninth year), he was listening to the reading of the fourth chapter of the second Epistle to Timothy. At the passage, ' I have fought a good fight ; I have finished my course,' &c., he exclaimed with emphasis, ' Oh! glorious ! '

" His gratitude to the friends who were constantly

ministering to his comfort seemed warmer than ever. Only two days before his departure, he dictated a note of thanks to one of them for what he termed her *persevering kindness*, and requested her to select a volume from his library."

On Wednesday, Aug. 24 (but two days before his death), his daughter read to him some hymns from a Collection received the night before, of which one of his sons was the editor, and the other the publisher. He spoke of them both very affectionately, and was much pleased with the hymns read. Two by St. Bernard drew from him the repeated and animated exclamation, " Beautiful! Beautiful!" One of these begins,

> " Jesus, the very thought of thee; " &c.,

the other, which, in the version given, is of recent appearance, is addressed to our Saviour on the cross :

> " Sacred Head! so bruised and wounded,
> With the crown of thorns surrounded,
> Smitten with the mocking reed, —
> Wounds which may not cease to bleed, —
> Hail! from whose most blessed brow
> None can wipe the blood-drops now:
> All the flower of life has fled,
> Mortal paleness there instead.

> " Thou this agony and scorn
> Hast for me, a sinner, borne —
> Me unworthy! all for me
> Were those signs of love on thee!
> Let me true communion know
> With thee in thy sacred woe;
> Give thee thanks with every breath,
> Jesus, for thy bitter death.

" When my dying hour must be,
  Faithful Shepherd, think of me;
  In that dreadful hour, I pray,
  Jesus, come without delay:
  All unworthy of thy thought,
  Guilty, yet reject me not;
  When my dying hour is near,
  Lover of my soul, appear ! "

Well did these words associate themselves with the dying thoughts of one whose whole religion drew its life from humble, trustful contemplation of the cross of Christ.

The next morning, he came down to breakfast and prayers as usual, but soon after began to feel some indisposition, which, however, his physician thought would pass off. In the course of the day, his illness increased, and he spoke but little, except in reply to questions. He showed signs of bodily pain, but his mental composure was perfect.

The next day, his breathing was labored, and throughout the day it was only with much effort that he could speak. The passage, " Like as a father pitieth his children," &c., being repeated in his hearing, he said with difficulty, "*I know it.*" He was now evidently sinking. Suddenly, the difficult breathing ceased; without a groan or a struggle, he " fell asleep."

It was ten minutes before nine o'clock in the evening of Friday, Aug. 26, 1859.

" Eternity and time
    Met for a moment here;
  From earth to heaven, a scale sublime
    Rested on either sphere,
  Whose steps a saintly figure trod,
  By Death's cold hand led home to God."

CHAPTER XVI.

1859.

FUNERAL SERVICES. — TRIBUTES TO HIS MEMORY.

THE tolling bells announced, next morning, to the inhabitants of Newburyport, that he was gone who had so long been with them. On the following Tuesday, the funeral services were held in the Second Presbyterian Church.

"The event was marked by more than usual solemnity and impressiveness.

"The bells upon the several churches of Newburyport commenced tolling at one o'clock, and, with brief intermissions, continued to toll until the remains were deposited in the grave.

"About one o'clock, a large number of clergymen, together with the relatives and friends of the deceased, assembled at his late residence on High Street, where prayer was offered by Rev. Professor Emerson.

"About two o'clock, the remains were conveyed to the Second Presbyterian Church, followed by carriages containing numerous relatives.

"At the entrance to the church, the funeral *cortège* passed between two files of clergymen, many of whom were scarcely less aged and venerable in appearance than the still form which they now reverently greeted with uncovered heads.

"The church was filled. Such of the seats as were not reserved for relatives and clergymen were occupied before the hour of the services. The pulpit was deeply draped with crape, and the recess in the rear surrounded with this emblem of mourning." *

Sorrow that they should see his face no more, holy triumph in the assurance that henceforth for him there was " a crown of righteousness," divided the emotions of that crowded, silent assemblage, and found worthy utterance in the solemn services. These were participated in by the pastors of the two Presbyterian Churches, by Rev. Drs. Withington and Dimmick of Newburyport, Rev. Daniel Fitz of Ipswich, and Rev. B. R. Allen of Marblehead. Of those thus united in affectionate tribute to his memory, one had stood by his side in the ministry forty-five years ; one had been long and congenially associated with him in Presbytery. The former (Dr. Withington) said, —

"Perhaps there never was a funeral where a man so beloved left behind him so tranquil a sorrow. His life was long : we follow him to its close as we follow the sun in one of the longest days in summer, and see it set in the softest radiance, almost without missing it, compensated by the light of the departure, and the brightness left behind. . . . Little need be said over the grave of one whose stone would be inscribed, by the consent of our whole population, THE GOOD MAN.

"There are difficulties in a long life, from the very fact that it is long. The man that lives long must be tried by all the temptations of youth, manhood, and age. To have at once a sober youth, an active man-

---

* Newspaper Report.

hood, and a cheerful old age, is a combination difficult, yet necessary to give fulness to the Christian life.

"Oh, may my latest sun shine as benignly on my head, as it did on thine, my father and my friend!

. . . "Over his coffin, I venture to say, DR. DANA IS NOT DEAD. Some men, when they are entombed, are gone forever. Of our departed father, we cannot help retaining the mental inscription. Let us give eloquence to his thoughts, now that he can speak to us no more; and let us remember that the most grateful tribute we can pay to his spirit, is to appreciate his counsels, and profit by his example."

Dr. Allen said, —

"Though I loved Dr. Dana as a father, and venerated him as a sage, and agreed with him in all his *theological opinions and positions*, yet this is not the place nor this the time to consider *these*. Other business has called us here to-day, as these mournful tokens — this house draped in black, this large circle of weeping friends, this immense gathering — clearly indicate. We have come to pay our tribute of respect to the departed, to drop the tear of affection into his coffin, and with hearts sorrowful, yet buoyant with Christian hope, to bear his venerable form to its last resting-place in the dust, in firm faith of a glorious resurrection when Jesus shall come.

. . . "He was endowed with a high order of mind. God designed him for a man of mark. His intellect was broad, comprehensive, acute, his faculties finely balanced, his judgment sound and reliable. These faculties had been cultivated and developed by a sound and fine education, not only in the schools and by the books, but also in his intercourse with the world in the important relations he sustained, and the posts of honor and of usefulness which he filled. And his moral and social endowments were no less marked than were his mental. His conscience was enlightened and tender; and it was stern, also, and unyielding, as to the right and the true. His heart was warm, generous, kind, sympathizing; his disposition amiable in the highest degree. That politeness and urbanity, that fear of wounding the feelings of others, that singular sweetness and affection, which so highly distinguished all his social intercourse, was no studied effort to please; it was the simple, spontaneous outburst of the inner man.

"And here we cannot but admire the grace, nay, adore it, which gave his heart so strong a hold on the truth as it is in Jesus, not only for his own sake, but for the sake of the truth and the Church; for, if this had not been the case, his peculiarly amiable disposition might have proved a strong temptation in contending, as he had to contend, for the faith, with those he loved; and he might have been led, in his fear to displease, and his dread of separation, to sacrifice the truth he so nobly defended. We thank God, through Jesus Christ our Lord, for his strong, enduring faith.

"Dr. Dana was a representative man, not only of the past, in the soundness of his faith and his conservative character, but, to a very great extent, of the present also, especially of the church to which he belonged and in which he ministered, where he stood as a patriarch among his brethren. That was a scene of deep interest when the Presbytery assembled in his dying chamber, once more to take him by the hand, to hear his last words of counsel, and receive his last benediction. Who that was there can ever forget it?

"Dr. Dana filled an important place in our country, outside his own church, as a patron of sound learning, and a friend of enlarged Christian benevolence. He was instrumental, with others, in the establishment of the Seminary of sacred learning which he so fondly loved, over which he watched as an official with intensest interest down almost to the close, and which retained his warm affections, and was remembered in his prayers, till that noble heart ceased to beat. In the promotion of the great missionary and other associations of Christian benevolence, which so distinguish our age and country, he took a prominent part. With the good they have accomplished he was identified; over it he rejoiced with exceeding joy. He long survived most of his noble compeers in that great work, and stood here as almost the only link connecting the present with the past.

"And now he is a glorified spirit with God. His labors, his trials, his anxieties, his sorrows, are over. He is now singing, with a louder voice, and in purer and more exalted strains, that new song of redeeming grace and undying love, which he so loved to sing on the earth. Oh, how much have we to thank and praise God for in his behalf! For his character, as a man, a Christian, and a minister of Jesus; for his long life of eminent usefulness; for the strength imparted in scenes of trial; the consolations, so rich and full, in the dark hour of domestic affliction, when his crushed heart wept out its sorrows (and in his long life many such scenes were his); for that placid and cheerful old age; for the bright shining of that noble mind, and the strong affections of that warm heart, down to the very close, which made his sick chamber any thing rather than a place of

21

gloom; for the gentle manner in which the silver cord
was loosed; for his calm and peaceful death, free from
all those presages and accompaniments which so often
attend the dread march of the last enemy — for all
this we thank and praise God. What other, what more,
could we ask for one beloved so much, and over whose
venerable form, so peaceful in its last rest, we so delight
to bend to-day!

"He is not dead; he has just entered into life; he
has entered the society of redeemed spirits; he has
again been united to his loved compeers in the Christian
pilgrimage who went before; he is in communion, face
to face, in glory everlasting, with that Redeemer with
whom he was identified on earth, united in the bonds
of an endless life, and to whose love and grace he owes
his crown of glory. Death is swallowed up in victory.
'O death! where is thy sting? O grave! where is
thy victory?'

"Dr. Dana lives. He lives in this community, where
he moved for so many years as a faithful servant of
Jesus Christ; he is cherished in the sacred memory
of all your hearts. The influence of his character and
his works is immortal. He lives in heaven; he has
exchanged the pilgrim's staff and weeds for the crown
of the conqueror."

At the close of the services, the long procession
passed to Oakhill Cemetery.

The Newburyport "Herald" of Aug. 31, says, —

"Long before the bells over the city began to toll,
telling that the last hour for connection of the living
with his mortal remains had come, the house began to
fill with the old and young from among his former
parishioners, and from the other societies of the city, —

with his townspeople and friends here, and with strangers from abroad ; all leaving their various avocations
to go to the house of mourning, and pay their last
tribute of respect to the great and good man — the
greatly good — who had fallen. The church in and
about the pulpit was draped in mourning, and a solemn
stillness rested upon the audience."

"It was pleasant to see" (says another writer),
"how universal and unaffected were the respect and
sorrow. A stranger must have known that a good man
had died, and that the loss was a public one."

On the following Sabbath, a commemorative discourse was delivered in the First Presbyterian Church
by the Rev. Mr. Timlow, his latest successor in the
Second Church.

Before and after the funeral, many spontaneous trib-
utes to his memory appeared in secular as well as
religious journals. A few lines selected from several
of these, may serve to show how general was the sentiment of veneration and affection toward him : —

"A great and good man has departed : the sun of
his life, like that of a long and bright summer's day, has
gone down to its beautiful setting. Three generations
in the community in which he lived have walked in its
light, and rejoiced in its blessed and holy influences.
His eminent talents were adorned by graces peculiarly
his own."

The following is from "The Boston Courier :" —

"Dr. Dana was an admirable scholar of the old school
of classicists and divines, an extremely elegant and
forcible writer of English, and has always been one of
the chief lights of the Presbyterian Church. His affectionate disposition and nice conscientiousness made him

a most faithful and valuable pastor; and in all the exercises of his office he was a model, as he had long been the patriarch of his denomination in this part of the country. Few clergymen were better known, none more endeared to a very extended circle. Dr. Dana was for many years minister of the First Presbyterian Church in Newburyport, afterwards President of Dartmouth College, and finally a resident of his early home; where, while unable to fulfil the regular duties of the ministry, he long officiated as a home missionary, and was received by multitudes as a welcome and venerated guest. No man ever lived a more exemplary and blameless life; and the memory of his goodness, of his amiable aspect, of his polished manners, and truly venerable appearance, cannot fade away from the minds of those who had the happiness to be numbered among his friends."

Another writes, —

"Dr. Dana was emphatically an old-school gentleman and divine. He was one of the most courteous and agreeable of men in his manners, and one of the most faithful and affectionate of pastors.

"As a writer, he was distinguished for simplicity and purity of style; as a thinker, for clearness and discrimination. He held with undeviating firmness to the doctrines of the Westminster Catechism, as interpreted by the old-school theologians. In fact, he was old school in every thing, — manners, divinity, and piety; and a better type of all these cannot easily be found.

"Few clergymen have been more widely known than the deceased; and it rarely falls to the lot of man to enjoy so large a share of respect, esteem, and honor, as has been awarded him by all classes and sects during his long, active, and useful life. Dr. Dana's appearance

, was very striking: his expansive forehead, intelligent eyes, intellectual features, and spirited expression, combined to inspire veneration wherever he was present. Of late, he has received great attention from his fellow-citizens, and strangers who have visited the city of his residence; and the closing years of his life have been cheered by those who will never forget his gentle and affectionate teachings." — *Boston Transcript.*

Another writer says, —

" The long and eminently useful life thus closed, the rare qualities of the deceased, and the reputation, so unsullied and extended, which he enjoyed among the last and the present generations, make something more than an ordinary obituary notice becoming and necessary.

" Though firm in his opinions, and uncompromising, if need be, in their expression, he was singularly urbane and prepossessing in his manners. No better specimen of the Christian gentleman could be found.

" He was universally beloved, and one of the few who had not an enemy."

From distant California, a correspondent of one of the Newburyport papers wrote, —

" I see by 'The Herald' that the venerable patriarch has gone to his rest at last. The Rev. Dr. Dana is dead. Like a shock of corn fully ripe, he has been gathered in. I have often heard the inquiry made of new comers from Newburyport, 'Is Rev. Dr. Dana living yet?' How well we remember that venerable form, that kindly face! But he has passed away after a long life of peculiar usefulness, and most honestly can we write his epitaph, — 'A GOOD MAN.'"

The notices of the religious press and of private cor-

21*

respondents, were too numerous for extended citation. One who had known him well * thus writes : "The image of Christ shone very brightly in your beloved and venerable father, and its lustre was admirably blended with that of fine natural qualities and high mental and social culture."

The Synod of Albany adopted the following resolutions : —

" *Whereas,* it has pleased God to call to his heavenly rest our venerated father, Rev. Daniel Dana, D.D., of Newburyport, Mass.: therefore *Resolved,* —

"1. That this Synod records its grateful acknowledgments to the great Head of the Church for the gift of this honored and faithful minister of the gospel, in whose character we have so luminous and expressive an exhibition of the sanctifying power of the truth, in whose laborious and heroic defence of the doctrines of our holy religion we have an instance of fidelity so worthy of our imitation, and in whose long and useful life so much was done under the divine blessing for the salvation of the world.

"2. That the fall of this standard-bearer in Israel reminds us of our own mortality, and that our dependence is not in an arm of flesh, but in the arm of the Omnipotent God, who is able to supply the instrumentalities needed to carry on his work; and hence our duty is to pray the Lord of the harvest to send forth more laborers into the vineyard."

Of more recent date is the following extract from the " Newburyport Recollections " of Mr. James Morss, son of the Rev. Dr. Morss, so long the highly respected

---

* Rev. John Proudfit, D.D., one of his successors in the First Presbyterian Church.

rector of the Episcopal Church in Newburyport. The lamented death of Mr. Morss occurred very soon after he had written thus: —

"The late venerable Dr. Dana, who so long went in and out among the people composing his congregation, was an acknowledged theologian, and eminent as a writer. In person he was slender, in air and manner he was mild and winning; and no passing events of exciting interest, whether personal or otherwise, could for an instant disturb his calm benignity. Towards him respect was awarded, as by common consent, for the splendor of his Christian character. I have always made it a specialty, when visiting your town during the later years of the life of our venerated friend, to honor myself by a call of respect upon him. But the grave now closes over his remains; and when earth to earth, and dust to dust, was pronounced or meditated at his grave, it probably never consigned to earth a casket which once contained a soul of purer and more heavenly aspirations. He was the friend of my kindred, and by them beloved, respected, and honored. He was the friend of man; and all who knew him were also his friends. He was a Christian soldier and a Christian patriot, whose devoted and prayerful utterances were ever for God and his country. *Requiescat in pace.*"

Thus have we traced his long day of life — from the dewy freshness of its morning, through its hours of alternating cloud and brightness, down to that serene and glorious sunset, to our eyes an attractive vision, to his, the dawn of an eternal day.

Not alone as a tribute to his memory has this record

been prepared; but in the hope that, ministering spiritual strength to others, it may subserve the holy purposes to which his life was devoted. May the divine blessing thus attend it !

It was remarkable how many who had been near to him in life, were not long separated from him in death. But a few months rolled by, and several clergymen with whom he had been for a long series of years associated, one of whom had spoken at his funeral; a beloved niece, long intimate in his family; his son-in-law, Rev. John M. C. Bartley, of kindred sentiments and spirit with himself, — were all numbered with the dead.   Lastly, his son, Daniel Dana, jun., of New York, who of all his children most resembled him in many striking traits, died at Newburyport, Feb. 12, 1861.

In the Oakhill Cemetery, on a spot from which spreads out a magnificent prospect of city and country, river and ocean (the spire and the tower of the two churches associated with his name are both in view), a chaste and beautiful monument bears these inscriptions : —

The Reverend

DANIEL DANA, D.D.,

OF BLESSED MEMORY.

Sixty-six years a minister of the gospel of Jesus Christ; of which sixty were in New-buryport.

Born July 24, 1771; *died Aug.* 26, 1859.

"A man greatly beloved." — Daniel x. 11.

"After he had served his own generation by the will of God he fell on sleep." — Acts xiii. 36.

———

How good, how kind, how upright and honorable, how firm in loyalty to truth, how guileless, how saintly, let those say from whose hearts the dear remembrance of the Christian pastor, the sympathizing friend, the affectionate father, can never fade away.

Resurgam.

RECOLLECTIONS OF DR. DANA.

BY W. B. SPRAGUE, D.D.

THE true index to the character is the life — we infer what a man is from what he does. Especially does this remark apply, where the outer man is only the spontaneous flowing forth of the inner — where no cunning and tortuous spirit is suffered to intervene to prevent the doings of the hands and the utterances of the lips from answering faithfully to the movements of the heart. It is hardly needful to say that it is the life of an eminently guileless, and, in the best sense, simple-hearted individual, that is narrated in the preceding pages; and it may safely be presumed that no one who has traced his interesting career, and marked his conduct in the various relations he sustained, and the various positions of difficulty and trial, of high responsibility and honorable usefulness, which he occupied, can fail to have a definite idea of all the prominent qualities of his mind and heart. Still, as his children, in whose wishes I recognize a law, have intimated a desire that I should sum up the narrative of his life, which is itself a fitting and grateful offering of filial devotion, by a brief estimate of his character, I cheerfully undertake the office which their kindness has assigned to me. It is due to candor, however, to state

250

that my acquaintance with this venerable man did not commence till I had been some years in the ministry; that my intercourse with him, though free and intimate, has never been more than occasional; though I have somehow felt that I had penetrated into the interior of his heart, and the embarrassment which I feel in writing about him, results, not from my being in doubt in respect to any points of his character, but from a conscious inability to transfer to other minds the impression which he has left upon my own. I shall attempt nothing beyond a mere outline.

Dr. Dana's personal appearance, if not imposing, was altogether prepossessing, and prepared one to find in his character the fine intellectual and moral qualities which an acquaintance with him was sure to reveal. He was rather above the middle height, and was symmetrically formed; though, in his latter years particularly, his head, as he stood or walked, had a slight inclination forward. In his countenance, it was difficult to say whether the intellectual or the moral had the predominance; but no one could see him without being struck with the expression of earnest thoughtfulness on the one hand, and intense benevolence on the other. There was a look of calm dignity, I had almost said of modest reserve, that could hardly fail to elicit a deferential regard, even from a stranger who should meet him in the market-place. His movements, without being particularly graceful, were simple and natural, and seemed to indicate a consciousness of having something to do. In his manners he was bland, quiet, genial, self-possessed — he was generally grave, though he had a vein of humor that occasionally flashed out in innocent merriment, rendering him quite the life of the social circle. It is presumed that his whole life might be safely challenged for a single act that could reasonably be considered as inconsistent with the dignity of either a gentleman or a Christian.

Dr. Dana's intellect was at once comprehensive, acute, clear, and thorough. In his investigations of truth, he descended to first principles, and, having planted himself first on a basis that he felt sure could not be moved, he gradually worked his way onward to a remote conclusion, each successive step bringing him into a brighter and still brighter light. He had the power of discerning the minute differences of things with great accuracy, and though he would sometimes hold a difficult subject to his mind for a long time in patient investigation, yet he would never leap at a conclusion in the dark, or suffer himself to be bewildered by a premature admission of what he could not see clearly. With his uncommon powers of analysis he combined a remarkably exact and cultivated taste — insomuch that his ordinary compositions would very well bear to be referred to the most rigid standard. His memory also was much more than ordinarily tenacious, and it was interesting to see how, even in his old age, the results of his early reading, as well as his long-continued observation, seemed to be entirely at his command. An extraordinary fondness for study had been among his earliest developments; and this did not become less as he advanced in life; and the consequence of this early and ever-enduring habit, in connection with the best opportunities for improvement, was, that he attained to a very high degree of intellectual culture. As his mind was originally cast in a mould of uncommon symmetry, so there was a due proportion maintained in the cultivation of his different faculties; and hence the whole intellectual man attracted your attention and admiration, rather than any one distinguishing feature.

Dr. Dana was, in some respects, highly favored in his moral constitution; though his moral character was so identified with his religious, that it is impossible to do justice to the one without taking into view the other. He had naturally warm and generous sensibilities: his heart was alive to the joys of friendship, and it vibrated in quick response to every note of sorrow. He united great gentleness with great firmness: his tones were always bland, his words and manner always kind, and it evidently cost him a sacrifice to take the attitude of an antagonist in any thing; but no flatteries could beguile him, no threats could intimidate him, into the semblance of a compromise of his own honest convictions. His firmness may have sometimes been mistaken for obstinacy; but it was not even akin to it. He was firm because he was conscientious — because he felt, that, come what would, God must be obeyed rather than man. He would not needlessly give offence to a mortal; but, if this must be the alternative to the following out of his honest convictions of duty, his course was so plain that he had no occasion to bestow upon it a thought. However he might differ from an individual in respect to religion or any other subject, he never felt himself called upon, for that reason, to treat him with coolness or discourtesy, or withhold from him any expression of good will, though he may have felt constrained to do what he could to convince him of what he believed to be his error. One of his most intimate and valued friends, as appears from the narra-

22

tive of his life, was the late Dr. Benjamin Abbot, long the accomplished and honored Principal of the Phillips Exeter Academy, who is understood to have held some form of Unitarianism; and though there is no doubt that Dr. Dana, in all fidelity to his convictions, conversed with him freely and earnestly on the points of difference between them, yet it is evident that their early friendship never lost any degree of its intensity, so long as they were both among the living.

It is scarcely necessary to add, in this connection, that Dr. Dana, in all his intercourse and deportment, was a fine example of Christian prudence. His tongue had never learned to utter harsh, or bitter, or even hasty words; but it had been trained to move in obedience to the law of kindness. He was always most considerate of time, and place, and circumstances, and never, by any random speech in a promiscuous company, run the hazard of giving offence or pain to any one present. He was social and communicative on all ordinary occasions, but he was sure to hold his peace when he had nothing to say. His cautious and conciliatory spirit, in connection with his acknowledged general wisdom, gave him great consideration as a counsellor; and in this capacity he was often put in requisition, and most successfully, not only to settle private controversies, but to restore harmony to contending and distracted congregations.

He possessed great natural sensitiveness; and possibly this sometimes took on a morbid form, and gave a sombre and desponding hue to some of his judgments and feelings. When he was called to the presidency of Dartmouth College, all his convictions and predilections were at first adverse to an acceptance of the appointment : but the earnest wishes of his friends and the friends of the college, together with their enthusiastic predictions of his complete success, proved an overmatch for his first decided preference, and he was brought, though most reluctantly, to the conclusion, that perhaps it was his duty to take the new position that was offered to him; though it is doubtful whether he was altogether free from misgivings when he accepted the appointment. The result of this movement seemed, perhaps, one of the most mysterious events of his life. Scarcely had the voice of gratulation in connection with the inaugural ceremonies died away, before his health became seriously impaired, his mind became cheerless and despondent, and he was oppressed by the gloomy conviction of his utter inadequacy to the duties he had undertaken; and after a very brief experiment, — too brief, many would have said, — in which he seems to have had little enjoyment, and to have thought that his hopes of usefulness were but poorly realized, he tendered the resignation of his office. Without deciding whether or not he reached a wise conclusion in this matter, it cannot be doubted that, with stronger nerve and more vigorous health, he would at least have waited longer before he retired from a place in which he had already become fixed, and for which his friends believed that he possessed high qualifications.

Dr. Dana was an eminently devout man. It was impossible to be in habits of intercourse with him, without feeling one's self in contact with a heart that was glowing with love to Christ, and in intimate communion with him. He did not make this manifest so much by set and formal conversations, as by those incidental and apparently unconscious outgoings, which, where the heart is full, nothing can suppress, and no one ever heard him pray, without feeling that he was not only at home in the exercise, but greatly delighted in it. Humility, faith, reverence, gratitude, every element of devotion, was beautifully represented in his fervent addresses at the throne of mercy.

He was, moreover, a model of Christian consistency. Sometimes men who talk much and pray much, after all do little; or else they do so much in the wrong direction, and in the wrong manner, that even Charity herself is obliged to pause before deciding upon their probable character. Not so with the venerable man who is the subject of these remarks: with him, prayer and alms, faith and works, went together — because he endeavored to conform every part of his conduct to the Bible standard, there were no unsightly protuberances in his character, — nothing to outrage a correct taste, or shock one's sensibilities, or suggest the inquiry, how so much that is good can consist with so much that is exceptionable. He was careful not only to cultivate every grace, but to cultivate each in due proportion; and thus it was, that even the world, and the most scrutinizing and captious portion of it, awarded to him the high praise of being a consistent Christian.

Dr. Dana was a well-read and able theologian. He had made theology his study from early life, and he always delighted in it. The system which he received in the beginning, was the same to which he held fast to the end: it was not only Calvinism as opposed to Arminianism, but Calvinism as opposed to Hopkinsianism, — the real, undiluted Puritan theology. Though he had a mind capable of profound philosophical research, he allowed philosophy little scope in settling or shaping the doctrines of Christianity. The one only inquiry which he was interested to answer was, " What saith the Scripture?" and that point once settled, his faith was as firm as a mountain. Wherever he thought he detected any departure from " the old paths," he always stood ready to bear his testimony against it, no matter how great the sacrifice it might cost him. But notwithstanding he contended so earnestly for the purity of the faith, he never seemed partial to the extreme technology of any school; and it happened, in one or more instances, that his own orthodoxy was temporarily at a discount, from the fact that he used either too sparingly, or not at all, some of the accredited religious phraseology of the day. His theological views were well defined, and as he held them with undoubting confidence, so he was ready to defend them with great skill at whatever point they might be assailed.

Dr. Dana was an admirable preacher. He had fine natural qualifications for the pulpit, almost the only drawback being the use of green spectacles, in consequence of an early and enduring injury to his eyes, by means of which the audience lost the inspiriting effect of his bright and animated eye. He usually preached from a manuscript, though he extemporized with great ease, and of many of his discourses, nothing beyond the starting outline was written. His voice was rich, sonorous, and mellow, and, in its full volume, was large enough to fill a church of the largest dimensions; though its tones were not greatly varied. He spoke with great fervor and unction, and showed evidently that he was absorbed in his subject, though he had but

22*

little gesture, and there was no approach to any thing
declamatory or boisterous. If his elocution was not
particularly graceful, it was highly effective — it was
the soul coming out in rich and earnest thoughts and
well adapted words. The matter of his preaching was
intensely evangelical. In the selection of his themes,
he always kept near the Cross; and, in his treatment of
them, he made no show of learning beyond what his
subject manifestly required. His preaching was happily
divided between the doctrinal, the practical, and the
experimental; or rather they all harmoniously com-
mingled in almost every discourse. He reasoned, and
often with great power; but his reasoning was so simple and luminous as to be within the comprehension
of the humblest of his hearers. He dealt in great
fidelity with the Church, drawing the line most carefully between true and false religion, and urging upon
all who had named the name of Christ, not only to
depart from iniquity, but to let their light shine. In
his appeals to the careless and ungodly, he was most
persuasive and impressive, and sometimes the terrors
of the law went forth from his lips in words of burning
import. It was impossible to listen to him without
being impressed with the idea that every sentence that
he uttered came from his inmost soul; and that he
knew no other motive in preaching the gospel than
to glorify his Master in saving the souls of his fellow-
men.

He was eminently qualified for the more private
duties of a pastor, and his heart rejoiced in the discharge of them. Constituted as he was with quick and
generous sympathies, with an ear and a heart always
awake and open to the tale of woe, he was like an

angel of mercy in the chamber of sickness, at the bed of death, and amidst scenes of bereavement; and it is no wonder that his services in this capacity should often have been sought, beyond the limits of his own immediate charge. He was emphatically the friend of the poor; and there is no doubt that it was this beautiful feature of his character that suggested to some of his friends, after he resigned his last pastoral charge, the idea of his being employed, as his strength might permit, as a minister at large; and probably it was this that predisposed him to accept their kind proposals. In this humble field, his sympathetic heart found objects enough to act upon. As the venerable man who had, for almost sixty years, been an object of grateful respect not only in his own city and State, but throughout New England, passed around from street to street, stepping into one wretched hovel after another, and leaving there his blessing in the form of words of tender sympathy, or Christian counsel, or fervent prayer, his name became deeply engraven on the hearts of those to whom he thus ministered; and no doubt some of them, in the grateful remembrance of those visits, have already heaped their benedictions upon him in a better world.

Dr. Dana was little disposed to put himself forward as a leader in deliberative bodies — his naturally modest and retiring spirit rather disposed him to keep himself in the background; and yet he could be active and earnest enough when he felt that the occasion required it; and his acknowledged remarkable soundness of judgment and prudent foresight gave great weight to his opinions, however briefly or casually expressed. Indeed, so much was he respected and

honored, that his very presence, even when he kept
silent, was felt to be an element of power.

Dr. Dana, as might naturally be inferred from the
intellectual qualities already attributed to him, ranked
among the best writers of his day. Most of his published works are occasional discourses, though he is
the author of two or three pamphlets which are of a
decidedly controversial character. He had great
facility at adapting himself to an occasion, and seemed
always to enter fully into the spirit of it, seizing, as if
by intuition, upon its most prominent characteristics.
In controversy, he never lost his self-possession, or
good temper, or regard to Christian decorum; but,
while he evidently wrote under a deep sense of the
importance of his subject, and of the responsibility
pertaining to the attitude which he had assumed,
he was always perfectly respectful in the treatment
of his antagonist. Even those who did not sympathize in the views which he was endeavoring to
establish, admired the carefulness and the candor with
which he stated them, as well as the force and discrimination with which he defended them. A crowning
excellence of his writing was the precision, simplicity,
and purity of his style — he had made the best English
writers a study, and had imperceptibly imbibed their
excellences, without attempting to imitate them.
Though there are many whose productions contain
more that is bold and striking, and to the common
mind attractive, it may safely be said there are but few
who more rarely or more lightly offend against good
taste and good logic, than Dr. Dana.

It is hardly necessary to add, that Dr. Dana was an
earnest friend of revivals of religion; and he labored

to promote them, by every legitimate means, to the extent of his ability. But he was, nevertheless, a strict adherent to all the principles of evangelical order; and would never, even under circumstances of the greatest excitement, consent to the slightest compromise of Christian decorum. He did not indeed doubt that much good is often accomplished where the great truth, that God is a God of order, is practically, to some extent, overlooked; but as he saw no warrant in the Bible, and certainly found none in his own inherent sense of Christian propriety, for the irregularities and extravagances which have sometimes been exhibited, even within the limits of his own communion, he felt constrained, wherever he met them, to resist them, as at least marring the revival with which they were connected, if they did not vitiate it altogether. He looked for the evidences of a genuine work of God's Spirit rather in a deep and all-pervading solemnity, than in an overflow of animal feeling; rather in the utterances of the " still small voice," than in the storm and the earthquake.

It is not too much to say of Dr. Dana, that he was one of the most able, devoted, useful ministers of the period in which he lived. Happily his early training was under the best influences; and that, with a naturally docile spirit and wakeful conscience, proved, under the divine care and guidance, an adequate security against all youthful aberrations. Neither he nor his friends ever had occasion to look back to a period in which he had even begun to walk in the counsel of the ungodly, or to stand in the way of sinners. Even before he became the subject of a spiritual renovation, he was uniformly exemplary in his conduct, and strongly attracted to himself all with whom he had intercourse. But, from the commencement of his Christian life, he seems to have been a shining light, ever shining brighter — as new spheres of usefulness successively opened to him, his heart expanded in broader sympathy with all the great interests of humanity, and his mind woke to a correspondingly higher tone of effort to promote the well-being of all who were within his reach. In the gracious ordering of Providence, his first and principal field of ministerial labor was one which, while, from the elevated tone of society in the neighborhood, it furnished excellent advantages for intellectual and social culture, was also admirably adapted to bring his various faculties into exercise in the best manner and to the best purpose. From the time that his connection with Dartmouth College ceased, the congregations to which he ministered were less prominent in their relation to the Presbyterian Church than that of which he had previously had the charge; but, even in these narrower spheres, his active and devoted life could not but tell powerfully upon the interests of truth and piety; and indeed, though he was eminently faithful to those who were under his immediate care, his example was always shining for the benefit of the whole community, and his general influence went out through innumerable channels to bless the Church and the world at large. It was impossible, that, with so meek and unobtrusive a spirit as he possessed, he should have ever put himself forward in any enterprise where he could labor with equal advantage in subordination to others; but his whole life, though noiseless as the dew, was a calm and steady course of efficient activity.

His influence in connection with different institutions; his influence upon the Christian ministry, especially in rebuking the vagaries of fanaticism in regard to revivals of religion; his influence in the higher walks of society, in inspiring respect for his office, and checking the tendencies to a perversion of God's gifts, and in the lower walks of society, by mingling with them as a helper and a comforter, and quickening their self-respect, and counselling them how to live, and directing their views upward, — his influence, exerted through these various channels and over these widely extended fields, must be seen in the light that shines beyond the dark valley, before any adequate estimate can be formed of it. But his great and good influence has survived him; and not only so, but it is rising, and deepening, and spreading like the light of Heaven; and, after centuries have rolled over his grave, his quiet and godly life on earth will still be perpetuated in the character and destiny of each passing generation. This thought is rich in consolation, when applied to any good man; but in reference to one whose whole life, as in the case of Dr. Dana, has been one steady, earnest, loving, protracted course of self-consecration to God and man, it comes upon us as a distinct benediction. When the secrets of all hearts shall be revealed, and each one shall be able to read, by the light that shines around the eternal throne, the history of the formation of his own character, no doubt multitudes who never on earth knew their obligation to him, will stand forth the glorified witnesses to his fidelity.

As Dr. Dana's course through life was marked by eminent usefulness, so he was eminently honored both in the Church and in the world. As he was incapable of all unworthy concealment, so he passed for just what he was — the judgment which the public formed of him was in accordance with what they saw; and they saw as little to censure, as much to approve and admire, as perhaps in any other man. He was not a time-server, nor a man who hesitated to give utterance to his convictions when he thought duty called, though it must be at the expense of differing with his best friends; but, even in such cases, his undoubted integrity and high conscientiousness could not but command universal respect. In every place in which he lived, the community loved and venerated him; and many were the tokens of good-will that came to him as well from those in low places as in high. As he advanced in years, especially as he drew near to the end of his course, while he moved about with patriarchal dignity, he was looked upon with the reverence to which a patriarch would be entitled. Whenever he appeared in any public body, especially in the Presbytery of which he was a member, his brethren instinctively testified their affectionate respect for his character, and their confidence in the wisdom of his suggestions and counsels. After he had become too infirm to leave his chamber, and was even confined to his bed, they made him a farewell visit, as they would have gone to the chamber of Abraham or Jacob, when he was gathering himself up to die; and that visit awoke both his faculties and sensibilities into lively exercise; and his lips, and his eyes, and his whole visage, became eloquent, and it really seemed as if he was transfigured before them. They were completely bowed under his tender and sublime utterances; and as he took them successively by the hand, confident that he should see their faces no more, his whole soul evidently impressed itself upon the last benediction. It actually seemed as if the Heavens had come down into that chamber to bear the waiting spirit upward. And when the day of his funeral came, the whole community in which he lived became a mourning community, — the addresses which were delivered over his coffin were a fitting tribute to his exalted worth, — a testimony that no ordinary light had been extinguished, — the prayers that were offered were the breathings of deeply smitten hearts — and the long procession that followed him to his last resting-place, instead of being a heartless and unmeaning pageant, proclaimed, silently indeed, but more impressively than words could have done, that Heaven had claimed one of the purest, brightest spirits that earth had to lose. And, as the news of his death went abroad through the land, many hearts were set to throbbing sadly that the guide of their youth, or perhaps the friend of their later years, was gone; while the whole Church mournfully realized that one of her strong pillars had been stricken down, one of her brightest stars translated to a higher sphere. The generation which he has left has already embalmed his memory; and future generations will take care that his name, his character, his services, are not forgotten.

I regard it as a signal privilege that I was permitted, for many years, to share the friendship and confidence of this venerable man. I think my acquaintance with him commenced in 1826, on occasion of my passing a Sabbath in Newburyport, when, by his request, I occupied his pulpit a part of the day. I was

23

struck with his extremely bland and unassuming manner, the great kindliness of his spirit, and the good
judgment that he evinced in respect to every subject
that we conversed upon. The next time I met him, if
my memory serves me, was in 1827, at the meeting of
the General Assembly of the Presbyterian Church at
Philadelphia, both of us being delegates to that body.
He appeared there with his characteristic modesty, and
I think his voice was scarcely heard in any of the de-
liberations; but it was evident that he commanded
general and great respect from the members. He
preached during the session, at least once; and I
believe that was the only time I ever heard him. His
discourse answered well to the description already given
of his efforts in the pulpit: it was a simple, logical,
luminous exhibition of one of the great truths of the
gospel, and was delivered in a style of simplicity and
earnestness that was to me quite irresistible. Here I
resumed my acquaintance with him, and, as we were
thrown much together during the two or three weeks
that the Assembly was in session, I had the opportunity
of observing more particularly his distinctive characteristics; and my intercourse with him at this time gave
him an abiding place in my heart. I found in him a
most generous friend, who never seemed to regard any
sacrifice that was involved in doing me a favor. In several enterprises, partly of a literary and partly of a religious character, he has rendered me most effective aid;
and he has done it so cheerfully that one might have
supposed that he was receiving a favor instead of bestow-
ing it. During several of his last years, I have paid him
an annual visit; and I can truly say that it has marked a
bright spot in the year: for I have reckoned it no com-

mon privilege to get a sight of his venerable form, and listen to his words of wisdom and kindness, and catch the breathings of his heavenly spirit. In these visits I have had the opportunity of observing what a model of dignity and tenderness and consideration he was in his own family; how the life of his children seemed but one unbroken ministration of filial love, while his mild and gentle presence, his beaming smile, and bright sayings, and fervent, child like prayers, made that house a scene of cheerful but hallowed sunshine. I saw too, from year to year, that he was becoming more and more unearthly in his feelings and aspirations; that, while his spirit lost nothing of its kindly and genial tone towards those around him, it was evidently all the time girding itself for its upward flight. In his family prayers there was a richness, a sweetness, a tenderness, the savor of which lingered with me long after I had left him; and, as his eye is not to rest upon what I write, I may be permitted to add that, on one occasion, I was awaked, at the dawn of day, by the fervent expressions of gratitude and praise which I heard going up from him as he lay in an adjoining chamber. In all my intercourse with him, I cannot recall a single harsh expression, or any thing that indicated the absence of a benevolent spirit, towards any human being. The last time I saw him, I perceived that the preceding year had done much to reduce his strength, but nothing to diminish the life and glow of his affections. I could see that he was looking at every thing in its relation to eternal interests. While he was cheerful and sometimes even playful, it was evident that the chariot in which he was to ascend was making ready for him, and that his preparation was fully made for stepping into it. Dear, venerable old man! I left him with some faint hope of seeing him again; but before the time for my next visit came, the silver cord had been loosed, and the veteran saint had gone home!

APPENDIX.

THE DANA FAMILY.

A FEW notices are subjoined, specially interesting to some who will read these pages.

In a letter to Dr. Dana, dated March 10, 1826, James Freeman Dana, Professor in the Medical Department of Dartmouth College, writes: " When I was in Cambridge last summer, I made some researches: the most valuable result of them was the finding of an old record, in the possession of the family of the late Chief Justice [Dana], and which had for many years been supposed to be lost. The original minutes are in the handwriting of the late William Ellery of Newport.

" *Richard Dana* came from England to Cambridge, being a French refugee. He married Ann Bullard of Cambridge, by whom he had four sons, Jacob, Joseph, Benjamin, and Daniel, and four daughters," &c. To this, Dr. J. F. Dana adds, " I have always heard, by tradition, that the family left France," &c.

In a letter to Joseph Dana, D.D., of Ipswich, dated Feb. 22, 1827, G. W. Dana, postmaster of East Poultney, Vt., says, " I have devoted much time, the summer past, in searching records in Boston and towns about there, and in corresponding on the subject of the Dana Family. My researches have resulted in tracing back to Richard Dana, who died in Cambridge, April 2, 1690, at an advanced age; was born in France, and fled to England in consequence of the edict of the emperor, passed 1629, &c. I have obtained from Cambridge Records the names and ages of Richard's children."

The writer adds, that " the old Dana Farm in Little Cambridge, now Brighton, one mile west of the post-office," where his (the writer's) grandfather was born in 1720, was still in possession of the family.

Francis W. Dana of Boston writes, Dec. 18, 1834, to Rev. Samuel Dana of Marblehead: " I have been for some time collecting records of the Dana Family in different parts of the country, &c. It appears that our family is of French origin ; our ancestor Richard having been born in France, fled from thence to England in consequence of some of the persecuting edicts of the Catholics, and thence came to America, and settled at Cambridge, Mass., supposed about 1640."

In an obituary notice of Stephen W. Dana of Troy, N. Y., (born 1786), he is said to be " a descendant of Richard Dana, a Huguenot, who left France at an early period in consequence of the persecutions there, and settled in England. He, with many other French Protestants, came to America."

Rev. J. J. Dana (son of Stephen W. Dana) has elaborately traced the family history.

Of the four sons of Richard Dana, *Joseph* had but two children, who both died young. *Jacob* was ancestor of Rev. Sylvester Dana of Orford, N.H. *Benjamin*, who married Mary Buckminster, was ancestor of Joseph Dana, D.D., of Ipswich, Hon. Samuel Dana of Groton, Professor James F. Dana, Judge Dana of Fryeburg, Judge Dana of Danville. *Daniel* was ancestor of Chief Justice Francis Dana, (father of Richard H. Dana, the poet), James Dana, D.D., of New Haven, Samuel Whittlesey Dana, United-States Senator.

Joseph Dana of Pomfret, Conn., son of Benjamin, and grandson of Richard, married, for his second wife, Mary, daughter of Francis Fulham of Watertown Farms, Weston, and widow of Jonathan Moore of Worcester. Their children were (besides two daughters) Deacon Jonathan Dana of Pomfret, Vt., who died, at the age of ninety years, May 13, 1827 ; and Joseph Dana, D.D., of Ipswich, Mass., who died Nov. 16, 1827, aged eighty-five.

It was the privilege of the writer of these pages to spend more than two years of his childhood with the younger of these brothers, and, when a student in college, to visit the elder.

At a later period, he paid a visit to his father's elder brother, Joseph Dana, Esq., long Professor in the College at Athens, Ohio. Vivid remembrance of the temperament and manners of these and other senior members of the family, in whom its distinctive traits would naturally be most strongly marked, confirms his conviction of its French origin.

———

Since the above was written, the Rev. John J. Dana has published (1865) a pamphlet of sixty-four pages, compiled with indefatigable labor and research, entitled, "Memoranda of some of the descendants of Richard Dana." From this we take the following : —

"It is believed that every person of the name of Dana in the United States, entitled to the name by birth,* traces descent from Richard Dana, who came to Cambridge in Massachusetts in the year 1640. Certainly no person has been found or heard of, so entitled to the name, who does not claim descent from him. He had no brothers, or other relatives of the name, who came with him.

"Not only does he appear to have been the sole progenitor of the family in America, but no trace has been found of the name in England, except among the descendants of his great grandson, the Rev. Edmund Dana, who removed to England about the year 1761, married there, and had a large family (see p. 54). The Rev. Edmund Dana said his name was everywhere regarded as a new one in England ; and Dr. Luther V Bell (see p. 62) made careful search in England, not only at the usual sources, but in catalogues, indexes to law reports, and elsewhere, with no success. It seems, therefore, safe to assert, that, if any of the name existed in England in the seventeenth century, they soon died out.

* Judge Bell states that in the southern part of New Hampshire are families bearing our name, who do so by authority of an Act of the Legislature, changing their former name to Dana.

" The writer knows of no direct and positive proof in writing that Richard was born in England; but the uniform tradition has been, that he came here from England, that he was born there, and that his father was a native of France, who emigrated to England on account of religious persecutions. A silver cup was in possession of Hon. Judah Dana of Fryeburg, Me., which tradition says was brought by the father of Richard Dana from France. Tradition adds that this emigration from France to England took place about the year 1629.

" We have no written proof of the pedigree of Richard. The only fact conflicting with the theory that his father came from France to England, is the coat of arms now in general use among the Danas in the United States. This coat of arms is found in the Herald's College as having been given about the year 1569, in the reign of Queen Elizabeth, to William Dane (as the name is spelt on the record), a sheriff of Middlesex and alderman of London, an iron merchant. The writer has no proof that this coat of arms was brought here or used by Richard, or used by his immediate descendants. The first known proofs of its use are soon after the Revolutionary War. Nor has the writer been able to hear of any proof of any connection between Richard and this William Dane of 1569. If the fact be that this coat of arms was given at the Herald's College in response to inquiries made there by some of our family several generations after Richard, without any proofs of pedigree connecting him with this William Dane, and so passed lately into use in the family, it amounts to very little. If there be any proof of its earlier and general use in the family, or of a pedigree of Richard, it is earnestly hoped it will be produced.

" There is no reason for connecting our name with that of Dane. The name of Dane is common in England and America, and is always a monosyllable. It means " the Dane," i.e., of Danish descent, in England. Our name, on the contrary, has always been a word of two syllables. No other mode of spelling it has ever prevailed than the present. Not only did Richard so spell it, but all his numerous descendants, scattered in all parts of the country, and without much opportunity for communication, are found to have spelt it uniformly Dana. In the Cambridge records, when written by other persons, it is found occasionally spelt Dany, and once (apparently, though the writing is obscure) Danae; but, however spelt or pronounced, it has always been a word of two syllables.* The names of Dauncy, Daneray, Dennie, &c., are found in England. The latter name is common in America ; but no descendant of Richard ever spelt his name in that way, nor has any person of the name of Denny, or Dennie, ever claimed descent from Richard Dana. It may therefore be considered as settled, that the surname borne by our common ancestor, Richard, was a word of two syllables, properly spelt Dana ; and that no person is found to have borne that name in America or England, entitled to it by descent, who is not descended from him.

" The date of Richard's settlement in Cambridge seems always to have been fixed at 1640. The writer has no documentary evidence of the date of Richard's birth, though in some late records it is placed at 1620."

* It was the universal custom of New England, until within fifty or sixty years, to give to the final *a* the English sound, as in *fate*. Our name would have been so pronounced when properly spelt, and was so pronounced under the general custom. This led to the occasional mis-spelling of the name, by persons who spelt from the sound only. Now the final *a* in proper names has the continental sound, as in *far*, and the spelling is less likely to be mistaken. In England, both syllables of the name have the sound of *a* in *far*.

THE REV. SAMUEL DANA.

The Rev. Samuel Dana of Marblehead departed this life Aug. 16, 1864, in the eighty-seventh year of his age.

The writer was privileged with a brief interview with him one year after his brother's death. He said, "I have thought with a great deal of pleasure of your dear father, — that in all his life he never gave me a word, no, not a look, that was unkind or unbrotherly."

From 1801 to 1837 (when ill health compelled his resignation), Mr. Dana was the beloved and devoted pastor of the First Church of Marblehead. In the sermon occasioned by his death, the present pastor, the Rev. B. R. Allen, thus speaks of him : —

"Mr. Dana possessed a strong, well-balanced, and lucid mind ; a large share of sound, practical wisdom ; and a deeply affectionate and most ingenuous heart. Having studied men as well as books, he was an accurate and discriminating judge of character. He was slow in forming his opinions, and maturing his judgments ; but, when reached, he adhered to them with great tenacity. His conduct in any given case was founded in principle, not inspired by impulse ; hence he was highly conservative. His morality and his philanthropy, which were high and broad, sprung out of his religion ; and his religion was derived solely from the Bible, as the revelation of God. Any religious opinion or doctrine, any scheme of philanthropy or ethics, which could show for its warrant the authority of the Bible, he embraced with all his heart ; while all those which failed to do this, he instantly, and with all heart, rejected.

"He was a generous man : whilst holding with great firmness

274

the truths which his faith or his intellect had received, and defending them with all his power, as a duty which he owed to Christ and his fellow-men, he was courteous and kind towards those from whom he was compelled to differ. Had he been less positive and firm in his faith, his generosity, his fine culture, his high social character, might have betrayed him into a sacrifice or a compromise of the truth; had he been less generous, his positive faith might have degenerated into bigotry. But the very nice adjustment of these two qualities of mind and heart made him what he was, — the bold uncompromising defender of the truth, and the perfect Christian gentleman.

" Mr. Dana was thoroughly educated, both in literature and theology. While his voice was feeble, the testimony to the richness of his sermons, in matter and composition, was universal; so that he was always listened to with attention and profit.

" Mr. Dana's domestic character was of a very high order. His affection and reverence for his parents, and his love for his brothers and sisters, resembled in depth and fulness that of the great Webster, more than that of any other man I know of. Dr. Dana, the father, like most ministers in New England, had a limited salary; and yet, like a true Puritan, next to their salvation by Jesus Christ, he sought as the first thing the thorough education of his children. Hence he often found himself in straitened circumstances. His three sons were liberally educated, and amply repaid, by their characters, their positions in life, and their usefulness, — all which the venerable father lived to see and enjoy, — all the anxiety and labor attending it. The subject of this notice fully appreciated his father's position, and deeply sympathized with it. Between the time of his graduation and that of his settlement, a period of about five years, Mr. Dana taught an academy, thereby accumulating some means to help himself and relieve his honored father from a large pecuniary embarrassment of thirty years' standing. He has recorded it as one of the happiest moments of his life, when he was enabled thus to lift off the heavy burden from the heart of that father whom he so tenderly loved and so profoundly revered.

" His amiable, devoted, and lovely wife, whom he most tenderly loved, and whom to know was to love, who was the partner of his joys and the partaker of his sorrows for nearly sixty years, was the first to be called home : she preceded him only a few months to his heavenly rest.

" How wise and kind is God ! He causes every thing to be beautiful in its time. How marked in the case of our venerable father's death ! The time, — the period of weakness and weariness and loneliness, after he had enjoyed, through a long life, all of earth there is to enjoy, — in his happy home, in the sweet communion of choice spirits, with his heart, even at the last, warming with fresh life towards those he loved. And the manner, — that sleep, how beautiful, how calm, how peaceful ! deepening and deepening as hour after hour passed away, until earth was absorbed, the river was crossed, and his eyes opened to drink in the immortal glories of heaven."

Anna, the last surviving daughter of Dr. Joseph Dana, closed a life singularly devotional and benevolent, at the paternal mansion in Ipswich, Feb. 13, 1866.

DR. DANA'S PUBLICATIONS.

Sermon the Sabbath after Ordination, Nov. 23, 1794.

Sermons on John vi. 29, and Eph. iv. 30, March 24, 1799.

Two Sermons on the National Fast, April 25, 1799.

Discourse on the Character of Washington, Feb. 22, 1800.

Sermon on the Death of Mr. Benjamin Moody, March 7, 1802.

Sermon at the Interment of the Rev. John Boddily, Nov. 4, 1802.

Discourse on Music, delivered at Boxford, Sept. 12, 1803.

Discourse before the Female Charitable Society, Newburyport, May 22, 1804.

Discourse on the Qualifications of Rulers, March 31, 1805.

Discourse on the Deity of Christ, July 31, 1810; Reprinted 1819.

Discourse on the Annual Thanksgiving, Nov. 26, 1812.

Address to the Merrimack Humane Society, Sept. 7, 1813.

Address to the Rockingham Sacred Music Society, Hampton. Oct. 6, 1813.

Sermon on the death of William Coombs, Esq., June 12, 1814.

Discourse on American Independence, and the Deliverance of Europe, July 4, 1814.

Sermon before the Gloucester Female Society for promoting Christian knowledge, April 18, 1815.

Sermon before the Merrimack Bible Society, July 27, 1815.

Sermon at the Ordination of the Rev. Levi Hartshorn, Gloucester, Oct. 18, 1815.

Sermon at the Ordination of Rev. Jacob Weed Eastman, Methuen, Dec. 13, 1815.

Sermon at the Ordination of Rev. Hervey Wilbur, Wendell, Jan. 1, 1817.

Sermon before the Massachusetts Society for promoting Christian Knowledge, May 28, 1817.

Address before the Phi Beta Kappa Society, Dartmouth College, Aug. 26, 1817.

Sermon at the Funeral of Rev. William Morrison, D.D., March 12, 1818.

Address at a Meeting of the Sabbath Schools of Newburyport, Aug. 16, 1818.

Sermon before the American Education Society, Sept. 20, 1818.

Sermon at the Installation of Rev. Henry Blatchford, Salem, Jan. 6, 1819.

Sermon at the Dedication of Church in Dedham, Dec. 30, 1819.

Sermon on the Death of Rev. Levi Hartshorn, Gloucester, Feb. 20, 1820.

Sermon before the Female Benevolent Society, Exeter, July 30, 1820.

Farewell Sermon to the First Presbyterian Church, Newburyport, Nov. 19, 1820.

Election Sermon, Concord, N.H., June 5, 1823.

Convention Sermon (on the Atonement), Concord, N.H., June 2, 1824.

Sermon before the New-Hampshire Auxiliary Colonization Society, June 2, 1825.

Sermon at the Ordination of Rev. W. K. Talbot, Nottingham West, N.H., Nov. 2, 1825.

Two Sermons on the Sabbath after Installation, Newburyport, 1826.

Sermon at the Ordination of Rev. Daniel Fitz, Ipswich, 1826.

Sermon at the Installation of J. Brown, D.D., Boston, 1829.

Sermon at United Meeting of Churches, Newburyport, 1832.

Sermon at the Ordination of Rev. John C. March, Belleville, 1832.

Sermon on the Death of Mrs. Harriott Putnam, 1832.

Address before the Associated Alumni of Dartmouth College, 1833.

Address before the Ipswich Female Seminary, 1834.

Sermon at the Installation of Rev. John M. C. Bartley, Hampstead, 1836.

Election Sermon, Massachusetts, 1837.

Letters to Professor Stuart, 1839.

Sermon Commemorative of William Bartlet, Esq., 1841.

Half-century Sermon, Newburyport, 1844.

Sermon on " The Faith of Former Times," 1848.

Sermon on " The New Song," 1849.

Sermon before the Presbytery of Londonderry, 1851.

Remonstrance addressed to the Trustees of Phillips Academy, Andover, 1853.

Introduction to " The Theology of New England," 1855.

Also, contributions to "Annals of the American Pulpit," Memoir of Rev. John C. March, Tracts, Lectures, and very numerous contributions (sometimes over the signature of Philalethes) to various periodicals and newspapers.

www.ingramcontent.com/pod-product-compliance
Lightning Source LLC
Chambersburg PA
CBHW030625030726
47497CB00006B/1641